*'If I had thought there was the least s
have been in it for all tl*

Robert Catesby is a man in despair. His father is dead and his wife is burning in the fires of Hell – his punishment from God for marrying a Protestant. A new King presents a new hope but the persecution of Catholics in England continues unabated and Catesby can tolerate it no longer. King James bears responsibility but the whole government must be removed if anything is to really change. And Catesby has a plan...

The Gunpowder Treason

Copyright © Michael Dax 2017

First Published in 2013 as "The Powder Treason" by Carter & Allan

This edition published 2017

The Author asserts the moral right to
be identified as the author of this work

All rights reserved. No part of this publication may be reproduced, stored in a retrieval system, or transmitted, in any form or by any means, electronic, mechanical, photocopying, recording or otherwise, without the prior permission of the publishers.

Set in Times Roman

This book is sold subject to the condition that it shall not, by way of trade or otherwise, be lent, re-sold, hired out or otherwise circulated without the publisher's prior consent in any form of binding or cover other than that in which it is published and without a similar condition including this condition being imposed on the subsequent purchaser.

Robert Catesby and the Gunpowder Treason

"A dangerous disease requires a desperate remedy"
- Guido Fawkes, 5th November 1605

Prologue

Sir Everard Digby was not the first to die. He would not be the last, either. The verdict of the court had been unanimous: every man would die a traitor's death. Only Digby had been allowed to speak and he had begged the court's forgiveness.

'I shall go more cheerfully to the gallows, if any of your lordships say you forgive me.'

'God forgives you,' they had responded, 'and so do we.'

It was a cold January morning. The route to St Paul's was lined with jeering crowds. Household Guards had been stationed at regular intervals. The authorities were taking no chances.

Digby had been strapped to a wickerwork panel in the courtyard of the Tower. The frame was tied to the back of a horse and the young knight had been dragged through the cobbled streets towards the place of execution.

A sizeable crowd had gathered in the churchyard.

Digby was cut free of the horse. He staggered to his feet and took a moment to regain his composure. He was a handsome, aristocratic man, athletically built and extravagantly dressed. The journey had been uncomfortable, but apart from a few cuts and bruises he was still in good shape.

Two guardsmen in metal breast plates escorted him across to the wooden platform. It was almost dawn now, though the sky was dark and overcast. He took a deep breath and clambered up the narrow stairway. All eyes were upon him as he reached the top of the steps. His face was pale and his hands were shaking. Fear was beginning to take hold, but Digby steeled himself. He could not allow his nerves to get the better of him.

Slowly, he knelt down and began to pray.

The crowd jostled impatiently but guards were on hand to keep the rabble in order. There would be no interference in the due process of the law.

A small fire had been stoked near the quartering block. The butcher stood ready there, sharpening his knives.

On the far side of the platform, a group of young noblemen had gathered expectantly. Most of these men Digby knew by sight. In happier times, he had even dined with one or two of them. Now the men had a solemn duty to perform. One of them stepped forward. 'We call on the prisoner to acknowledge his fault and accept his punishment.'

The words echoed across the churchyard and the audience cried out for a response.

Digby quickly collected his thoughts. A speech was expected. It was part of the spectacle. He had given the matter some consideration in the days since the trial and had prepared a few words. The crowd quietened in readiness. 'I do not believe I have offended God in my actions,' he told them. 'All that I have done, I did for the good of my fellow Catholics and the cause of my religion. However, I freely admit that I have broken the laws of this land and I am willing to accept the consequences.'

An Anglican clergyman stepped forward. 'Will you pray with us, my lord?'

Digby waved the man away. 'I will pray with none but those of my own religion.' He turned back to the crowd. 'I ask any here of the Catholic faith to pray with me now, as I go to my death.' He crossed himself and knelt down at the edge of the platform, closing his eyes once more and mouthing a silent prayer.

When he had finished, he stood up and bowed to the various gentlemen congregated on the scaffold. Friends, peers of the realm, fellow knights; he acknowledged them all with courtesy and respect. His nerves had dissipated and for a few moments Sir Everard Digby seemed his old, extravagant self.

A ladder was propped against the side of the scaffold. It was a double ladder, wide enough for two men. The executioner stripped off Digby's clothes, leaving him naked but for his shirt, then tied his arms firmly behind his back and escorted him to the ladder. Digby placed a foot on the lowest rung and began to whisper the mantra he had heard many others use before him. 'O Jesus, save me and keep me. Jesus, save me and keep me…' With these words, and with the help of the hangman, he started to climb the ladder.

At the top of the scaffold, the rope was hanging loose. The hangman mounted the cross-beam and pulled the cord to one side. Digby allowed him to fasten the noose around his neck. Then the executioner pushed him from the ladder and for a moment he was suspended in mid-air. The rope had been kept short and the drop was not sufficient to break his neck. The hangman was under orders not to let him die too quickly. But the noose tore savagely at his throat. A few seconds of agony were soon ended, however. The hangman, sat at the top of the scaffold, leant forward and cut the rope with a knife.

Digby fell in a heap to the floor. The drop was only a few feet, but he landed badly and his head struck the wooden platform. For a few seconds, the young knight was left dazed. Two noblemen came forward to assist him. Rising to his feet, he was escorted to the far side of the platform, where the butcher stood ready with his sharp knives.

Still somewhat disorientated, Digby was laid out on the quartering block. His shirt was pulled open. A slash of a knife castrated him. He cried out as the blood spurted between his legs and his private parts were held up for the inspection of the crowd. A fire was still burning to one side. The butchered genitalia were tossed into the flames and the onlookers clapped enthusiastically. Digby screamed again. The executioner had set to work a second time, slicing through the flesh lining his stomach and pulling out the entrails. His heart would be next, then his arms and legs. Finally, his head would be sliced from his body and held aloft for the delight of the crowd.

Digby could feel his consciousness fading fast. Oddly, the pain was not all-encompassing. His mind was too fogged over to properly register the screams of his nerve endings as the beating heart was ripped from his chest. Blood splattered across the platform. The executioner held up the quivering organ.

'This,' he proclaimed, 'is the heart of a traitor!'

With his dying breath, Digby whispered two words:

'*You lie!*'

Part One
The Plot

"Shall we always, gentlemen, talk and never do anything?"
– Thomas Percy, May 1604

Chapter One

'I'm going to kill him,' Thomas Percy growled. He swung his leg over the top of the horse and thumped down onto the gravel. 'I'm going to kill the lying bastard.'

Robert Catesby took a step backwards.

Percy drew his sword – an expensive, finely wrought blade – and advanced on his oldest friend.

Catesby was lost for words.

Thomas Percy was a giant of a man, with a rugged face, restless eyes and a shock of prematurely white hair. He cut an imposing figure, even in repose. When anger gripped him, however, he could frighten the devil himself; and anger had gripped him now.

Percy drove the sword toward his friend. 'I'll take this blade and I'll shove it right through his lying Scotch belly.' The tip of the sword pressed hard against Robert Catesby's stomach.

'I believe you!' Catesby exclaimed, his breath forming a cloud in the cold winter air. He held up his hands in mock surrender, but could not keep the smile from his face.

Percy never did anything by halves.

Catesby had been crossing the courtyard from the chapel when he had caught sight of his older friend. Percy had been passing through the gatehouse, ducking down and battering his heels into the body of his latest purebred stallion. The poor creature had slowed to a trot to pass underneath the arch, but Percy had been determined to cover the last few yards as rapidly as possible. The reluctant animal had stumbled into a canter, bounding up the gravel driveway, only to be brought up sharply by an ungrateful master before it had managed to hit its stride.

Thomas Percy liked to make an entrance.

He sheathed his sword and his eyes flashed a cursory greeting. Percy was a regular visitor to Ashby St. Ledgers and his arrival, however unorthodox, was always welcome.

'It's good to see you.' Catesby grinned, looking up. Even at six feet tall, he was the shorter of the two men. 'Perhaps we should go up to the gatehouse?' If Percy wanted to vent his anger, it would be better to do it in private. Catesby's mother would not thank him for bringing a raised voice into the house while she was entertaining.

He summoned a groom to stable Mr Percy's horse, then quietly led its fuming owner back up the pathway to the main gate. Catesby was not surprised at his friend's anger. He had already heard the news and he could scarcely believe it himself.

The gatehouse straddled the low archway leading onto the estate. It was a half-timbered affair with a brick-built base. Catesby often used the house when he wanted to discuss matters of a sensitive nature. He led Percy up the narrow stairs to the main room. It was cramped and poorly lit. The walls were oak-panelled. A fire-place stood opposite a small table in the centre of the room. Catesby gestured for Percy to take a seat at the table. A servant scurried past to light the fire.

'You've heard about the proclamation then,' he said.

The other man snorted, taking the proffered seat. There was really no need to ask. Everybody had heard about the proclamation. Shockwaves had spread across the whole of England. 'It wasn't enough for that scoundrel to announce his utter detestation of the Catholic faith,' Percy spat. 'He's now restored every single bloody law that bitch-queen Elizabeth put on the statute books.' He jumped to his feet and marched over to the window. 'It beggars belief, Robin. How could one man be so duplicitous? After all he promised us. And promised me, Robin. In person.' Percy clenched his fists. 'I went all the way up there. To that bloody country. Half a dozen times, I went, just to speak to him.'

'I know,' Catesby agreed. 'You've been going on about it for two years.'

Percy had been acting on behalf of his patron, the Earl of Northumberland. It was closer to three visits, Catesby recalled. Percy had always been prone to exaggeration.

'He looked me straight in the eye and said "all my loyal subjects will have freedom of conscience." "Nobody will be persecuted for their religious beliefs." Easy enough for him when Good Queen Bess was still alive. He could promise the moon.' Percy returned to his chair and leaned across the table. 'But now we've put him on the throne, he doesn't give a toss about anyone but himself.'

'We were foolish,' Catesby admitted, 'investing as much hope in him as we did.' It had seemed reasonable at the time. James was married to a devout Catholic. His mother had been a Catholic. Why would he not be sympathetic to the Catholic cause?

'*I* was the fool,' Percy exploded. 'There was I, coming back from Scotland, telling everyone how wonderful the man was and how fantastic it would be when the old hag died and this genius of a monarch ascended the throne of England. And now he stabs me in the back. Publicly humiliates me. I tell you, Robin, I'm going to kill the lying bastard. I swear. With my bare hands, if I have to.'

There was no doubting the anger in Percy's eyes.

'I believe you,' Catesby whispered.

'At least with Elizabeth, we all knew she'd drop dead at some point. And without a direct heir, there was always the possibility of something better. But with this Scotch beggar there's no hope at all. Better to kill him now, before his miserable progeny takes root and we're stuck with them forever.'

Catesby sat back. 'So what's the plan?' he asked, unable to hide the scepticism in his voice. 'You gain an audience with His Majesty and then just…attack him?' He looked away. 'They'd have you in irons before you could even draw your sword.'

'I could always try shooting the bastard. A stray musket ball, when he's out hunting. Or if the worst comes to the worst, I could just strangle him. I can get close. I have connections.'

'They'll hang you for it.'

'Do you think I care?'

'*I* care, Thomas. If you're going to throw your life away, you might as well die doing something worthwhile.'

'What could be more worthwhile than strangling a Scotsman?'

Catesby leaned forward. 'Thomas, you've got to think these things through. There's no point rushing headlong into… assassination. I understand your frustration. Lord knows, I feel exactly the same. But for goodness' sake, think this through. Even if you do kill him, what then? There are his children to consider. Prince Henry. Elizabeth. Even that half-wit Charles. What do you think the Privy Council will do? They'll put a child on the throne and Robert Cecil will continue to run everything on their behalf.' Cecil was the King's most important advisor. 'He was practically running the country anyway when Elizabeth was dying. Do you want him to carry on? Because that is exactly what will happen. Just killing the King isn't enough. It's the whole administration that is at fault. If you're going to be a traitor, Thomas, you might as well betray the whole body, not just the head.'

Percy stared at his friend suspiciously. 'You've got a plan.'

Catesby suppressed a smile. 'Just an idea. Nothing more at present.'

The other man leaned in. 'So tell me about it…'

Catesby shook his head. He would say no more for now. Percy was too headstrong. 'Give me time to work things out properly,' he said. 'Then I'll tell you everything.'

It had started with a book.

Catesby had always been interested in theology. He kept a small library at his home in Northamptonshire. The books were well hidden. It did not do to have such things on public display. One particular volume had been neglected for some time. Catesby had come across it one chilly afternoon.

A thin film of dust covered the book. He picked it up and began to skim through it idly. It was a familiar work, which he had first read some years previously. The details, though, had faded from his mind.

Settling down before the fire with a flagon of Spanish wine, a particular paragraph caught his eye. It was part of a chapter focusing on a well-worn dilemma: the sanctity of the Confessional when a criminal act was being confessed. To illustrate the dilemma, a hypothetical example was presented, involving the use of gunpowder. Catesby took a sip from the goblet of wine and frowned.

He read on to another chapter, but try as he might he could not stop his mind from wandering back to the earlier idea. The words of the elderly theologian had somehow struck a chord. For the next two hours, Catesby could think of nothing else.

For years, he had been searching for an answer to the problems of Roman Catholics in England. Every day, since the death of his wife, he had focused on nothing else. And now here was the solution, printed out for him, as if he had been meant to find it. It was Divine Providence. It had to be.

He placed the book down on a small table and stared at the flickering flames behind the metal grate.

A portrait hung above the fireplace; a painting of a young woman, finely dressed, smiling serenely. Looking up, Catesby caught the gaze of the figure in the picture.

Catherine.

It was six years since she had died. Dear, sweet Catherine. Catesby had been a different man back then. He had fallen in love and no sacrifice had seemed too great. Catherine had been beautiful and rich but she had also been a Protestant. With all the fecklessness of youth, Catesby had abandoned his principles and married her for love. Given time, he thought, he would be able to convert her to the True Faith. But Catherine had proved as committed to her beliefs as he was to his; and in the end, it was he who had compromised. At Catherine's insistence, their first son, William, had been baptized in an Anglican church.

And God had punished him for it.

William had died in infancy. Not long after, Catesby's father had also died. And finally, within a year, so had his wife. It had been a harsh lesson. There could be no compromise in matters of religion.

The pain did not get any easier with the passing of time. Whenever he looked at the portrait, Catherine's smiling face rebuked him somehow. Sweet Catherine. She was burning now, in the fires of Hell. Catesby shuddered at the thought. He was responsible for her predicament. It had been his duty to show her the error of her ways, but he had failed his wife and now she was lost forever. It was his fault.

With trembling hands, he rose to his feet and placed the textbook back on the shelf.

Catherine would not have approved of this new idea. Catesby was certain of that. He did not know if he approved of it himself. He was not sure if the idea was workable, less still if he would have the courage to carry it through. But a seed had been implanted; and once there, he knew, it would be impossible to dislodge.

His wife would not have approved; but perhaps, Catesby felt with a desperate sadness, she would have understood.

Chapter Two

The second letter was more insistent. Tom Wintour was needed in London, on a matter of the greatest urgency. It did not matter if he was ill, he must come at once.

Tom had been in the grip of a heavy fever but when the second letter arrived he dragged himself out of bed, pulled on his riding boots and headed out into the snow. His friends needed him. Illness or no illness, he would not let them down.

Perhaps the fresh air might do him some good.

Tom was a short, stocky fellow with a well rounded face and a neatly trimmed beard. A respectable looking man in his early thirties, he was comfortable on horseback but disliked riding in winter. The journey to London was never pleasant at this time of year. Frost lined the bridleways and the air was bitterly cold. He wore a heavy winter cloak, but the wind cut through it easily.

At Lambeth, he met up with Jack Wright and Robert Catesby. Jack was staying across the river at a small inn on the Strand. Catesby had a lodging on the south bank. It was Catesby who had written the letter. The two men greeted Tom enthusiastically. Catesby was a distant cousin; Jack Wright a childhood friend. The men towered over him – they were both ridiculously tall – but Tom had long since grown used to the physical disadvantage.

'I'm sorry to drag you all the way here from Huddington,' Catesby apologised, his eyes flashing with energy and good humour. 'Are you feeling any better?' Catesby was a couple of years younger than Tom, a warm and charismatic man with a ready smile and a kind heart. Tom loved him like a brother. If the fellow had any fault, it was rashness. He would get an idea into his head and would not let it go.

'I'm fine,' Tom replied, as the three men settled down together in the drawing room of Catesby's Lambeth residence. 'Fully recovered, I think.' It had been a hard journey from Worcestershire but the exercise had served to revitalise him.

Jack Wright was not convinced. 'You still look a bit peaky to me.' Jack was a sturdy, well-built Yorkshireman in his mid thirties. He lacked the boyish looks and natural charm of Robert Catesby, but made up for it in good humour.

'I've just been feeling a bit down lately,' Tom admitted wearily. 'It's not my health. It's just...' He glanced at Catesby, who was sitting on a hard wooden armchair opposite the main window. 'Everything is turning sour, Robin. I don't know what to do. With everything that's going on here...I'm beginning to think it might be better just to leave the country. To go back to Flanders.'

Catesby was appalled. 'Tom, you can't leave now...'

The other man shrugged. He had thought long and hard, but he could see no alternative. 'If our own King is against us, what hope can we possibly have?'

Catesby was having none of it. 'This is the time when we need to stand up and fight.'

'I would happily fight, Robin, if I thought it would do any good. But what can we do? Kidnap the King? Lead an armed revolt? It's been tried. It doesn't work. Not if the people are too frightened to make a stand. Face facts, Robin. We are too few and too isolated. We can do nothing without foreign aid. And the Spanish don't want to help us. Not since the ceasefire. I know. I spoke to the Spanish Envoy when he came here last year.'

'They haven't finalised any terms for a permanent treaty,' Catesby pointed out. 'The Spanish could still act on our behalf.'

'Stranger things have happened,' Jack admitted, scratching his neck idly.

'And even if they won't help, we can still act on our own.' Catesby was becoming energised now. An idea was clearly bubbling beneath the surface. 'There is one way we can be sure to succeed, without any outside assistance.'

'And what's that?'

The man paused for a second. He had obviously been working up to this moment. Catesby was nothing if not a performer. 'To destroy the government,' he said, simply. 'To kill the King and his ministers all in one go.'

Jack laughed. 'Of course! We'll just gather them together and blow them all up. Couldn't be simpler!'

'Mr Wright, that is exactly what I'm suggesting.'

'I was being facetious.'

'Yes, but think about it. When is the one time when the whole of the government is gathered together?'

'Well...the opening of Parliament.'

'Exactly. Don't you see?' Catesby leaned forward in his chair. 'It's almost as if the place had been designed for their punishment. The King gives a speech. The lords gather together to formulate laws against us. And all the while, underneath, we'll have stockpiled enough powder to kill every single one of them.'

'Gunpowder?' Tom's eyes widened.

'Why not? Barrels of the stuff. We set them off and the whole government is brought down in a single instant. Think of it. Cecil, the King, the lords. Every last one of them.'

Tom could not believe what he was hearing. 'But that's cold blooded murder! My God! Hundreds of people would be killed.' He shook his head in disbelief. 'I can't believe you would even suggest such a thing.'

'I do suggest it.'

Tom was horrified. 'Robin, how could it possibly serve God to spill that much blood?'

'If our enemies are destroyed...'

'Our enemies, maybe. But what about all the innocent people who would die? The Catholic peers. Our friends, Robin. Lord Monteagle. Lord Mordaunt. Thomas Howard. Good men. Are you going to kill them all as well?'

'If necessary.'

Tom stared at his cousin in dismay. 'Your soul would be damned forever,' he breathed. 'And mine too if I agreed to it.'

'Not if it was for the greater good. A few lives lost could make all the difference. And it's not our friends we're aiming to kill. We can always warn one or two of them away. It's the malignant majority who sit in that House. Think of it, Tom. We could bring down the whole government in a single action.'

'People will hate us for it,' Tom pointed out. 'For killing so many people.'

'Not if we succeed.'

'And how are we supposed to get hold of all the powder? How would you smuggle it inside without being seen?'

Catesby grinned. 'That's the clever part. We dig a tunnel. Rent a house opposite the House of Lords and smuggle the powder underneath through a mine shaft.'

Tom was lost for words. 'Do you know anything about mining?'

'We can find someone. Forget the details. We can work all that out. But the *principle*. Think of it, Tom. If the whole government is brought down in one go, we'd be sending out a signal to the whole world. There'd be nothing to stop us from restoring the True Faith to the entire country.'

Tom closed his eyes. He was having difficulty grasping the scale of the idea. Emotions were clouding any kind of rational judgement. He took a moment to calm himself. He had to consider the matter objectively. 'All right,' he replied at last. 'I admit that the destruction of Parliament would hit at the root of the problem. If your plan succeeded, there would be absolute chaos.'

'And with a little planning, we would be better placed than anybody to exploit that.'

'But what if it *didn't* succeed, Robin?' That, surely, was the most important question. 'What if it failed at the last moment? Plots *do* fail. It's almost in their nature to fail. And *if* it did, we'd be giving the authorities a perfect excuse to crack down even more. They hate us now. If we tried to kill the King and *failed*, the people would take it out on every Catholic in the land. We'd be condemning all our friends and they would be condemning us for bringing it down upon their heads.'

Catesby threw up his arms. 'What choice do we have, Tom? The longer this disease is allowed to endure, the more difficult it will be to cut it out. We must strike now, or the war will be lost.'

Jack Wright had been listening carefully to the argument. 'What about the Spanish?' he suggested. 'They might not be planning an invasion, but they might be able to put some pressure on the King.'

Catesby glanced across. 'Religious toleration, you mean?' He sounded doubtful.

'It might be worth another try,' Jack thought. 'Rather than this. If the Spanish can persuade the King to be more lenient towards us, we might not need to do anything quite so radical.'

Catesby considered for a moment. 'You mean, get the Spanish to include a clause in this peace treaty they're going on about...?'

Tom leapt at the idea. 'I'll go to Flanders,' he resolved. 'I'll speak to the Constable of Castile. He might listen to reason.' Don Juan de Velasco was the man who would be negotiating the peace treaty on behalf of the Spanish Government. 'I'll try to persuade him. He'll be sympathetic, I'm sure he will.' Tom was doing his best to sound enthusiastic. Anything would be better than Catesby's plan.

'Even if they won't compromise the treaty,' Jack said, 'they might be able to persuade the King to let us *buy* our freedom.' The idea of English Catholics paying for liberty of conscience was not unreasonable. It had been tried elsewhere, with great success.

'It's worth a go, I suppose,' Catesby admitted, thinking the proposal through. 'I promise you, Tom, if there's any realistic way of resolving this problem peacefully....'

'I'll go to Flanders,' Tom repeated, emphatically.

'We might as well have one last stab,' Jack agreed.

It would not be difficult to put forward a convincing argument. Tom had the necessary contacts and the legal training.

'And while you're out there,' Catesby added, 'if you find anyone you think might be able to help us with this other matter, bring them back with you. Especially anyone with mining experience.'

Jack had a suggestion. 'Actually, there is a man. An old school friend of mine. Should know a bit about that sort of thing. He's career military; been out there for years. He might be able to help us.'

'Make the Constable your priority,' Catesby said. 'And if Velasco won't help us, well then. We will just have to help ourselves. Are you with me, Jack?'

Jack Wright sighed. 'I never wanted an easy life. Agreed.'

'Tom?'

Tom Wintour looked away.

'Let's at least give it a try, Tom. Work out the details. Bring the threads together. If it turns out be impractical, so be it. What do you say?'

Tom took a deep breath. 'All right. I'm with you, Robin. In this and in anything else.'

Chapter Three

London had not witnessed such extravagance in living memory. Thousands of loyal subjects had gathered on the streets to catch a glimpse of His Majesty King James as the slow procession made its way from the Tower of London to the Houses of Parliament. It was a glittering occasion. The most important men in the land, dressed in their finest clothes, accompanied the King through the winding, cobbled streets of old London town.

At St Paul's Cathedral, there were speeches and musical performances. Wooden platforms had been erected in the church yard and tributes were enacted by the finest players, musicians and orators that England had to offer. Ben Jonson made a speech. Danish minstrels performed traditional melodies in tribute to Queen Anne. The newly anointed King's Servants, headed by the actor Richard Burbage, performed extracts from the recent works of his fellow artiste, Mr William Shakespeare.

At the centre of it all, beneath a canopy held aloft by the Gentlemen of the Privy Chamber and sitting astride a handsome Spanish horse, was King James of England. At thirty six years of age, James Stuart had the natural authority of a man who had been sovereign in his own country for the whole of his adult life. He was not a handsome man. His eyes were small and heavily lidded. His nose was bulbous and a short, wispy beard did nothing to accentuate his appearance. And yet, in his fine clothes, riding a dazzling white jennet and exuding a calm, statesman-like solemnity, he looked every inch the wise and noble monarch.

Catesby watched with trepidation as the procession made its way through Charing Cross towards Whitehall.

In the King's wake, mostly on foot, came the lords and other nobles. Behind them were the artisans and King's Servants. Guardsmen kept the crowds at a distance, but there was no sense of threat or displeasure. If anything, a feeling of euphoria had gripped the streets. Small children darted through the crowds to keep up with the King and to catch a glimpse of Prince Henry, the royal heir. Henry was the darling of all England. The ten year old boy was one of the star attractions of the day. Queen Anne, riding beside her husband, waved regally to the cheering crowds.

It was all a marked contrast to the Coronation, which had taken place the previous year. Catesby had been away from London at the time. Fear of plague had kept most people out of the capital. The Archbishop of Canterbury had been keen to conclude the ceremony as quickly as possible. There had been little pomp and few speeches; and it had rained hard from dawn to dusk. The State Opening of Parliament now, in such an extravagant fashion, was an obvious way of recompensing the crowds. It was, in effect, the true Coronation.

It was also the time, Catesby knew, in which the future direction of the kingdom would be decided. He pushed through the crowd as the King drew up outside the Houses of Parliament.

Parliament Square, in ordinary times, was a seething mass of street traders, tenement houses, drinking establishments. There were slums and brothels and all manner of immoral opportunities, clinging like lichen to the surface of the Parliament building. The Household Guard could clear a path through the centre but there was little control over the periphery; and little desire for it. This, Catesby knew, would act in his favour. Anonymity, so difficult in the country, was so much easier in proximity to the seat of government.

James's speech that afternoon would set the tone for the whole session. Catesby was determined to be there. A small number of lesser gentlemen were often allowed to watch proceedings from the near end of the chamber. Catesby was hoping to chance his luck.

He made his way hurriedly towards the House of Lords. If necessary, he could drop a few names and offer a few coins. Now more than ever he needed to hear what King James would say and he needed to hear it in person. If the speech was as vindictive as Catesby feared, then his presence here would serve as a useful prelude to later events.

He would know precisely what to expect when the second Parliament opened the following year.

Even now, Catesby hoped it would not come to that. He had been sincere in telling Tom he would prefer to find a peaceful means of achieving Catholic liberation. The powder plot had to be a last resort. Catesby did not hold out much hope with regard to the Spanish, but there was a slim chance that the King's words thus far had been a political manoeuvre, to placate the Protestant extremists. James had, after all, shown some courtesy towards Catholics in the first few months of his reign. Fines had been remitted and a handful of priests had even been released from prison.

Catesby arrived at the entrance to the Upper Chamber. Here, the lesser nobility would be admitted to the House. A clump of eager gentlemen were haranguing the guard on the door.

'You're too late,' the gruff fellow informed them bluntly. 'We're full up.'

Catesby grimaced but he was not surprised. It had always been unlikely that he would gain a place on this of all days. The would-be Catholic conspirator would have to wait like everybody else to read a transcript of the proceedings.

He moved away from the crowd and took hold of the golden crucifix he always wore around his neck. Out of sight of the guard, he whispered a short prayer.

The next few minutes, he knew, would decide the future of all England.

Sir Everard Digby was bursting with pride as he entered the Upper Chamber for the first time. A fanfare was sounding, heralding the arrival of King James. Digby was standing to the right of the King, dressed in a colourful long-skirted doublet and a heavy sleeveless cloak. In his hand he carried the slender pike that marked him out as a Gentleman Pensioner. The other bodyguards stepped forward and together they escorted King James – dressed in long, flowing robes of white and red – to the ornate jewel-encrusted throne which dominated the far end of the chamber.

The House of Lords was bristling with activity. Bishops jostled for position with Barons and Earls in all their finery. The nobility of England had turned out in force. On a less formal occasion, Digby would have waved a greeting at one or two of them. There were friends here as well as colleagues. Elaborately dressed commoners from the Lower Chamber filled up the extra capacity but the babble of noise and hearty conversation had died the moment the fanfare had begun.

Digby had grown used to an element of pageantry. A distinguished young man a few weeks shy of his twenty-sixth birthday, he was already a popular figure at court. His conspicuous good-looks and easy charm had endeared him to even the most rabidly anti-Catholic of King James' courtiers. Even Digby, however, had been taken aback by the sheer scale of events that morning. It was the grandest, most extravagant spectacle that England had witnessed in a generation.

And the fact that he was standing here at all, protecting the life of the King of England, seemed utterly preposterous.

Digby had first met King James about a year previously. The King had been on his way south to claim the crown after the death of Elizabeth. Various dignitaries had gathered at Belvoir Castle to greet their new ruler and to his surprise Digby had been one of those singled out for a knighthood. Mary – his wife – had been utterly speechless. That a Protestant King, in one of his first acts on English soil, would ennoble a known Catholic simply beggared belief. And on St George's Day too. It was more than he could ever have hoped for.

They had been heady days, those first few months after the death of the old Queen. Everything had seemed possible. The whole country had pledged its loyalty to the new King and several prominent Catholics had received royal favour.

Digby had felt blessed back then. In Mary he had the best wife that ever a man enjoyed. His first child had just been born; a son, Kenelm, now barely a year old. And for a time it had seemed that the old enmity between Protestant and Catholic was being put aside forever.

The mood had soured eventually but Digby had not given up hope in the new administration. The proclamation in February had been a slap in the face but it was probably more of a rhetorical flourish than a statement of intent. Now that Parliament was in session, King James would doubtless abandon the rhetoric and revert to the natural balance and good judgement he had shown in the lead up to the Coronation. Everything would be well from now on.

King James took his seat beneath the covered throne and the lords seated themselves quietly on the rows of benches along either wall. Digby was not the only Catholic in attendance this afternoon. There were still one or two brave lords who publicly professed their faith and many others who pretended to be Protestants but still practised the old religion in the privacy of their own homes.

Digby took his place to the right of the throne. Another Pensioner, pike in hand, stood to the left, whilst the excited peers and commoners settled down to hear the King's opening address. Digby, facing forward, was more excited than any of them.

King James looked up, a hint of amusement flickering across his podgy face. 'Firstly,' he began, 'I wish to deliver my thanks to you all for your gracious welcome and for your support.' James spoke with a mild Scots lilt that was by no means unpleasant to the ear. It had none of the guttural choke of some of his less refined Scottish courtiers. 'This kingdom of ours is truly blessed. It is blessed in the union of two ancient and famous kingdoms and it is blessed in the peace and stability that the Lord in my person has kindly bestowed upon it. God has looked kindly upon us all.'

The peers murmured their agreement.

'But all the blessings in the world are as nothing, my lords, if God is not moved to maintain our prosperity.'

Digby kept his head facing forward but his attention did not waver from the speech. This was the point, surely, where the King would address the subject uppermost in everyone's mind.

'On matters of religion,' he declared, 'I have already made my thoughts abundantly clear. There is but one religion permitted by law. This is the True Religion, to which I adhere. But when I first arrived in this country, I discovered another religion – a private sect lurking within the bowels of the nation. These people call themselves "Catholic" though in truth they are nothing of the kind. They are papists. Servants of the Pope in Rome. And the Church they follow – this "Mother Church" – is an institution riddled with infirmities and corruption.'

Digby blinked uncertainly.

'Since coming to this country,' James continued, 'I have shown great tolerance towards these "Catholics", even remitting the fines for those who refuse to attend our lawful church services. I certainly do not consider them to be my enemies. But I would like to teach them the error of their ways.'

Digby swallowed hard. The speech was not going the way he had expected.

'The ordinary papists, who are quiet and peaceable and merely ignorant of the True Religion, have nothing to fear from me. I would be sorry to punish their bodies for the error of their minds.'

'But as for the clergy and any other corrupt persons employed under the colour of religion, I will not suffer them to remain in this kingdom. Their false doctrine seeks to divert my subjects from their rightful allegiance to the crown.'

'I therefore urge my bishops and clergy to be more vigilant and diligent than you have been hitherto to win over these souls to the True God. And I say to the papists: do not presume too much upon my leniency. I will not allow your religion to grow again. I will tread down your errors and wrong opinions. If you are good subjects, then I am a friend to you. But if you seek to erect your religion again on these shores then I am your avowed enemy.'

The lords thundered their approval.

Tom Wintour had spent the last few days in London, navigating the routine bureaucracy involved in all foreign travel. There was no telling how long it would take to arrange a meeting with the Constable of Castile and it was possible he would be in Flanders for several weeks. Luckily, his employer Lord Monteagle was a good friend and was happy to grant him a leave of absence. This was in the run up to the State Opening of Parliament. A licence was also required for any trip abroad. Tom had arranged an interview with the relevant government official and – when asked the reason for his journey – had replied that he was thinking of becoming a soldier. This was an entirely plausible excuse. Tom was unmarried, after all, and as a second son had inherited little on the death of his father. Such gentlemen often went to seek their fortunes on the battlefields of Europe. The passport was granted without comment.

A few days later, having finally crossed the channel, Tom arrived in Bergen and met up with Hugh Owen, an ageing Catholic exile. The genial Welshman had taken considerable pleasure in introducing him to the Constable of Castile. In return for this small favour, Owen had asked for an account of the meeting once the audience was concluded.

Tom dutifully reported back to him at the man's comfortable lodgings in Bergen. The plump sexagenarian listened carefully whilst Tom recounted the arguments he had placed before the Constable and then outlined Velasco's seemingly warm response.

'He told me he'd been commanded by the King of Spain to do everything possible to help counter the persecution of Catholics throughout Christendom. He said as a Christian, he felt it was his moral duty to do so.'

Hugh Owen sat forward in his chair. 'But he made no specific promises?'

'No.' That, of course, was the sticking point. 'Although he did seem sincere in what he was saying.' As far as Tom could tell, the Spanish Constable had appeared genuinely troubled by the account he had given of events in England over the last few months.

Owen was sceptical. 'I've been dealing with the Spanish for a good few years and I'm telling you, boy, they care little for anything other than their own well-being. They won't do anything to help you.'

Tom resented the Welshman's tone. He had had some experience of the Spanish court himself and he was well aware of their limitations. All he had been asking for was a bit of pressure on behalf of English Catholics. A few words added to a treaty, nothing more. But even this appeared to be too much for the Spanish crown and the request, he now realised, had been smothered in polite but evasive diplomacy.

Hugh Owen had come to the same conclusion. 'It seems you have had a wasted journey Mr Wintour,' he lamented.

The Welshman was probably right.

'Tell me honestly, Mr Owen. If the Catholics of England were to do something by themselves, do you think the Archduke would offer assistance?'

Owen raised an inquisitive eyebrow. 'Why? Is somebody planning something?'

'Not that I know of,' Tom responded, a little too quickly. 'But...if the situation worsens, somebody's bound to try something.'

'That's true. There are always plots brewing in England. And in Wales, come to that. But as regards the Spanish, the straight answer is: no. Not a chance. They're all so focused on peace with the English they wouldn't even consider talking about anything else.'

'That's what I thought.' Tom let out a gentle sigh.

'What will you do now? Head home, I take it?'

'I suppose so. But there is one other thing you might be able to do for me…' Catesby had given Tom a second task, if the interview with Velasco came to nothing.

'Of course, my boy. Name it.'

'Have you ever heard of a gentleman by the name of Guy Fawkes…?'

Chapter Four

Horses were clattering up the road towards Baddesley Clinton

Half a dozen servants had gathered in the drawing room to hear Father John Sugar conduct the regular service. An altar had been set up and candles had been lit in preparation for the morning Mass. Sugar was dressed in his usual purple robes with a small cross on a chain hanging from his neck. He was a kindly middle-aged man with a narrow, bearded face and a friendly expression. Baddesley Clinton was a modest country house a few miles north of Warwick and Sugar had always made a point of stopping off here whenever the opportunity arose.

His manservant – a slender, nervous fellow by the name of Robert Grissold – was carrying a silver goblet containing the communion wine and a platter of unleavened bread. Grissold moved carefully along the line of worshippers, supplying the bread and wine as Father Sugar directed. The priest had spent most of his time ministering to the poor since his return to Warwickshire but when circumstances allowed he greatly enjoyed conducting prayers and worship at the comfortable thirteenth century manor house.

Sugar was so intent on delivering the service that he failed to register the noise of the horses in the courtyard. His attention was abruptly seized, however, when a young stable lad burst into the room.

'Soldiers!' the boy exclaimed anxiously. 'Pursuivants! They're coming up the lane!'

The Father shuddered involuntarily. The authorities had been cracking down on suspected Catholic activity but until now he had been lucky enough to avoid their attention.

Anne Vaux – the mistress of the house – was on her feet at once. A stocky, plain faced woman in her early forties, she had been kneeling in line ready to receive the sacrament. Now she leapt forward, grabbing the candlesticks from the table and pulling away the cloth. 'Hide everything!' she commanded, gesturing the servants to their feet. 'Don't let them into the house!' It was not the first time the forces of law and order had raided Baddesley Clinton and Anne Vaux knew exactly how to react. All evidence of the Mass would have to be cleared away. If the soldiers caught so much as a glimpse of any religious paraphernalia they would tear the place apart. And if they caught sight of a priest...

'Robert! Hide your master. Quickly!'

Robert Grissold knew the drill. The nearest priest hole was located in the west wing. Grissold bundled Father Sugar hurriedly towards the door. 'Upstairs!' he whispered, leading the flustered priest through the house and up the steps. Behind them, the soldiers were already banging on the front door.

'We have a warrant!' one of them bellowed. 'Open up in the name of the King!'

The best access to the priest hole was from the sacristy above the kitchen. A narrow shaft led down to a dark tunnel that ran the whole length of the west wing. 'It used to be a sewer,' the servant explained, as Father Sugar slipped out of his priestly robes and grabbed hold of the thick rope. 'This is where they used to throw their waste, I'm afraid.' The priest handed the vestment to Robert Grissold then awkwardly descended the shaft. There was a splash as his feet hit the ground. The water here was ankle deep.

Grissold followed his master down the rope.

The tunnel was dark and claustrophobic. Vile odours infected the damp air. A heavy stone slab had been fitted to the wall at the bottom of the shaft but water still trickled in from the moat. The priest shuffled along. At least there was some space to move about. Most priest holes were scarcely bigger than the priests they were intended to conceal. This tunnel could hide several people at a time. At some point, it had been adapted for just that purpose. Anne Vaux had made a career out of protecting members of the priesthood.

The two men stood silently as the soldiers thundered into the house. There were four of them in all – pursuivants; priest hunters – rough ill-educated thugs clomping about with their swords drawn. Father Sugar hoped Anne Vaux had had time to clear away properly. The pursuivants would search everywhere. Tables were being moved already; cupboards ransacked; beds overturned. Even the sheets would be checked to see if they were still warm.

And Anne Vaux – brave Anne Vaux – was protesting bitterly all the while.

'We'll be all right, Father,' Grissold breathed, trying to reassure his master. 'They've never found anyone yet.'

But there was no telling how long the search would continue.

Long wooden oars sliced through the putrid water, propelling the small rowing boat slowly upstream. It had been a long journey from Greenwich. Tom Wintour pulled the oars towards his chest and scanned the river ahead. Navigating the Thames was never easy. Hundreds of vessels made use of the crowded waterways and collisions were a constant threat. Tom could swim well enough, but he had no desire to end up in the murky depths. A couple of mouthfuls of fetid Thames water had been known to kill a man. At least, that is what he had heard. He angled the boat towards the bank and prepared to pull up. 'Almost there,' he said.

The small vessel drew up alongside an outhouse, adjacent to the lodgings where Catesby resided. On the opposite bank stood the Houses of Parliament. Some perverse sense of humour must have inspired the man to take rooms in Lambeth, in full view of the buildings they intended to destroy. Perhaps Catesby wanted to keep his enemies in constant sight, as a reminder of the seriousness of what was being planned.

A wooden doorway faced the river and a crude ladder descended into the water. Tom rose up unsteadily and grabbed the ladder with one hand. He took hold of the mooring rope with the other and secured the boat to one of the lower rungs.

A servant had opened the door at the top of the steps. It was Catesby's manservant, Bates. Tom knew the fellow well and nodded a greeting. Bates proffered a hand and he gripped it firmly, clambering up the steps and through the narrow doorway. A second man grabbed the ladder from below.

Bates showed the new arrivals through to the main house.

Catesby was seated at a desk, absorbed in a large, leather bound volume. He jumped to his feet when Tom entered the room. The two men embraced warmly.

Tom's companion stood back and waited to be introduced.

'Forgive me,' said Tom. 'Robin, this is Mr Guido Fawkes. Mr Fawkes this is my good friend Robert Catesby.'

Fawkes bowed his head. 'I'm pleased to make your acquaintance, Mr Catesby.'

'Likewise. I have heard a lot about you.'

The two gentlemen stood for a moment, quietly evaluating each other. The men were of roughly equal height; each about six feet tall. Catesby was better looking, but Fawkes' reddish brown hair and muscular build drew the eye more readily. He had made a good impression on Tom Wintour. The man seemed sober and intelligent. Sir William Stanley, his commanding officer in the Low Countries, had also spoken very highly of him.

Sir William had arranged the introduction. They had met at Ostend and Tom had asked Mr Fawkes to return with him to England. Fawkes had been given no specifics. All he had been told was that some friends of his wished to discuss some important matters. When Tom had mentioned Jack Wright, Mr Fawkes had readily agreed.

'Come in. Please.' Catesby gestured. 'Both of you. Make yourself at home.' He shouted through the door for refreshments to be brought up. 'I was just reading a bit of Martin Del Rio, before you came.'

Tom picked up the book. The title was engraved on the frontispiece: *Disquisitionum Magicarum*. He had heard of the book, of course – it had been published back in the nineties – but he had never actually read it. Something about the sanctity of the Confessional. Catesby was always one for delving into the more arcane theological matters.

Fawkes was offered a chair and the three men sat down together. 'How did you get on in Flanders, Mr Tom?' Catesby asked. 'Did you get an audience with Don Juan de Velasco?'

The housekeeper entered, carrying a tray which she placed down on the table. Three cups had been laid out beside a jug of lemon juice. Catesby filled the cups and handed one to each of his companions.

'I spoke to the Constable at Bergen,' Tom explained, after taking a quick mouthful of juice. 'He was very understanding. I told him how difficult things were for us here and how the situation seemed to be deteriorating.' He repeated the report he had earlier given to Hugh Owen. 'But I have to be honest, Robin, I don't believe he will do anything at all.'

Catesby frowned. 'What's your opinion, Mr Fawkes? By all accounts, you've spent a lot of time in the Low Countries.'

'Indeed I have, Mr Catesby. I have a great deal of affection for the Spanish nation. They are a pious and methodical people. But they are not swift to act. And war has somewhat depleted their resources. They are anxious to finalise the peace treaty as quickly as possible, so that they can concentrate their efforts on stabilizing their own territories. Mr Wintour is right. The problems of English Catholics are remote to them. I do not believe they will intercede on our behalf.'

The room fell silent for a moment. Tom took another swig of lemon. 'What about Parliament?' he asked. 'Have there been any developments while I've been away?'

A shadow passed across Catesby's face.

'I heard about the King's speech,' Tom admitted.

'That was only the beginning. The whole machinery of Parliament seems to be geared against us. A new Bill was introduced just yesterday, at the behest of King James himself. We are to be excommunicated, Tom. Declared outlaws in our own country.'

Tom put down his cup. 'My God.'

'It's true. I could scarcely believe it myself.'

Mr Fawkes was appalled. 'Even the Old Queen would not have stooped that low.'

'Our children will be disinherited,' Catesby continued. 'Our debtors will be free of any obligation to pay us our dues and we will have no recourse whatsoever to the law. The state has made us criminals, Mr Fawkes, through no malice on our part.'

Tom Wintour stared at the book lying open on the table. 'So we have no option, then.' He looked up at Catesby, hoping his friend might offer some alternative vision.

'They have left us no alternative, Tom. We are criminals now. We have no obligations to anyone but ourselves.'

'To ourselves and to God,' Mr Fawkes added gravely.

Chapter Five

It had been some years since Father John Sugar had last had a permanent residence. The middle-aged priest was hurrying on foot along a narrow country lane. He was rarely able to stay more than a couple of nights in one place. Robert Grissold was following closely behind, glancing nervously from side to side. They had left Baddesley Clinton half an hour earlier but it would not do to be out in the open for any length of time.

A track took the two men via Chessetts Wood and across country until they reached the old Warwick road. 'We should hurry,' the priest suggested. 'We don't want to be out in the open when it starts to get dark.'

Grissold nodded grimly.

Father Sugar was used to being on the move. He had trained abroad, at the English College for Catholics in Douai, but after his ordination he had returned to England and taken on the role of itinerant priest. It was a harsh life but a satisfying one, preaching to a disparate flock of farmhands, servants and labourers across three counties. Sugar had met Grissold through a mutual friend and the two men had travelled together ever since, moving from village to village, house to house. The local people would provide all the food and shelter they required. Even the poorest of his flock would offer to mend his clothes or share what little bread they had. His only regret was the caution he was forced to display. He had to rely on word of mouth and personal introductions. Spies were everywhere and the authorities would pay handsomely for any information regarding the whereabouts of a Catholic minister.

'There's another path a couple of minutes north of here,' Grissold said, peering ahead to a curve in the track. The old Warwick road was rarely free of traffic. An elderly woman came into view, dragging an empty cart along the battered stonework. 'That'll take us straight to Bushwood, Father,' he added.

The priest and his servant had spent the better part of six hours trapped beneath the manor house at Baddesley Clinton. It was the closest that either of them had ever come to being caught. The two men had huddled together in the cold and the damp with no light and no provisions; and no idea how long their incarceration might last. Pursuivants had been known to lay siege to a building for three or four days. They would starve a priest out; or let him die from dehydration. Luckily, Anne Vaux had managed to convince them there was nobody there. The soldiers had left Baddesley Clinton mid-afternoon but Anne had waited a further hour before sounding the all clear, just to be on the safe side.

'Did they do much damage?' Father Sugar had asked her, as he clambered awkwardly out of the shaft.

'A little, Father. Nothing we can't put right. But I had to give them five shillings to get rid of them.'

Sugar smiled ruefully. It was often the way. 'Robert thought he recognised one of the voices,' he said. They had heard a lot of shouting and sneering from the soldiers, even from the bottom of the tunnel.

Anne Vaux nodded. 'I think it was your cousin.' She glanced at Robert Grissold, who had followed his master back up to the sacristy. 'Judging by the description you gave me. He must have had a tip off you were here.' The servant shuddered, stepping out onto the floorboards. Father Sugar gave him a hand as he steadied himself. Grissold was not the bravest of souls and his cousin Clement was particularly unpleasant. 'He's gone to search your uncle's place in Rowington. That's what he said, anyway. You'd better not go back there tonight. It won't be safe.'

'We can't stay here either,' Father Sugar said, wiping the dirt from his shirt sleeves. He paused and considered for a moment. 'I suppose we could head to Bushwood Hall.' A man named Catesby owned a small mansion house a few miles west of Rowington. The priest had met the fellow several times, though he was rarely in residence. His servants were all good Catholics, though. It would be an ideal place to hide out for a day or two. 'Robert knows the way. It shouldn't take more than an hour and a half.'

The two men had left Baddesley Clinton shortly afterwards.

It was now late afternoon. All being well they would reach the estate long before sun down, but they would have to be careful with the traffic. The Warwick road was invariably busy at this time of day. People on foot could be safely ignored, but horses might easily spell trouble. Sugar could already hear the sound of hooves approaching from the north. He pulled Grissold from the track and the two men huddled out of sight as a solitary rider trotted past – a messenger, by the look of him; a scruffy fellow on a tired horse delivering post to Rowington or Warwick.

When the man had gone, the priest came out from behind the bushes and dusted himself down. He smiled reassuringly at his servant. 'Let's get on,' he said, moving back onto the road. As he stepped forward, he caught his foot inadvertently on a jagged stone and suddenly found himself sprawling across the track.

Just then another horse galloped into view from the south.

Grissold rushed forward to help his master but the horseman had already seen them. 'Stay where you are!' the man bellowed. Other horses were following from behind; four of them, hurtling back up from the village. It was the same group of men who had raided Baddesley Clinton that morning. Sugar scrambled to his feet but the soldiers were already upon them.

The man who had cried out jumped down from his horse and quickly drew his sword. Grissold was standing stock still, paralysed with fear. Sugar made for the trees but the other pursuivants had already dismounted and he hesitated when he saw them closing in on the servant. Two of the men were now sprinting in his direction. Before the priest could turn round, they had launched themselves through the air and brought him crashing down onto the grass verge.

Sugar did not struggle as the two men secured his arms behind his back.

The leader of the group had come to a halt in front of Robert Grissold. He was a lofty, well-built fellow of about thirty, with a long black beard and a lopsided smile. Grissold recognised him at once. It was his cousin Clement.

Father Sugar was pulled onto his knees at the side of the road.

'Well, well, well.' Clement grinned sourly. 'What have we here, Robbie, my lad? This wouldn't be a priest now would it?'

One of the other soldiers had grabbed the crucifix the Father was still wearing around his neck. He waved it at the other man by way of confirmation.

'Father Sugar, I presume?' the burly pursuivant enquired with mock courtesy.

The priest said nothing.

Clement stepped forward and struck the minister a glancing blow across the cheek. 'No point denying it, Father. There'll be plenty of people who'll be able to identify you.' He shook his head. 'And here you are on the open road, spreading your lies throughout the entire county.'

'I am a man of God,' Sugar protested.

'You're a man of the Pope,' Clement snarled, turning away in disgust. 'Get him out of here. Let the magistrate deal with him.'

The other pursuivants pulled the priest to his feet and dragged him over to the horses.

Clement moved back to his cousin, who was still standing frozen to the spot in the middle of the road. 'But what about you Robbie lad?' he asked, peering over Grissold's shoulder from behind. 'What are you doing in the company of scum like that?'

'Father Sugar is my master,' Grissold stammered.

The other man shook his head in disbelief. 'You always were soft in the head.'

'He's a serving man,' Sugar protested, as one of the soldiers began tying the priest's wrists to the saddle of a horse. 'He has done you no harm. Let him go. It's me you want.'

Clement scratched his beard. 'What do you reckon, lads?' He grinned, circling around his cousin and coming to a halt directly in front of him. Grissold could feel the man's breath on his face. 'I did grow up with the little sod.'

The soldiers murmured non-committally. They were more interested in the priest.

Clement grabbed his cousin by the shoulders, spun him around and pushed him back towards the foliage at the edge of the road. 'For your mother's sake, Robbie,' he said, chuckling good-naturedly. Grissold stumbled forwards, losing his footing and falling into the undergrowth. He landed heavily in a clump of nettles and cried out as the prickles stung at his hands and face.

The pursuivants laughed.

'Go on, Robbie. Be off with you,' his cousin ordered, turning away dismissively.

Grissold swallowed hard. His hands were bright red but he dragged himself back onto his feet and wiped the mud from his breeches. 'I'll not leave the Father,' he insisted.

Clement turned back to him, baffled. 'You want to be hanged with the priest?'

Grissold closed his eyes. 'I will not abandon my master.'

The other man shrugged. 'Your choice, Robbie.' He clicked his fingers and gestured an underling forward. 'I told you he was soft in the head.'

The candles flickered in the back room of the *Duck and Drake*. Jack Wright was grinning from ear to ear. 'It must be ten years!' he exclaimed, embracing his old school friend.

'More than that,' Guido Fawkes suggested.

Jack pulled back and clutched the other man's shoulders. 'You haven't aged a day!'

Fawkes denied the assertion. 'I do have one or two battle scars…'

Jack laughed. 'Don't we all? It's good to see you, Guido.'

The two Yorkshire men fell silent for a moment.

Robert Catesby cleared his throat and invited them to join him at table. He had already asked the ostler to make sure they were not disturbed. Several large flagons of beer were laid out on the table before them. 'Can I get either of you a drink?' he asked rhetorically.

Catesby had been the first to arrive at the inn. He had brought Mr Fawkes. Tom Wintour had a room here on the first floor, but Jack had only just arrived.

Catesby had rarely seen the Yorkshireman so animated. Jack Wright was a quiet fellow, as a rule.

'How is your brother?' Fawkes asked, taking his seat. Tom passed him a tankard of ale.

'What, young Kit?' Jack grinned. 'He's fine. He said he'd met up with you in Spain. Told me all about your adventures in the Low Countries.' He chuckled. Since leaving school, Fawkes had spent the better part of a decade as a soldier, fighting for the Archduke Albert in the Spanish Netherlands. 'You must be an expert swordsman by now,' he concluded.

Fawkes disagreed. 'There isn't much swordplay on the battlefield these days. It's all pikes and muskets, I'm afraid. I rarely get the chance to practise proper swordsmanship.' He spoke with some regret. The rapier, most people agreed, was a more appropriate weapon for a gentleman than a musket or a pike.

'Remember all the scraps we had at school?' Jack asked, his eyes fogging over with the memory.

Fawkes clearly did remember. 'You always beat me,' he lamented. 'You and Robert Middleton.'

'He was better at it than I was.' Jack grinned. Then he frowned. An unwelcome memory had bubbled to the surface. 'Did you hear what happened to him?'

Fawkes nodded gravely.

'I know you two were very close.'

The soldier looked away. 'His sister wrote me a letter. Two weeks after he was hanged.' Fawkes shook his head. 'He'd only just been ordained. He said it was the happiest day of his life.'

'Poor sod.'

'He was such a gentle soul. And they hunted him down like a dog.'

Jack took a mouthful of beer. An awkward silence descended upon the room.

Tom Wintour cleared his throat. 'Jack's still a master swordsman,' he said. 'He's probably one of the best in the country now.'

Jack Wright denied this vehemently. 'Well, I have at least improved a little with age.'

'Mr Wright and Mr Percy tour the length and breadth of England picking fights with people.'

Jack beamed. 'Thomas picks the opposition and I do my best to defeat them.'

'Where *is* Mr Percy?' Catesby wondered, from the other side of the table.

The old scoundrel had known about the meeting for several days. Catesby had confirmed the time with him and had stressed the importance of the occasion. It would be the first time that all the plotters had gathered together. They would not be discussing business – a common tavern was not the place to embark on such a noble enterprise – but it would be an opportunity for everyone to meet Mr Fawkes. The pious soldier would be a vital component of the plan and it was important that the others got to know him properly.

When Percy finally deigned to put in an appearance, the group was busily discussing the insularity of the Spanish. Tom was lamenting their apparent obfuscation when the white-haired older man was shown into the chamber.

Thomas Percy frowned, catching the last few words as they faded into the background. 'Shall we always, gentlemen, talk,' he scowled, 'and never *do* anything?'

Catesby rose to his feet. 'Thomas, glad you could find the time to join us.' The other drinkers stood up to greet the new arrival. 'This is Mr Guido Fawkes. He's an old school friend of Jack and Kit's. Mr Fawkes, this is my good friend Thomas Percy.'

Percy grunted a cursory greeting. It was clear he was not in the best of moods.

'Mr Percy's my brother-in-law,' Jack declared. 'But don't hold that against me.'

Percy gestured to his friend. 'Robin, can I have a word?'

Catesby allowed himself to be led aside. At the table, Tom Wintour resumed his seat and continued the point he was making.

In the corner, Percy was as blunt as ever. 'This is really pissing me off,' he hissed. 'I've been waiting for weeks to hear back from you. You said you had a plan. Just hold fire, you said. Let me work out the details and then we'd be in it together. And then I arrive here and you're still talking about the bloody Spanish. How long am I supposed to wait? How long before we take some action? Until Parliament publishes another Bill, ordering mandatory castration?'

'Thomas, have a little faith in me. I meant what I said. I just needed a little time. But we're here now. Everything's been worked out.'

'You have a plan?'

'I have a plan. Jack and Tom approve.'

Percy glanced at his two friends. They were listening intently to something Mr Fawkes was saying. 'You've told them already?'

'We've discussed the matter in private.'

Percy's eyes began to harden. 'You've told them and not me?'

'I just needed to be sure...'

The older man pulled away angrily. 'You don't trust me! My God. After all we've been through...'

'Thomas, for goodness' sake. You're as dear to me as my own son. Of course, I trust you. I would trust you with my life.'

'So what do you need to be sure about?'

'I just…I felt we needed to be certain there were no other options.'

Percy frowned. 'You mean this ridiculous peace treaty.'

Catesby nodded.

'The Spanish won't lift a finger. They only care about themselves.'

'I had to be sure. I sent Tom to speak with De Velasco in Flanders. But it was a complete waste of time.'

'I could have told you that for nothing.'

'Tom wanted to be sure. *I* wanted to be sure.'

'Well, I'm glad we've satisfied you're conscience. Now perhaps we can start doing something ourselves.'

'That is my intention.'

'And about bloody time! So tell me. What is this wonderful plan of yours?'

Catesby raised a finger. 'Not here.'

'What?'

'I told you before. This is just a friendly get-together. We'll discuss things in detail at the weekend.'

'Oh, for – '

'It's for the best, believe me. I want everyone to swear an oath. Of secrecy.'

'So you really *don't* trust me.'

'Thomas. It's not you. It's all of us here.' Catesby glanced back at the table.

'Mr Fawkes, you mean?'

'Exactly. He seems a reliable fellow and Jack vouches for him. But an oath will underline the importance of what we're about to do.'

'We can take an oath here.'

Catesby shook his head. 'I want to do it properly, on the Sabbath. Then we can consecrate the whole enterprise by taking Holy Communion. We are doing this for the right reasons, Thomas. The sacrament will help to underline that.'

Percy let out a growl of frustration.

'Come on!' Catesby teased. 'It's only a few days. We take the oath, go to Mass, and then all will be revealed.'

'This Sunday?'

'I swear.'

Percy looked away in disgust. 'All right. In three days.' He closed his eyes. 'But this had better be good.'

Chapter Six

Catesby swallowed the thin wafer Father John Gerard placed in his mouth and took a sip of wine from the silver goblet. He closed his eyes. The liquid felt warm in his throat. Consecrated wine had an unusual taste. There was something reassuring in that. Catesby was eating the flesh and drinking the blood of the Lord Jesus Christ; no amount of repetition could alter his sense of awe at this everyday miracle. He had the greatest respect for the many priests, Father Gerard among them, who regularly conducted Holy Communion. It was a dangerous service. Catholic rites had been outlawed in the time of Elizabeth and the penalties were severe.

Catesby had a particular affection for Father Gerard. He vividly remembered the time, many years before, when the priest had been caught and imprisoned in the Tower of London. The government had been determined to discover the whereabouts of the Jesuit Superior, Father Henry Garnet. When Gerard had refused to help them, the priest was put to torture. He had kept the secret, though, and soon after had managed to escape from the Tower. Catesby had given him sanctuary at his house in Uxbridge and a strong bond had formed between the two men.

Father Gerard was currently residing at the home of a Mrs Herbert, near St. Clement's Church. It was a stone's throw from London Bridge. Before the sermon, the five plotters had met up to swear their oath. Mrs Herbert had happily provided a quiet chamber on the ground floor and had promised to call them when Father Gerard was about to start the service.

Percy was impatient to get on with things. The white-haired rascal grabbed the prayer book as soon as Catesby had produced it. Taking the book in his right hand, he knelt down and read out the oath. "'I swear by the blessed Trinity and by the Sacrament I am about to receive, never to disclose the secret matter proposed to me this day, nor to rest from the execution of it unless given leave by others here present.'"

Fawkes followed Percy, repeating the same words with quiet solemnity. Then came Jack Wright, Tom Wintour and finally Catesby himself. Of the five, only Fawkes and Percy remained in ignorance of the plot. But that would soon change.

As Catesby finished swearing the oath, the bells of St. Clement's chimed the hour and Mrs Herbert knocked gently to inform them that Mass was about to begin.

Catesby could not have timed it better.

The men went up together to join Father Gerard and several servants who had assembled to hear the service. Taking Communion now sanctified the oath and legitimised the plans the group were about to discuss. The five would-be plotters knelt in a short row as Father Gerard completed the ceremony.

The priest knew nothing of Catesby's embryonic plot. It was better this way. Father Gerard would not accept the necessity of what they were planning. Better to keep quiet for now, until the details had been finalised. But the Church would have to be told eventually.

Percy was last in line to receive the sacrament. Catesby glanced across and saw that the older man's attention was beginning to waver. Catesby grimaced. Percy was allowing his understandable curiosity to distract him from proper contemplation of the Eucharist. The man had never learnt the virtue of patience. He had too much energy for his own good, though Catesby did not doubt his piety. Percy was a good Catholic and a loyal friend. His energy would serve the plot well, if it could be properly harnessed.

Tom Wintour was kneeling to their right, his short, solid frame bent forward in gentle meditation. Tom had been a bit of a wild child, too, in his younger days, though it seemed scarcely credible now. Catesby smiled at the thought. Tom Wintour, the dissipated youth. He had certainly strayed from the path of righteousness – drinking heavily and consorting with prostitutes – but he had found his way again in his late twenties and the light of religion had calmed him, giving him a new maturity.

After the sermon, Catesby exchanged a few pleasant words with Father Gerard and then slipped back down to the private chamber Mrs Herbert had provided. Percy was already there. Jack and Tom arrived with Mr Fawkes. Catesby let these two expound the details to the newcomer, whilst he himself outlined the plan to his older friend.

Percy's eyes widened quickly. 'I take my hat of to you, Mr Catesby,' he breathed, when the other had finished. 'There was I, all set to murder one individual and all the while you were plotting to blow up half of London.'

'Just Parliament, Thomas. Just the vipers in their nest.'

'It's an audacious scheme,' Fawkes admitted, across the room. 'But I think it could be made to work.'

'We'll give it our best shot,' Jack agreed.

Tom Wintour, as ever, was cautious. 'There are a lot of details that would need to be worked out,' he said. Catesby was relying on his cousin to identify any flaws in the plan. The man possessed a remarkably logical mind. 'For a start, will we be able to rent a house close enough to Parliament?'

'I made a few enquiries while you were abroad,' Catesby said. He had scouted the area during the State Opening of Parliament. 'There's one house that seems ideal. It's in Parliament Place, directly adjacent to the Upper Chamber. I've looked into the leasing. It's currently rented to a Mr Henry Ferrers. If we could obtain that lease from him, everything would fall into place.'

Percy raised a hand. 'I know Henry Ferrers. He's an antiquarian. Dreadfully dull man. Rented Baddesley Clinton to the Vauxs a decade back. Didn't make much of an impression on me, I have to say. But I can't imagine much difficulty brow-beating him into giving up the lease. He is a Catholic, after all.'

'Do you know who *owns* the building?' Tom asked.

Catesby nodded. 'John Whynniard. The Keeper of the King's Wardrobe. He owns a few properties around there. I can't see that he would object to Mr Percy as a tenant.'

At that, Percy raised an eyebrow. 'You want my name on the rental forms?'

'It's all right, Thomas. I don't expect you to pay for it.'

'I'm more than willing…'

'It makes sense for you to do it,' Catesby explained patiently. 'I already have the place in Lambeth. It might raise awkward questions if I was seen to be renting two properties in close proximity to the Houses of Parliament; even if they are on opposite sides of the river.'

'Robin's right,' Tom agreed. 'It would attract less attention if *you* took out the lease. And if Mr Fawkes acted on your behalf, that would minimise any suspicion. Guido has been out of circulation for so long, nobody would recognise him.' That was part of the reason Mr Fawkes had been brought into the conspiracy in the first place.

'I have no objection to that, gentlemen,' the Yorkshireman agreed.

Jack scratched his head. 'He's not completely unknown. People might recognise the name, if not the face.'

'I could adopt an alias,' Fawkes suggested. 'Perhaps I could act as Mr Percy's servant.'

'So long as you don't expect me to pay you!' Percy exclaimed. Catesby rolled his eyes and Percy looked away. 'I agree. It's a good idea.'

'What name would you use?' Jack asked his friend.

Fawkes considered for a minute. 'Mr…Johnson? John Johnson?'

Percy snorted. 'Well, it's certainly nondescript. All right, Mr Johnson, consider yourself under my employ.'

'It does mean a considerable risk,' Tom pointed out.

Fawkes nodded. 'I realise that, Mr Wintour. But I did have an idea what I might be letting myself in for. And the oath is sworn.'

'All right,' Tom agreed, clutching his hands together. 'Assuming the house is rented, the next obstacle is acquiring the powder.'

'I think I can take care of that,' Catesby said. 'A lot of the mills are over-producing at the moment. They're happy not to ask too many questions if you pay them well enough.'

'Who'll provide the funding?' Tom asked.

'I'll cover it for now.'

'Can you afford it?'

'The authorities haven't managed to rob me of my entire estate thus far.'

'I'll chip in too,' Percy added, a little resentful of the earlier remarks. 'Where I can. I might be able to divert a bit of rent money at some stage.' Percy collected rents on behalf of his patron, the Earl of Northumberland. It was almost expected that some of the money would go astray.

'And then there's the matter of the tunnel,' Tom said.

Catesby looked to Mr Fawkes. 'I gather from Tom that you have some experience in this area?'

Fawkes nodded. 'A little. Munitions are more my field. But I do have some experience, yes.' Mining had long been a staple feature of siege warfare. Fawkes leant forward in his chair. 'Gentlemen, there are three main difficulties in laying down a mine. The first problem is waste disposal. We need to get rid of the earth and the rocks.'

'If we get the Whynniard house, that shouldn't be a problem,' Catesby responded. 'It's about forty yards from the river. We can dump stuff there during the night. Nobody will see.'

'The second problem is noise. We'll be using shovels and picks and we won't be digging at any real depth. Therefore, we will have to find some way to muffle the sound.'

'Or some excuse to explain it away,' Percy suggested.

'The third and largest problem will be drainage. Whenever you dig a tunnel, especially close to a river, water will always seep in and fill up the hole. We need to find some way to remove it.'

Catesby waved the problem away with his hands. 'We can deal with that,' he insisted.

Tom was less certain. 'It might be a problem with the powder though. If it gets damp, we won't be able to set it off.'

'The powder won't be stored in the tunnel. I'll stockpile the supplies at Lambeth. Then we can keep it in the house and move it through as late as we possibly can. My main concern, Mr Fawkes, is whether the idea is practical in principle?'

Fawkes sat back. 'It's certainly possible.'

Percy grinned suddenly. 'I can't believe we're actually planning this. Just the *scale* of it.' The older man could barely contain his enthusiasm. 'We'll blow the beggars right back to Scotland.'

'I told you to have faith in me,' Catesby chided.

'Robin, how could I have ever doubted you?

Chapter Seven

The black stallion broke into an impressive gallop.

Thomas Percy lashed at the animal with a leather whip, but still he could not get it up to full speed. It was not the horse's fault. There were too many carts and pedestrians cluttering up the roads out of London. And no matter how hard he yelled at them, nobody ever seemed to want to get out of the way. Percy whipped the animal again and kicked hard with his heels.

It was better up north, he reflected. A man could gallop for hours along the border without encountering another rider. And Percy would be up there soon enough, now that his business in London was concluded.

It had not taken much effort to persuade Mr Henry Ferrers to give up the lease. The mention of Percy's patron, the Earl of Northumberland, had been more than sufficient. Mr Ferrers was anxious to do anything to assist such a high-ranking individual. In some ways, Percy was disappointed. He had had a lot of experience in persuading people to leave their homes and it was much more enjoyable when they tried to be difficult.

Percy's new servant, Mr John Johnson, had gone to collect the key from the landlord, Mr Whynniard. The rent had been set at twelve pounds per annum. This was a bit steep, but Percy had not been in a position to bargain. In any case, it was Catesby who was spending the money.

Mr Fawkes would look after the property for the time being. Percy had other business.

Syon House was about eight miles from the centre of London. It took him less than forty minutes to reach the home of his patron. A two hundred acre estate had been carved out on the north bank of the Thames. Percy was a frequent visitor here. It was the ideal place to discuss business. The Earl of Northumberland had sent him a summons the previous afternoon; a brief and uninformative note. Presumably, Northumberland wished to discuss his imminent departure. Percy would be heading north in a few days, to collect the rents on behalf of his employer. He was looking forward to it.

It had been nine years since Sir Henry Percy had conferred on him the role of Constable of Alnwick Castle. The appointment had been an act of pure nepotism. Percy was a distant cousin and it was expected that the Earl would show his kinsman some kindness. Percy had repaid the favour by applying himself rigorously to the job. Over the years, it had been a profitable enterprise for both of them. Northumberland was not interested in the niceties of the law. His only concern was the extraction of money from his tenants and Percy had always been given full authority to use whatever methods he saw fit. He would evict troublemakers on the slightest excuse – regardless of whether he was legally entitled to do so – and was more than happy to use force whenever he felt it was required. It was a job that could have been invented for him and in the summer months, when London was best avoided, it was the perfect activity for a man who was still very much the poor relation.

'Ah, Thomas!' Northumberland exclaimed as Percy was shown in to the reception hall. 'I wanted to speak to you, before you left.' The Earl was a stern, unfriendly man of about forty. He was softly spoken and had a distracted air which seldom endeared him to others. 'A position has become vacant which I think might suit you.'

Percy was intrigued. 'My lord?'

'In addition to your current duties, of course.' He paused. Though not unintelligent, Northumberland often needed time to collect his thoughts. 'I'm in need of another Gentleman Pensioner,' he continued, at length.

So that was it. Percy could not stop the smile from forming on his face. 'And you want *me* to take the position?'

'You'd be the ideal man,' the Earl insisted. 'It's about time you moved up in the world.'

'I don't know what to say.' Percy was genuinely flattered. It was an honour to be asked. More than that, it was an unparalleled opportunity. The Gentleman Pensioners were the King's ceremonial bodyguard. Joining the band would place Percy within a few yards of the King on almost a daily basis – and with a huge pike in his hand. Outright assassination would be easier than ever.

Percy grinned. Then he frowned. Bloody Robin, he thought. Why did he have to come up with such a good alternative plan…?

'You would have to reside in London for a part of each year,' Northumberland continued, softly. 'You already have lodgings, don't you?'

'I've...just rented a new house in Westminster,' Percy admitted. Being a Pensioner would provide the perfect excuse, even if the property had been leased in advance of the appointment.

There was just one problem. Public servants had to swear an oath, proclaiming the supremacy of the Protestant Faith. It was mandatory for anyone taking up public office. Catesby had dropped out of university specifically to avoid the problem and Percy was not about to compromise his religious beliefs either, no matter how advantageous the new position might be to Catesby's latest scheme.

'My lord, can I be frank?' Percy looked down. For the sake of the Earl, he would have to phrase his concerns more delicately than usual. 'I wouldn't feel comfortable accepting this position if it necessitates the renunciation of my faith.'

Northumberland bit his lower lip. 'I understand your concern, Thomas.' He waved a hand dismissively. 'However, I think we can dispense with the oath on this occasion. I do have full authority where the Gentleman Pensioners are concerned.' Northumberland's appointment as captain of the brigade had been seen as extremely positive by the Catholic community, at a time when there had still been some optimism surrounding the new King. Though the Earl had publicly renounced Catholicism, it was widely felt that he was still a Catholic at heart. No doubt this was why he was prepared to waive the oath for the sake of his cousin.

'I am very grateful, my lord.'

Northumberland put a hand to his ear. 'What was that?'

Percy raised his voice. 'I'm very grateful, my lord!' The Earl – on top of his many other faults – was also a little deaf.

'So you'll accept the position?'

Percy bowed his head. 'With eternal gratitude.'

Northumberland managed a smile. 'Good. That's settled then.'

The noose had all but garrotted Father John Sugar. The mild-mannered priest had been cut down from the gibbet and carried fully conscious to the quartering block with the rope still in place around his neck. Only when the man's head had been hacked from his body by a particularly clumsy executioner did the twitching stop and the rope fall away to the floor.

The hangman lifted the decapitated head aloft. '*This*...is the head of a traitor!' he proclaimed. The crowd cheered enthusiastically.

But not everyone on Gallows Hill was cheering.

In a gold-trimmed doublet and long purple cloak, Sir Everard Digby murmured a silent prayer for Father John Sugar. The middle-aged priest had shown great courage and dignity on the scaffold. The least Digby could do was to whisper a few words to see him on his way. Not that the Father really needed any help. The man had stood confidently before the crowd, gazing up at the early morning sky. 'I shall be up there soon,' he had said, as the sunlight flickered across his pale, calm face.

Digby had stopped at Warwick on his way home for the summer. It had been a relief to get out of the capital. The young knight had been growing increasingly disillusioned with events at court. Every day seemed to herald the introduction of yet more anti-Catholic legislation. But there was some good news: his wife Mary had written to tell him that she was expecting another child and he was eager to return home, to make sure that she was being properly looked after.

He had put up at an inn on the outskirts of Warwick and when he had heard about the hangings taking place that morning he had felt duty bound to attend. He could not allow a man of God to go to his death without at least one friendly face in the crowd.

Sugar's body was removed from the platform and the gibbet was quickly prepared for the next victim. By now, some of the crowd were beginning to drift away. They had come to see the priest and the prospect of watching a servant being garrotted was not enough to keep their interest. A few dozen spectators remained, however, happy to witness any disembowelment so long as it was unpleasant. They looked on with barely disguised glee as Mr Robert Grissold was marched before them onto the platform.

Grissold was a slender, nervous fellow in his late twenties. Digby had heard all about him from the customers at the inn. Grissold was of yeoman stock, they said, not a gentleman like

Sugar. He had been captured on the road near Baddesley Clinton. The magistrate had offered the servant his freedom, but only if he renounced Catholicism. This was common practise – there was little point in hanging the hired help, after all – but to his credit Grissold had refused. And now he would die alongside his master.

Digby admired the man's courage and hoped he would have the strength to see it through. People often took fright at the sight of the gallows and it was difficult to predict how anyone would react when the time came, especially a serving man.

Grissold had seen the rope that was being prepared for him. The thick hemp was lying flat at the base of the scaffold. This was the moment of truth. Digby crossed himself mentally. But there was no need to worry. Grissold bent over and picked up the rope. He moved across the platform and gently dipped the end of the noose in some of the blood now congealing on the quartering block. Another sign of solidarity with his master.

Digby quietly nodded his approval.

Grissold walked over to the gibbet. The executioner – a bluff, ugly fellow in a blood stained tunic – fastened the rope around his neck. Grissold took a step up onto the ladder and began to address the crowd. His voice was thin and uncertain. 'Good people, I ask you to bear witness…'

'Speak up!' some oaf yelled from the crowd.

'I ask you to bear witness,' Grissold stammered, 'that I die here not for theft or murder, but for my conscience.' His voice was barely audible now. The man was trembling visibly, but he forced himself to continue. 'I would like to forgive all those who have persecuted me and to forgive my executioner, who is merely carrying out his duty. If I have offended God then I ask His pardon and the pardon of any who have suffered at my hands.' He looked across nervously at the quartering block, where Father John Sugar had met his end a few moments before. 'And now I commend myself to the mercy and protection of our Lord Jesus Christ.'

'You won't be seeing him where you're going!' somebody else yelled. 'Bloody heathen!'

Grissold moved up the ladder.

The crowd had quietened, savouring every last moment.

Digby looked on in horror. It had been bad enough watching a man of God go to his death; but to see it done to some poor servant who had never hurt anybody…it was sickening. He steeled himself, determined to see it through to the end.

The executioner pushed Grissold from the ladder. The man's eyes bulged and his body danced as he struggled for air against the tightening noose. Digby did not allow himself to blink. There was a look of sheer terror on Grissold's narrow face. It barely diminished as the seconds turned into minutes and the gruesome dance continued. Even in the face of certain death his body fought for its life, thrashing left and right. But gradually the muffled cries began to subside and soon all that remained was the occasional awkward twitch. At last he died, though the broken body continued to swing beneath the crude wooden scaffold.

Digby said a quick prayer under his breath. He kept his face calm, but his body was shaking with barely suppressed anger. This was the truth of Protestant England. This was the reality behind the King's words in Parliament.

He took a lungful of air and quickly regained his composure. The remnants of the crowd were beginning to drift now, their blood lust satiated, at least for the time being. Digby turned away as they cut the limp body down and carried it across to the butchering block. At least the hangman had had the decency to let Grissold die by the noose.

The servant was now a martyr and would meet his maker with his head held high.

The same could not be said for his executioners.

Chapter Eight

'I wonder if I might say a few words,' Father Henry Garnet asked, clearing his throat politely. He unfolded a letter lying on the edge of the table and rose to his feet to address the other diners. 'I have received some correspondence from Father Claudio Aquaviva in Rome, which I would like to share with you.'

Robert Catesby downed the last of the sherry and focused his attention on the Jesuit priest. Servants were clearing away the remains of dinner. It had been an exceptional meal. A wide variety of meats and fresh vegetables had been provided for the honoured guests, alongside a copious supply of sack. It was rare for so many members of the Society of Jesus to be gathered together in one place and it was right to celebrate the occasion.

Catesby's presence amongst the priests was a happy accident. He had come to White Webbs to visit his cousin Anne. It had been the Jesuits who had insisted he join them at table. Catesby felt honoured to be dining in such august company.

He glanced around the table. The priests were looking up expectantly at Father Henry. The faces were familiar, though none of the men wore priestly robes. A stranger at table would not have taken them to be holy men at all. The Jesuits knew the value of discretion.

Father Henry opened a leather pouch and drew out a small pair of spectacles, which he perched on the bridge of his nose. He was a thin-faced man in his late forties. His beard was grey and rectangular; his hair closely cropped. Catesby had known him for many years and was somewhat in awe of the man. Father Henry glanced through the letter in his bony hands and provided a quick summary of the contents.

'His Holiness has expressed his devout desire that English Catholics should live in peace and accept the authority of our sovereign King James. He is particularly keen that we, the members of the Society of Jesus, should make this clear to the Catholic community at large.' Father Henry glanced up. He had become England's Superior of the Society of Jesus some twenty years earlier, when his predecessor, Father William Weston, had been captured and imprisoned. At that time, there had been few

Jesuits in England. Now, thanks in part to Father Henry's efforts, scores of Jesuit priests were in hiding across the country. Half a dozen were sat listening respectfully to him even now.

None of them had yet heard about the execution of Father John Sugar.

Henry Garnet removed his reading glasses and looked up at the other diners. He was warming to his theme now and had disregarded Aquaviva's letter. 'We as guardians of the True Faith in England have been expressly forbidden from involving ourselves in any action which might disrupt the legitimate government of this country. It is up to us to ensure that this injunction is clear in the minds of every Catholic under our care, so that we may continue to exercise the patience and restraint that our circumstances demand. The ultimate conversion of our King and this country to the Catholic faith must be left to Providence and the hand of God.'

Catesby listened to the priest's words with growing disbelief. He had always admired Father Henry but it was wrong of the man to present this argument as any kind of papal declaration. It was the opinion of one man in Rome and a man furthermore who clearly had no understanding of the persecution English Catholics were having to endure. Catesby had long been deferential to the priesthood. They were better educated and far wiser than he was. In any other circumstances, he would not have dared to speak a word in opposition. But this time, as the Jesuits began to rise from the dinner table, Catesby could not hold his tongue. 'There are good men,' he said, doing his best to keep his voice level, 'throughout this kingdom who have grown tired with the treatment they have had to endure. Such men will not readily accept the teaching of restraint.'

Father Henry frowned, surprised to hear him talking in such a forthright manner. Catesby was renowned for his reticence in the company of priests.

'They are asking,' he continued, 'if there is any authority on Earth that can take away from them their natural right to defend themselves from the aggression of others.'

The other Jesuits, who had been moving away from the table, held back at the sound of his voice. Father Oswald Tesimond – a large, ruddy-faced gentleman who served as Catesby's confessor – was paying particular attention.

'They speak scornfully of a doctrine which robs Catholics of spirit and energy, leaving them weak and vulnerable to the predations of the Protestant extremists. Our situation, they say, is worse than slavery. Our peaceful endurance of such atrocities seems, to such men, beyond any rational belief.' Catesby's voice had been growing steadily louder. 'Why else do our enemies treat us with such contempt? Why else do they refer to us as "God's lunatics"?'

Father Henry placed a gentle hand on Catesby's shoulder. 'It is a sign of our strength, Robin. They may persecute us, they may even kill us, but they can never destroy our faith. We will endure, my dear Robin, and we will prevail, so long as we do not allow ourselves to be distracted. That is the will of God.'

Catesby looked down at his feet and nodded reluctantly.

'Come, let's go through to the garden,' Father Henry suggested. 'I was planning to play some draughts this afternoon. Would you care to join me?'

'Why not?' Catesby did his best to smile. It had been foolish to lose his temper. He should not have spoken out, not in these circumstances. 'I'll be out in a minute.'

He stood and watched as Father Henry left the dining hall. Father Oswald Tesimond stood for a moment at his side. Tesimond was closer to Catesby's own age. 'You've changed, Robin,' he declared. 'Since your wife died.'

Catesby could not deny it.

'I know the memory is still painful to you. These things never really go away.'

Catesby gripped his hands together tightly. He looked down at the golden crucifix hanging from his neck. 'I'm grateful, in a way. I was too distracted in those days. But when…Catherine died, it put things in perspective. It forced me to decide what was really important. It's a lesson I've never forgotten, Father.' He lifted the crucifix to his mouth and kissed it gently. 'Every day not spent furthering the cause of Catholicism in this country is a day wasted.'

'You're a good man, Robin. But you can't take the problems of the whole world upon your shoulders.'

Catesby looked down at the floor. 'I shouldn't have spoken to the Father in that way.'

'Father Henry is a man of great wisdom. He'll understand.'

'He's been a light for all of us for as long as I can remember.' Catesby closed his eyes. 'I just get so wound up sometimes. When people go on and on about *perseverance*. Does the Father really expect us to sit back and do nothing? To waste our entire lives just waiting for things to change all by themselves?'

'We must trust in the wisdom of God. Father Henry is right about that, Robin. He sees these things more clearly than we do. He has the benefit of many years of experience. We could learn a lot from dear Henry. You must have *faith*, Robin. Faith above all else.'

The horses' hooves thudded across the dry stone as Guido Fawkes and Jack Wright made their way slowly northwards. It was a warm July afternoon. Clouds were gathering in the sky above them but the threat of rain seemed remote.

The two friends had been riding solidly for four days and the journey was proving interminable. The roads seemed to deteriorate the further north they travelled but the terrain was growing more familiar now and their destination could not be far away. It had been years since Fawkes had last come this far north but one did not forget the countryside of ones youth. He had been away from home too long.

His mother still lived in York, not far from where he had grown up. Fawkes had not seen her in over a decade, though they had written on occasion. His father Edward had died when he was eight years old and he had lost contact with his two sisters. His mother had later remarried but he had not taken to his step-father and had spent the last ten years abroad fighting for the Archduke Albert. After his return to England in April, Fawkes had scarcely been out of London. But now Parliament had ended, the Whynniard house had been properly locked up and it was better for everyone if he left the capital. There was no point compromising his anonymity this early in the proceedings. Jack had been heading north anyway to visit his wife and the time had seemed right for a family reunion.

The jovial swordsman had pulled ahead slightly as the lane meandered upwards and Fawkes trotted to catch up. At the top of the hill, a corpse was swinging from a crude gibbet. Jack was staring thoughtfully at the body, which had clearly been hanging there for some time. Flies were swarming around the desiccated corpse. Another victim of the King's justice. Perhaps this one deserved it. Who could tell?

Fawkes drew alongside and the two men continued on down the hill.

'Did you hear they executed another priest?' Jack asked, breaking the long silence. 'John Sugar. At Warwick, just recently.'

Fawkes had heard about it. 'It's a bad business,' he said. 'Killing a clergyman like that.' No-one could object to the hanging of criminals. A thief or a murderer had to be punished. It said so in the Bible: an eye for an eye. But executing a priest just for ministering to his flock – that was not justice; it was cold-blooded murder. 'I've witnessed some terrible things,' he said. 'On the battlefield. Friends killed. Bodies being ripped apart. But that's war. You're a soldier. It's *necessary*.' He shook his head. 'But to kill a man who never hurt anyone. A man following his conscience in the eyes of the Lord. It's barbaric.'

Jack nodded. 'It's happening all over, unfortunately.'

More blood on the hand of King James. Fawkes grimaced. But what could anyone expect from a Scot? He had been one of the few people who had objected to the accession of King James from the start, regardless of the man's attitude towards Catholics. There was something fundamentally wrong in placing a foreigner on the throne of England. And particularly a Scotsman. Fawkes had never liked Scotsmen and he had met his fair share of them during his childhood in Yorkshire. He had resolved to do something about the new King long before meeting up with Tom Wintour, but like Tom Fawkes' instincts had led him towards the Spanish. Now Catesby had offered them an alternative vision and Fawkes had grabbed it with both hands.

'At least we have a date now,' Jack said. Parliament had closed at the beginning of July and would not open again until the Seventh of February. 'That gives us six months to prepare.'

'I gave Mr Catesby a list of tools and essential equipment, before we left. But I fear he does not fully appreciate the difficulties involved in digging a mine.'

Jack frowned. 'Can't be that difficult to dig a hole, can it?'

'You'd be surprised. It can take many days, weeks even, depending on the type of earth. And in London we'll be dealing mostly with rock and stone. And it is hard physical work, too, of a kind Mr Percy and the others will not be used to.'

'We'll manage,' Jack stated confidently. He grinned. 'You never know, we might strike gold while we're down there.'

'It is not a subject for frivolity. Digging a tunnel can be an extremely dangerous venture. I have seen men die in such circumstances. The walls cave in, the roof collapses. It is not a pleasant way to meet your maker.'

'That's why we've got you to help us.'

'Even the most experienced of men can misjudge the stresses involved. Tunnelling is a difficult business. It only takes one mistake to kill a man.'

Jack shrugged. 'Still. Better than dying on the end of a rope…'

The countryside around Coldham Hall was flat but colourful. Catesby had borrowed a horse from the stables of Ambrose Rookwood and the two men had spent the afternoon out riding. It was a warm, autumnal evening but a gentle breeze served to cool the two horsemen as they raced across the Suffolk countryside. Catesby had seldom ridden a finer horse – Ambrose's stables were justly famous throughout England – but he had trouble keeping pace with his younger friend. Ambrose Rookwood was an expert rider and took pleasure in outpacing even the most accomplished of his companions.

Catesby had an ulterior motive in visiting Coldham Hall. 'It isn't illegal,' he protested, after broaching the matter directly. 'And the Spanish need all the help they can get.' The two of them had arrived back at Ambrose's lavish country house and were leading their horses into the stables.

Ambrose stifled a laugh. 'You are joking, surely.' The gifted horseman was a few years younger than Catesby and several inches shorter. He was a cheerful fellow, with an easy going manner and an unfortunate taste in clothes. His brightly coloured doublet and fine silk hose never failed to catch the eye.

'It's nothing to laugh about,' Catesby said. 'Why shouldn't I take a regiment to Flanders?'

A groom was waiting ahead of them to tether the horses, but Ambrose waved the man aside. He liked to take personal care of the animals. 'You really want to be a soldier?' he asked, his voice scarred with gentle scepticism.

'Why not? I've always been attracted to the idea.' That much, at least, was true. Catesby had often thought about going abroad and fighting with his fellow Catholics as Mr Fawkes had done. But somehow leaving behind a Protestant England had always felt like a betrayal. Now, of course, he had no intention of doing any such thing. But it was a useful smokescreen. 'And we are at peace,' he pointed out. 'Why shouldn't we give military assistance to our new allies?' The King had given his consent, albeit reluctantly. With the peace treaty now formally signed, the sovereign could hardly refuse.

'So you'll be fighting with Archduke Albert?' Ambrose guessed, tying up his horse and patting it gently on the nose. The animal shuffled across to a water trough and began to slurp at the murky liquid.

Catesby glanced across the stables. The smell of manure and fresh hay pervaded the yard. 'If I can get enough men together. And supplies. I'll need lots of horses, of course. Muskets. Shot. Plenty of powder.'

'I can help you with the horses,' Ambrose volunteered, spreading an arm to indicate the stables as a whole. 'And the powder, as a matter of fact.' He moved over to Catesby's horse, taking hold of the reins. The animal allowed itself to be led across to the far side of the yard.

Catesby smiled inwardly. That was exactly the response he had been after. He watched as his friend carefully tethered the horse. Ambrose, he knew, had connections to a prominent powder mill in the Midlands.

'It won't be cheap, of course,' he said. 'How much were you thinking of?'

'Well. About four hundredweight.'

Ambrose started. 'Good God! Are you planning to invade France as well?'

'No. But I want a good supply of munitions.' There was no point in ordering small amounts. Catesby would use a number of suppliers, but each would have to provide a substantial quantity of gunpowder. The House of Lords was, after all, an enormous building and the quality of powder could vary considerably from mill to mill. The more of it that was stored away, the greater the probability of success. 'I don't want the men under-equipped. I'll pay whatever's required.'

'Oh, I'm sure I can get hold of it. Now the war's over there's bound to be a surplus. Just give me a bit of time. When were you intending to leave?'

'Not until next year,' Catesby said. He could continue to use the camouflage of a Spanish regiment for some months, acquiring various resources from different, unwitting assistants. By the time anyone began to question its non-appearance, the plot would already have reached its climax. 'I'll probably store the powder in London,' he added, 'if you can get it there.'

'That shouldn't be a problem.'

'And if you can keep your eye out for more horses as well, I'd be very grateful.'

'Certainly.' Ambrose shook his head, perplexed. 'I never imagined you becoming a soldier.' He laughed. 'So what rank will you take?'

Catesby grinned. 'I think a captain will suffice. I'm considering asking Sir Charles Percy to command the regiment.'

'Northumberland's brother? I'm sure he'd jump at the chance. Shall we head back inside?'

Catesby nodded. The two men left the stables and crossed the courtyard towards the main house.

Catesby felt a stab of guilt about lying to his friend. Ambrose was a good man and did not deserve to be deceived in this way; but the deception was necessary. The fewer people who knew about the plot, the less chance there was of discovery. And Catesby had not been entirely dishonest. The gunpowder would certainly be used for the furtherance of Catholic interests.

He smiled. He had the men. He had the house. And now he had the powder. Everything was falling into place.

Part Two
The Tunnel

"…they worked by day, digging out the earth from the mine…"
– Father Oswald Tesimond, Narrative

Chapter Nine

The streets around Parliament were swamped with pedestrians. It was early October. Now that the cold weather was on its way, people were returning to the capital city. Traders had reopened their shops, coaches were rattling through the streets with their usual abandon and the taverns were filled with drunken customers.

Guido Fawkes had taken a boat across the Thames.

The muscular ex-soldier was returning from Uxbridge after an extended meeting with Robert Catesby. As autumn drew on, the plotters were becoming anxious to start work on the mine. Catesby had already arranged for tunnelling equipment and other supplies to be stored at his residence in Lambeth. The matter of the gunpowder was also in hand. All that remained was to check up on the accommodation in Westminster.

The boatman pulled up at the quayside and Mr Fawkes handed the fellow a few pennies. He jumped from the boat and made his way up the steps towards Parliament Place.

The house was situated less than two minute's walk from the river bank. It had been left empty for the duration of the summer. The metropolis was invariably deserted during the hottest months, for fear of plague. A particularly nasty outbreak the previous year was fresh in people's minds. Now, though, in autumn, the capital was coming back to life. It was the perfect time to return.

Fawkes had not stayed long in York. His mother had been in good health but she had been caught up in her own affairs and he had been too distracted to show much more than polite interest. His spirits had been buoyed, however, by a visit from Jack's younger brother Kit. The two men had been in the same year at St Peter's School and their shared reminiscences had proved to be the highlight of the trip. Fawkes had returned south in a considerably better frame of mind.

Arriving at the front door, he reached down and fumbled for his key. There were people about, but no-one was paying him any attention. Not that it mattered if they did. What could be more natural than Mr John Johnson returning to London to open up his master's house in readiness for the gentleman's return to Westminster?

Fawkes was getting used to playing the servant. It was no great stretch. He had actually been a footman, briefly, in his youth and a decade in the army had made him comfortable taking orders. He was no commoner, however. His father had been a Court Registrar in York and he had been a lieutenant in the army of Archduke Albert. At the time of his resignation, Fawkes was on the verge of being promoted to captain. Not bad for a thirty-four year old free school lad from Stonegate.

He inserted the key into the lock and frowned. The wooden doorway was not secured. It was not even properly closed. Somebody was inside the house. He blinked, nervously. Only one other person had a key to the door – the landlord, Mr Whynniard. Perhaps he was here, looking over the place for some reason of his own. But there were voices coming from within the property; several voices in fact. Cautiously, Fawkes pushed open the door and stepped into the hallway.

The voices grew louder. An argument was taking place; some kind of debate. One man – a well-educated fellow by the sound of it – was pontificating noisily. He had a deep, gravely voice and a peculiarly strangulated accent. It sounded almost Scottish.

Fawkes clutched his hands nervously. He hated the Scots.

The voice was definitely coming from the living room. Other voices were murmuring agreement. There had to be half a dozen people in there, at least.

Fawkes reached for the door handle. He had no idea what to expect, but he quietly pushed open the door.

It was not a large room. In truth, it was not a large house. A heavy oak table dominated the interior. A fire was blazing in the hearth. Tobacco smoke filled the air. And sat around the table in a disorganised muddle were a dozen or more bewigged gentlemen. Lords. Peers of the Realm.

The babble of noise ceased abruptly. The men turned to stare at Mr Fawkes. For a moment, there was silence. Fawkes felt like an intruder in his own house. Then one of the gentleman rose angrily to his feet. 'Who the devil are you?' he demanded, in a thick Scottish brogue. 'What are you doing here?' It was the man Fawkes had heard speaking a few moments before.

For a second, the ex-soldier was lost for words. A dozen Members of the Upper Chamber were staring at him, waiting for a response. 'I...my lords, I...forgive me. I hadn't...'

'Who are you?' the Scottish man demanded again.

'John Johnson, my lord. My master rents this house. I wasn't expecting...'

'Your master?' another fellow exclaimed. 'Ah, that explains it.' Judging by the accent, this one was also from north of the border. 'Well, I'm afraid you're out of luck, Mr Johnson.' The man sat back in his chair. 'We've requisitioned the place. Temporarily, you understand. Mr Whynniard has kindly allowed us to hold our discussions here. Bit of a conference, you know. There wasn't really anywhere else available.'

Fawkes gaped at them. It took a few moments for him to digest the information. He knew the house was sometimes used as a robing room when Parliament was in session. Mr Whynniard had warned him of that when he had first collected the key. But the landlord had said nothing about the place being used out of season.

'What are you...discussing?' he asked.

'Unification, of course,' the first man snapped, still upset at having been interrupted.

Fawkes tried not to grimace. So that was it. That was the reason they were all here. The King had been making noises about "unification" ever since the Coronation. It was a crazy idea. James was trying to mould Scotland and England into a single sovereign nation. He was going to call the place 'Britain', by all accounts. Nobody was taking the idea seriously, but the King had clearly brought these gentlemen together, out of season, to discuss the matter. That was why the house was suddenly filled with Scotsmen. It was a catastrophe. They would stink the place out.

Fawkes did his best not to let his feelings show. He was supposed to be a servant and he would act like one, no matter what his private opinions. 'How...long will these deliberations last?' he asked, politely.

'Oh not long. A few weeks,' the second lord responded. 'If your master needs a bed for the evening we'll try not to disturb him after nine o'clock.'

Fawkes took a deep breath. 'That's very considerate, my lords. Thank you.' He backed out of the room and closed the door behind him. The debate resumed at once.

Tom Wintour had ridden over from Uxbridge as soon as he had received the letter. He was more bemused than shocked. Fawkes had met up with him at a nearby tavern and in a private room the soldier had filled him in on all the details.

Tom scratched his head. The situation was too bizarre for words. At least the plot itself had not been compromised. 'They had no idea who I was,' Fawkes reassured his companion. 'They couldn't possibly know anything of our intentions.'

Tom gave a quiet sigh. 'It's just as well Robin stockpiled the gunpowder at Lambeth. If we'd stored it at the house the whole scheme might have been uncovered before we'd even begun.' He shivered at the thought. 'Once the lords are out of there, we'll have to make sure there's a proper guard twenty four hours a day. We can't afford to have people wandering in and out when they feel like it.'

Fawkes nodded. 'But do we simply wait until they finish their deliberations?'

Tom shrugged. 'What choice do we have?'

In the early hours of Tuesday morning, Robert Catesby brought the last of the supplies across the river. It had taken nearly two days to transfer the materials from Lambeth. Catesby had managed to acquire most of the equipment Mr Fawkes had requested: picks, shovels, buckets and a large quantity of timber to act as supports for the mine. The transfer took place under cover of darkness. There was less chance of being seen in the early hours of the morning. Fawkes took watch at the Whynniard house, making sure that the coast was clear while the rest of the plotters transported the goods across the Thames.

The lords had completed their discussions on the Sixth of December, the previous Thursday. Fawkes had watched them leave the lodging with some relief. No firm conclusion had been reached about this new "Britain", but no firm conclusion had been expected. Unification was nothing more than a pipe dream. Unfortunately, the lords' presence in the Whynniard house had put back the conspirators' plans by several weeks.

Jack Wright took the oars on the last trip across the river. Timber had been piled high in a small rowing boat. At Parliament Stairs, Catesby helped them transfer the wood to a battered-looking cart, which was wheeled up the forty yards to the house. The contents were then quickly smuggled inside.

Fawkes locked and bolted the door behind them.

'That's the last of it,' Jack declared happily 'We'll be stuck here now till Christmastide.'

Thomas Percy grimaced, taking in the limited dimensions of the lodging house. 'It's smaller than I remember,' he said. His white hair brushed the low wooden beams supporting the ceiling.

Catesby was stacking the last of the wood in a corner. 'We'll manage,' he said. 'We did agree, Thomas. From now on, we stay put.' It would be dangerous for any of the plotters to be seen wandering around in the vicinity of the house. Apart from Mr Fawkes, they were all known Catholics. If any of them were observed entering the lodging, people would assume a Mass was being held; and that would bring the authorities down on them at once.

The picks and shovels had already been carried through to a small vault beneath the main living area. Empty barrels stood ready to gather up the earth.

Catesby lit a candle and made his way down the narrow steps. The others followed closely behind. The floor of the cellar was solid stone. Catesby grabbed a pick axe resting gently against the far wall. 'Gentlemen,' he said. 'Let's get to work.'

Chapter Ten

'I'm too old for this,' Thomas Percy complained, crouching down on his hands and knees. It was ridiculous. The tunnel was scarcely big enough for a child. Percy was well over six feet tall – the tallest of a tall group – and being forced to work in such constrained conditions was already beginning to test his patience. He didn't mind a bit of mud and he could deal with the cuts and bruises well enough. It was the strain on his back that was really taking its toll. The tunnel was simply too cramped. It was impossible to manoeuvre, let alone to get comfortable. The mine was cold and damp and there wasn't even room to swing an axe properly.

Percy moved forward into the hole and promptly banged his head on the roof. He swore loudly as several large clumps of earth struck him from above.

'Keep your voice down!' Tom hissed from the other end of the tunnel. Away from the house, there was no telling who might be able to hear them.

Tom was hacking away at the rock face with a crude iron pick axe. He had been going at it for well over an hour, building up a small pile of rocks in the mud. Once Percy had taken over the job, Tom would collect the rubble and move it back up to the entrance, a job becoming more difficult with each passing day. The further the embryonic tunnel extended the more effort was required to remove the detritus.

Percy had scrambled half way along. 'It's all right for you,' he whispered, pulling closer. 'You're only a short-arse.' He wiped the soil from his hair and flinched as his hand caught a splinter from the wooden beam suspended above his head. He glared up at it.

'Did you bring the rags?' Tom asked.

Percy nodded, grabbing a bundle of discoloured fabric from over his shoulder. The rags were damp and mud spattered. He untangled the various pieces and slapped them down onto the floor of the tunnel, where they quickly became saturated with water.

Mr Fawkes had warned them about this. There was water everywhere here. It was disgusting. Even Percy's hose were wet through. But such were the perils of digging a tunnel so close to a river. The water would accumulate gradually over the course of a day. The rags would soak up most of it, though, and the droplets could be squeezed into empty jugs or wine flagons and then removed. It was just like bailing water out of the bottom of a boat.

'Gunpowder won't last five minutes in these conditions,' Percy lamented, abandoning the rags and pulling himself awkwardly forward to exchange positions with Tom at the end of the mine.

The plan had been to place the powder in the tunnel some time before the State Opening of Parliament. That way, only one person would have to stay behind to light the fuse. With conditions as they were in the mine, however, the gunpowder would almost certainly break down. To keep the material fresh, it would have to be transferred at the last possible moment. And that meant several of the plotters remaining in London until the Opening itself.

So much for forward planning.

Percy picked up the axe and glanced back at Tom. 'What time's supper?' he asked.

Each evening, there were long discussions, when the men were not sleeping or dumping material into the river.

Percy had clashed with Tom from the outset on one issue: the fate of the Catholics who sat in the House of Lords. Tom wanted to give specific warnings to various friends, including his employer, Lord Monteagle. Percy was adamant that nobody should be warned. 'Why take the risk?' he demanded.

The plotters kept their voices low, for fear of being overheard, but the discussions were no less vigorous for that.

A late supper had been prepared by Mr Fawkes, a simple meal of bread, baked meats and hard-boiled eggs, with a flagon of lemon juice to wash it all down. The men ate hungrily as they talked.

Catesby, who had considered the matter for far longer than any of them, was still undecided. 'Probably better to err on the side of caution,' he said. 'The fewer people who know what we intend, the less chance there is of failure.' He reached forward and cut a piece of bread from the loaf on the table. He was more concerned to discuss the aftermath of the explosion. This was the vaguest part of the plan so far. 'We can't simply proclaim ourselves sovereign just because the King is dead. We'll need a figurehead. And somebody whose legitimacy is not open to question.'

'Who were you thinking of?' Tom enquired.

Percy was chomping away at a meat pie on the other side of the table. 'There are only three choices,' he declared, gulping down a large chunk of meat. 'The three children – Henry, Charles or Elizabeth.'

'The oldest son will probably be attending Parliament along with his father,' Catesby said. 'So that rules him out. He'll almost certainly be killed in the blast.

'Do we know for sure he'll be there?' Tom asked.

The other man nodded. 'The King will want Prince Henry with him. It's a big occasion. The prince will be there at the Opening and he'll die with the others when we fire the powder.'

'So that leaves Charles and Elizabeth,' Percy said, swallowing another piece of pie. The princess was the older of the two children, but Charles was male and second in line to the throne. So far, the little prince had made few public appearances. 'If he's at Richmond, there's no problem. I can grab hold of the sprog as soon as the powder's blown.' As a Gentleman Pensioner, Percy had access to the Royal Bedchamber. 'No-one's going to question me in those circumstances. If anyone asks, I'm protecting the little bastard. I have a few friends who'll help me out if I give them the nod. A couple of horses on standby and I'll have the little brat out of London before anyone's any the wiser.' Percy wiped a few stray crumbs from his beard and poured himself a glass of lemon juice. He certainly sounded confident. 'We can proclaim Charles as King and appoint a Catholic knight to act as Lord Protector.'

'What about Princess Elizabeth?' Tom asked. 'If Charles were to attend Parliament along with his brother then she'll be next in line.'

Catesby had considered this. 'She's staying at Combe Abbey. That's not far from Ashby St. Ledgers.' He picked up a hard-boiled egg and cracked the shell on the edge of the table. 'If Charles is out of the picture, then it shouldn't be too difficult to abduct Elizabeth instead.' The eight year old was Catesby's preferred choice. Girls were always more pliable than boys. 'We could gather together some men for a hunting expedition,' he suggested. 'No one will question a few old friends going hunting on Dunsmore Heath. Then as soon as we hear the King is dead, we descend on the Abbey and take the princess by force.' He pulled off the shell of the egg and discarded the bits in the fire. 'With Parliament destroyed, we can take control of the whole country. And Elizabeth will give us the legitimacy we require.'

'We'll need lots of men,' Tom pointed out. 'And money.'

'Plenty of horses too,' Jack added.

'They'll come,' Catesby said. 'When people hear what we've done, they'll flock to our side. Mark my words, gentlemen, when the King dies, the whole country will rally to our cause. We'll have all the men and money that we need.' He leaned forward in his chair. 'If the powder goes off, everything else will fall into place.'

Tom Wintour was trying not to think about the roof. He was crouched on his knees halfway along the tunnel, his body slicked with perspiration and his hose saturated by the muddy water. A solitary candle flickered within a metal lantern. He glanced upwards. The light from the flame barely illuminated the jagged wooden beams suspended above his head. The mine had been propped as best they could manage but even with heavy timber in place the danger of collapse was ever present.

In his dreams Tom had been in just this position. He had been heaving a rock into a small barrel when suddenly there had been a loud roar and everything had gone black. Jack had cried out but then there had been silence. Tom had been trapped in the tunnel, all alone, unable to move, with the water gradually rising around him. He had woken in a cold sweat, on the wooden floorboards, struggling for air.

He squeezed out the rags and tried to think about something else. Muddy brown water sloshed into the ceramic jug. At least he had been able to get some sleep. The others had not been so lucky. Conditions in the lodging were cramped to say the least and tempers had occasionally flared. It was not easy for any of them. He wound the cloth tightly then reversed the pressure and forced the last few drops of water into the container.

Ahead of him, Percy was banging away at the heavy rock face. The poor man was sweating like a dog. He was stripped down to his breeches and was covered in dirt from head to foot. Percy hated the work – his ageing body was peppered with bruises – but he did not allow his dislike to diminish the energy he applied to the task.

Despite his advancing years, Percy had always displayed the greatest enthusiasm – and made the most noise – when swinging an axe. 'Bloody hell!' he exclaimed suddenly.

Tom peered forward into the gloom. 'What's the matter?'

There had been a loud thump before the cry. That was nothing unusual. Percy was forever banging his head. But this time, it was something different. 'More rock!' Percy called back, bitterly. 'It looks completely solid.'

Tom grabbed the lantern and scuffled up towards the end of the mine. He squeezed alongside his older friend and touched the far edge of the tunnel with the back of his hand. 'It's certainly hard,' he admitted. He tapped the surface gently with his fist. 'That's not rock. I think it's a wall.'

Percy's eyes widened. 'Parliament wall?'

Tom was not sure. 'Hang on a minute.' He shuffled back along the tunnel to retrieve the damp rags, then used the moisture from the cloth to wipe away some of the soil from the rock face. The regular construction provided a definitive answer. It was the outer wall. Tom grinned. 'That's Parliament, all right.'

Percy was ecstatic. 'We've done it!' he exclaimed. 'We've reached the foundations!' He looked again at the wall, his eyes gleaming triumphantly. Their goal was nearer now than ever. He placed a grimy hand on the heavy stonework. 'I wonder how thick it is.'

'Mr Fawkes reckoned about three feet.'

'Move back a bit,' Percy said, grabbing hold of the pick axe. Tom shuffled out of the way, while Percy swung the axe with both his hands and smashed it into the wall. There was an impressive thud. He leaned in and let out a hiss of disappointment. The pick axe had barely made an impression on the stone.

Tom tried to look on the bright side. 'We've got six weeks to get through it,' he pointed out.

Percy grimaced. 'Just when I thought we were getting somewhere...'

Guido Fawkes hurried across the street towards the Whynniard house, clutching a small bag to his chest. He had only been out for a few minutes, but the pious Yorkshireman was anxious to get back to his companions. Arriving at the door, he fumbled for the key and let himself into the building. It was warmer inside. The heat from the fire had spread across to the entrance hall. 'Only me,' Fawkes called out, removing his hat. It was a connacled capotain in black felt. He took a moment to latch the door, then placed the hat on a stand and unhooked his cloak. Hanging up the dark garment, he made his way into the living room.

Jack had been keeping watch while he was out. Fawkes' old school friend had been happy to cover for him while he had popped out to replenish a few essential items. Jack was sitting close to the window, sword in hand, looking out onto the street. 'It looks busy out.'

'It is.' Fawkes moved across to the table and placed the small shopping bag down upon the hard wooden surface. There was not much inside the bag: just a few candles brought from a nearby store and some fruit from the market. Nothing suspicious. There had been a lot of people milling about. 'Everyone's out buying food for Christmas,' he explained.

'People always leave it to the last minute.'

The clomp of feet heralded the arrival of Catesby from the cellar. He ducked down to pass through the low door frame. There was a huge grin on his face. 'Guido, we've hit the wall!' he exclaimed. 'We've hit the foundations!' He moved across to the table. Percy and Tom entered the room behind him.

'Drinks all round!' Percy bellowed.

The others hissed at him to keep his voice down.

Catesby grabbed a jug of sack and began to pour out a few cups. 'We might just meet our deadline after all,' he announced, handing the drinks out to his companions.

'I think that's more than likely,' Fawkes agreed, accepting a cup. The former soldier was itching to pass on his own news. 'As it turns out, we have a lot more time than we originally envisaged.'

Percy frowned. 'What do you mean?'

'I was just about to tell Mr Wright. There's been a proclamation. Parliament has been prorogued until the autumn.'

'You're joking!'

'It's true enough, Mr Percy. I read the proclamation myself. It's nailed to a tree just outside the palace. The lords have some concerns about the plague lingering. They want to make certain everything has died down before they begin the next session.'

Catesby swallowed a mouthful of sherry. 'So Parliament won't open until – what? – Michaelmas?'

'Thereabouts,' Fawkes confirmed.

Percy flopped down into a chair, 'So I needn't have worked so bloody hard after all.' He drained his cup in one gulp and held it out for Catesby to refill.

'The work needed doing,' Catesby said, pouring out some more of the sherry.

'We can take a break now, though, can't we? At least over Christmastide?' Percy looked up imploringly. 'Go back to our own lodgings for a few days. I can't face another night on that floor. My back is killing me.'

Catesby poured himself another drink and nodded happily. 'I think we deserve a short rest. Until Twelfth Night, at any rate.' He raised his cup. 'Gentlemen. We've done a good job. We should be proud.'

Percy slurped at the sherry.

'But there's a lot still to do…'

Chapter Eleven

Mr Fawkes left the lodging on the Second of February and took a small rowing boat across the Thames. Twenty large barrels of gunpowder had been stock-piled at Catesby's Lambeth residence on the opposite side of the river and the time had come to transfer them to Westminster. Each drum weighed just over a hundred pounds. The quality of powder was notoriously variable, but the plotters had managed to gather more than a ton of the stuff from a variety of sources. Such a quantity could not fail to destroy the Parliament building. Like as not, it would be the single biggest explosion England had ever seen.

Fawkes arrived at Lambeth some hours after sunset. Catesby had asked the veteran soldier to oversee the transfer of material. It would take some time, but it was better to do it now, when there was less urgency. A twenty-four hour guard and an extra lock at the Whynniard house would ensure there was no repetition of the Scottish Unification fiasco and it made sense to have all the danger located in one place.

'Take as long as you need,' Catesby had said, when Fawkes was preparing to depart. 'I'll send my man Bates along to give you a hand.'

The two of them had crossed the river together.

Thomas Bates had been fetching and carrying on behalf of the conspirators for several months, without ever being told the reason behind it. The servant was no fool however and had begun to suspect something serious was afoot. Catesby had therefore brought him in on the details of the plot.

Bates was not the only new recruit. Jack Wright's younger brother Kit had also joined, to help with the digging of the mine. At the Lambeth house, too, a Mr Robert Keyes had been enlisted to look after the gunpowder. Keyes was a cousin of Ambrose Rookwood, the man who had unwittingly supplied some of the barrels they were now transporting.

This burst of recruitment at the end of the year had been agreed by all concerned. Thomas Percy was grateful for anyone who could reduce the amount of digging he had to endure; and the new conspirators were all family men who were deemed to be utterly reliable. Each of them had sworn the oath of secrecy. Only Bates, as a lowly servant, was not connected to the others by blood, but Catesby had spoken warmly of the man's piety and commitment.

It took an hour and a half to get the barrels up from the cellar. Once at the door, Fawkes could roll each one onto a brewers' sling. With a man at either end, the wooden containers could be lifted with comparative ease.

Robert Keyes, meantime, was down at the bank side, arranging material to disguise the drums while crossing the river. Keyes was a tall, red bearded fellow of about forty. His clothes were poorly made and his face rugged. He was not a rich man but he was honest and dependable; and an extra pair of hands was always useful. He arrived back at the lodging to find Fawkes and Bates already manoeuvring the first barrel towards the door. 'Everything's set,' he told them.

The rowing boat down at the waterfront could only realistically carry three barrels at a time. The containers would be rested on the central beams to keep the powder clear of the bilge water. The last thing anyone wanted was the gunpowder getting damp.

Outside the house, everything was black. They had chosen a good night to begin their work. A few candle flames could be glimpsed through window frames facing out towards the river. Otherwise there was no light at all. Even the slim crescent of the moon was obscured by clouds. In the distance, a church bell chimed. It was a quarter to midnight.

Fawkes nodded to Bates and each man took one end of the brewers' sling, which they lifted to their shoulders. The load was heavier than Fawkes had anticipated. He gritted his teeth and carefully took the lead.

Robert Keyes held a dim lantern aloft and accompanied the men as they made their way across the small garden towards the river bank. Fawkes trod carefully. The terrain was a little uneven and frost had rendered the grass slippery and dangerous. At the river's edge, there was barely enough light to make out the steps which descended to the water where the boat was moored.

Keyes gave a hand as the men manoeuvred the barrel onto the gently rocking vessel. Once the first drum was in position the trio returned to the house to collect the others. When all the barrels had been safely stowed, Mr Keyes untied the mooring rope and threw the line across to Mr Fawkes, who had positioned himself on the near side of the boat. Thomas Bates was on rowing duty. At a nod from Fawkes, he leaned forward and dipped the oars into the water.

The Thames air, always noxious, now felt stilted and cold. Fawkes shivered. Scarcely a sound could be heard, bar the gentle lapping of the water at the edges of the boat. Slowly, the vessel pulled way. He glanced ahead. A thin mist was spread out before them. There were bound to be other boats on the Thames, even at this hour, but it was too dark to see anything properly. They would have to be careful.

The light from Keyes' lantern was barely visible now on the southern bank. A few minutes later, it had faded from view altogether.

There was a loud scraping noise coming from above.

Tom Wintour put a finger to his lips. Bates had already stopped working and was staring at the roof in alarm. The stone edges of the Parliament wall served to accentuate the strange sound as it reverberated through the tunnel. Bates had mentioned hearing a noise a few minutes earlier but Tom had paid no attention. The manservant was always quick to take fright. Now there could be no doubt. Earth was sprinkling down on them from above and the scraping sound was getting louder.

Tom looked up at the roof of the mine and frowned. He had heard odd noises before but nothing quite like this. He wiped the dirt from his face. It was as if something heavy were being dragged about directly above their heads. But that was ridiculous. They were still hacking through the outer wall. The only thing above them was solid rock. And it was not just the scraping sound. Now that he was listening carefully, he thought he could hear footsteps as well; and voices whispering.

A sudden fear gripped him. Had the worst happened? Had somebody discovered the tunnel? Tom shook himself. That was absurd. The noise was coming from above, not behind. In any case, Mr Fawkes was standing guard in the front room and would have raised the alarm if anybody had tried to get past him. No, thinking logically, the movement had to be coming from somewhere up ahead, inside the Parliament building. A store room, perhaps. Or the chamber of the Upper House itself.

Bates was becoming agitated. Even in the dim candle light, panic was clearly visible in the servant's dark blue eyes. Tom gestured at him to keep calm. Whatever was happening, they could not afford to make any noise. Better to abandon the mine temporarily and return to the house.

More soil was becoming dislodged from above. Tom looked up again. This part of the tunnel had not yet been fully propped. If the movement continued as before then there was a danger that the roof might collapse on top of them. He signalled for Bates to follow him back towards the entrance. They needed to get out of the tunnel. And quickly.

Tom tried to shuffle his body around but it was an awkward manoeuvre in the confined space. Suddenly a large clump of stone became dislodged from the roof. All at once earth and rock were raining down from above. The stone smacked hard, striking Tom a heavy blow across the left shoulder.

Bates cried out from behind as part of the ceiling caved in on top of him. His lantern was knocked over, extinguishing the candle and plunging the tunnel into darkness.

Soil continued to shower down from above.

Tom felt the earth thudding into his back. There were clusters of heavy rock too, smacking forcefully into his mud-soaked torso. He struggled not to cry out, clasping his hands desperately over the back of his head to protect himself as the heavy soil began to envelop him. In a few seconds it was all over.

Tom opened his eyes and took a deep breath. He was lying prostrate, with layers of rock and soil pressing down upon his spine. But he was still alive. There was space above his head and there was air to breathe. Somehow he had not been completely buried. 'Mr Bates?' he whispered, trying to glance back but in the process dislodging several large clumps of soil from the top of his head. Bates could not have been more than six feet away from him when the roof had fallen in. 'Thomas?' he called again, slightly louder. 'Are you all right?'

The servant groaned. 'I…I think so, sir.'

'Thank God.' They had both been very lucky.

Tom made an effort to move his body but there was a stabbing pain in his right shoulder. He flinched. At least there was some motion there. He did not appear to have broken any bones and there was still some feeling in his hands and arms. It was a miracle he had not been more seriously hurt.

From behind, Thomas Bates was beginning to extricate himself from the mess of rock and earth. The man coughed awkwardly.

'We need to get out of here,' Tom hissed.

Noises could still be heard coming from above. Scraping sounds and footsteps. Had anyone heard them crying out? It scarcely mattered now. The priority had to be to get out before the rest of the roof collapsed on top of them.

Tom groped forward, his fingertips exploring the constricted terrain as best they could. Had the avalanche blocked their retreat? He could certainly feel a large chunk of rock nestling somewhere up ahead of him. It was probably the piece that had struck his shoulder. Luckily it was too small to block their exit.

He reached forward and grabbed hold of the stone. It was surprisingly heavy – too heavy to lift in the narrow confines of the tunnel – but with the right amount of pressure it might be possible to shift it to one side. Tom steeled himself and gently began to rock the stone. Every movement of his arm sent a stab of pain through his shoulder but he bore it as best he could. It took a few seconds to edge the rock to one side. That left enough of a gap for a man to squeeze through. 'Let's go,' he whispered, dragging his body forward. His hands searched carefully above his head, feeling for the safety of the heavy timber that propped the rest of the tunnel.

Thomas Bates followed on slowly from behind.

At the entrance to the mine, Jack Wright was still working cheerfully, utterly oblivious to events down below. The quiet, smiling Yorkshireman had been replenishing the barrels of waste material that had been lifted out of the shaft earlier on. The first he knew of any problem was when he heard Tom Wintour grabbing the ladder at the bottom of the pit. 'That was quick!' he exclaimed as Tom's head popped up at ground level. Then Jack caught sight of the blood. 'What happened?' He proffered a hand and Tom pulled himself up onto level ground.

'Part of the roof collapsed,' the shorter man explained. 'There was some kind of noise. It must have dislodged the earth.'

Behind them, a severely shaken Thomas Bates was starting to climb the ladder.

Jack frowned. 'A noise? What sort of noise?'

Tom shrugged. 'I only wish I knew.'

Chapter Twelve

A workman was dragging a large sack of coal through a narrow doorway. The man's face was black and his hands were covered in dirt. He was having some difficulty with the bag; the coarse fibres were wedged tightly against the frame of the door. The fellow was pulling with all his strength, but to little effect. A second worker – younger but equally grimy – was struggling to load another huge sack onto the back of an oversized cart, which was parked awkwardly on the near side of the street. A dozen bags of coal had already been loaded up onto the cart. A bored horse stood waiting on the cobblestones. The man grunted and finally thudded the new sack on top of the others.

Guido Fawkes was watching so intently that he failed to see the other labourer struggling behind him. When the coal sack finally came free of the door, the workman was propelled backwards and suddenly collided with Mr Fawkes a few feet from the door frame. The old soldier stumbled forward and it took him a moment to recover his balance.

'Sorry about that!' a voice called from behind. Fawkes turned. The workman had planted his sack down in front of the door and was wiping the sweat from his brow. 'Bloody thing!' he said, in a thick West London brogue. ''Scuse my language.'

'I was just coming around to see what all the noise was about,' Fawkes volunteered. He had rushed out onto the street as soon as Tom Wintour had raised the alarm. 'My master resides in the house just along there,' he added.

The workman wasn't interested. 'Just shifting a few sacks of coal,' he said. 'Shouldn't be much longer. That's almost the last of it.'

Fawkes nodded politely. That explained the scraping noise. The two workmen were shifting coal from inside the building; quite a lot of it, by the look of things. They must have been dragging the sacks across the floor and the vibrations had somehow caused a partial collapse of the tunnel. Luckily, neither man had been seriously injured. But where on Earth had all the fuel been stored? He peered in through the doorway. 'There's a cellar in there?' he asked.

'Well, an undercroft. Just across the corridor.'

Fawkes frowned. Nobody had mentioned there being any kind of store room. He had assumed the conspirators were digging directly beneath the Upper Chamber.

'Who does the room belong to?' he asked.

The workman scratched his head. 'Well, strictly speaking, Old Man Bright. But he's just popped his clogs, so it's all got to be cleared out now.' He shook his head sadly. 'The business has gone belly up and the mistress wants it out of there. Can't afford the rent no more, you see.'

'I see.' Fawkes pursed his lips. An opportunity was presenting itself here. 'I wonder if it would be possible for me to take a look?' he asked, impulsively.

The workman let go of the bag and raised an eyebrow. 'You want to see the store room?'

'My...master is looking for somewhere to store wood,' he improvised. 'If the lease is available, he might consider renting it. My name is Mr Johnson, by the way. John Johnson.'

'Pleased to meet you, Mr Johnson. Renting it, you say? It's a bit big for storing firewood, if you don't mind me saying so. But you're welcome to have a look.' The man grabbed his sack again. The other labourer was just returning to the door. 'It's just through there, Mr Johnson. Ned'll show you the way.'

The younger worker glanced at his colleague, removed his hat, then gestured for Mr Fawkes to enter the building.

'It's directly beneath the Upper House,' Fawkes told them.

Thomas Percy stifled a laugh. The plotters had gathered at the *Duck and Drake* Inn, where Tom now had his lodgings. The landlord had arranged a private room at the back of the inn and Catesby had provided supper for the group at his own expense. All eyes were currently focused on Mr Fawkes, who was giving them an account of his findings. He was an odd fellow, Percy thought. Tall, muscular, but somehow anonymous. The name John Johnson suited him down to the ground. He was more like a servant than a soldier; reserved and formal.

'It's looks to be about eighty feet long,' the man was saying. He was sitting at the far end of the table, near Jack and Catesby. 'But only about twenty-five feet across.'

Tom Wintour frowned. 'So who exactly owns the place?'

'Mr John Whynniard. At least, he's the one who has responsibility for it. It's on the ground floor and has easy access from the street.'

Percy was fiddling with a small clay pipe. He was having difficulty containing his amusement. 'Let me get this straight.' He grinned broadly 'This room is directly above the tunnel we've just spent the last three months digging?'

Fawkes shook his head. 'Not quite, Mr Percy. It's a few feet beyond the end of the tunnel as it currently stands. But it is above the point we'll be at once we've broken through the outer wall.' Despite weeks of effort and additional manpower, the small group had so far only managed to hack through eight feet of stone. The Parliament wall had been considerably thicker than Fawkes' original estimate.

'And now it's empty?' Percy asked. He pulled out a pouch of tobacco and filled the end of his pipe.

'As you say. But after what happened to Mr Wintour it occurs to me that if somebody else fills the room with coal the entire floor might collapse on top of us.'

Percy did not see the problem. 'So. We acquire the lease and put the powder in the basement. If it's directly beneath the Upper Chamber, it'll save us all a hell of a lot of digging. And we won't run the risk of being buried alive.' He rose from his chair and moved across to the fire to light his pipe.

'But wait a minute,' Tom interrupted. 'How can we be sure the store room is secure? Can it be locked? How many doors are there?'

All eyes returned to Mr Fawkes. 'There appeared to be three of them. I was reliably informed they could all be locked. Nobody goes into the undercroft apart from the people renting it out. That's why we didn't hear anybody above us until they started to clear it. From what I can gather, most people don't even know it's there.'

'We certainly didn't,' Jack Wright muttered.

Percy was more enthusiastic. 'We could stockpile the powder in there and cover it up with bundles of wood or coal,' he suggested. 'Fill the place up with household goods. Charcoal. Anything. It's got to be better than all this bloody mining.' Percy was a clear decade older than most of the other conspirators and he had found the work particularly tiring. There had been days, over Christmastide, when he had barely been able to walk.

'I don't like the idea of the powder being stored in such an accessible place,' Tom declared uneasily. 'At least if we keep it underground, nobody would be able to find it.'

'But it isn't underground *now*,' Percy pointed out. 'And it isn't likely to be. Not until the last minute.' He returned to his seat and took a long, slow drag from the pipe. 'The stuff is no less safe at the Whynniard House. Who knows when some other bloody ridiculous committee will want to start using the place?' Even with a twenty-four hour guard and assurances of privacy from Mr Whynniard, the powder would always be vulnerable outside of Westminster. 'Why not hide it in plain sight? Isn't that what people always say?'

Tom was having none of it. 'It's too much of a risk. We shouldn't change our plans at this late stage.'

Percy looked away. 'What do you think, Robin?'

Catesby had been silent for some time, listening to the debate; but now, it appeared, he had reached a decision. 'If the place can be locked and we can smuggle the powder in without arousing suspicion, then I think it might be a good idea.'

'But Robin –'

'Though I also agree with Tom. We need to be assured of complete privacy. I suggest that on the morrow Mr Percy and Mr Johnson make a formal visit with a view to renting the cellar.'

'I'll tell them my wife's coming down to London,' Percy volunteered, his face partially obscured by tobacco smoke. 'That should convince them. I'll say we're going to start using the house and I need somewhere to store firewood.'

'And when you look around, I want you to pay very close attention. See how secure you think the place is. If everything looks all right, then speak to Mr Whynniard and we can take it from there. But *only* if the place is secure.'

Jack Wright pushed the drum towards the centre of the room. The wooden barrel was three-quarters full. Jack had hacked most of the stone out of the tunnel himself. There was some earth in the drum, too, but it was mostly rock. The barrel had been the last to be lifted out of the mine before Tom had sounded the alarm. Now the contents would be returned to the depths, where they rightfully belonged.

Tom Wintour was standing over the hole, peering down at the deep, dark tunnel. In his left hand, he held a small lantern, but the light barely illuminated the cramped cellar. Tom had mixed feelings about abandoning the mine. Digging it had proved more difficult than any of them had anticipated, but they had persevered, using the simplest of tools and their own brute strength. Now, that same strength would be used to destroy everything they had accomplished.

Jack sat down on top of the barrel and scratched his head. 'Crazy, isn't it? All that hard work, all for nothing.'

Tom nodded. 'It's the most difficult thing I've ever done. But Thomas is right.' He sighed. 'It could take us weeks to break through that wall and dig out a space underneath the storeroom.' Work had been slowing down considerably in any case, as the plotters had gone off to attend to other matters. Even the help of Jack's brother Kit had done little to redress the balance. 'Better to move all the powder directly beneath the Upper Chamber. It's got to be more secure there than in this house.'

'Less coming and going too,' Jack agreed.

Tom brought a hand up to his face. He felt tired. The hard work had taken its toll on all of them. His skin felt raw and his hands seemed to be permanently covered in mud. 'I just wish we could have rented this cellar in the first place,' he lamented. The discovery of the undercroft at this late date had been more disturbing to him than the partial collapse of the roof. 'I don't know, Jack. Have we thought all this through? We spend so much time working out the details, and then something like this happens. How could we not *know* about a room directly beneath the House of Lords? It's ridiculous. And it makes me worry about...well, what other things we may have missed. There seem to be so many variables.'

Jack stood up and put a hand on Tom's shoulder. 'Robin knows what he's doing. The powder's already set. What could possibly go wrong?' He gestured to the wooden drum. 'Come on, Mr Tom. Give me a hand with this.'

Tom placed his lantern on the ground and took hold of the far side of the barrel. They had briefly considered retrieving some of the wood used to prop the tunnel, but the danger of collapse was too great to make it worth the risk. All they really needed to do was cover over the entrance and that could be done with the minimum of fuss.

Together, the two men tipped the contents of the drum over the edge of the hole. The earth and stones poured into the gap, scraping the walls and creating a small mound of rubble at the bottom of the shaft.

Jack lifted the base of the barrel and made sure all the earth had been emptied out. Then he gestured to a second drum, lying in a corner of the room beside the lantern. This barrel was only half full. After they had emptied it out, the two men would set to work with the shovels. Perhaps a bit of earth would be needed from the garden, but it would not take long to fill in the hole.

In a couple of hours, all being well, there would be no trace left of the mine.

Part Three
Powder

"I would to God I had never known of the Powder Treason"
- Henry Garnet, 28th March 1606

Chapter Thirteen

Father Henry Garnet took a sip of red wine and sat back from the table. 'You've been avoiding me, Robin,' he chided.

It was a Sunday afternoon. Catesby had been invited to dine with the priest at the Jesuit's private lodgings on Thames Street, just west of the Tower of London. It had been a long while since he had seen Father Henry and as they were both in London it would have been churlish to refuse the invitation.

'I'm sorry, Father,' he apologised. 'I have been going to Mass each week. But I've been so busy recently.' It was a lame excuse. The truth of the matter was, Catesby had been avoiding him. After the unfortunate confrontation at White Webbs the previous summer, he had been determined to steer clear of the priest. Father Henry had continued to peddle the same demands for Catholic restraint to anyone who would listen but Catesby had no desire to lose his temper with the middle-aged Jesuit. Father Henry deserved better than that.

'I've heard all about your latest venture,' the priest commented, with an approving nod. 'Most commendable.' Like many others, Father Henry believed Catesby was planning to establish a regiment to fight alongside the Spanish in the Low Countries. The idea had been circulating for some months now and it was hardly surprising that the Father knew all about it. It was a useful lever; now, more than ever.

Catesby's cousin Tom was still having difficulty coming to terms with the idea of innocent people dying at the opening of Parliament. He was insisting that at least some of the Catholics who sat in the House should receive a warning to stay away on the day of the blast. Catesby had considered the matter long and hard, but the more he thought about it, the more he came to believe that it would be better not to tell anyone at all. Any friendly hints given in advance might scupper the whole project, if one of the peers took it upon himself to alert the authorities. At the same time, he understood his friend's misgivings. Catesby also felt uneasy about causing the death of so many Catholic men. How could he wilfully set in motion a plan that would kill so many innocents? Some of them were close friends and he would rather take his own life than raise a sword against them.

It was a moral dilemma that Catesby felt ill-equipped to resolve. Could he be justified, killing those innocents, if it was for the greater good of the Catholic church?

The matter had plagued the conspirators for months now; all except Percy, whose zeal was commendable but slightly disturbing. Tom Wintour had finally suggested a means of resolving the matter. 'Speak to Father Henry,' he had said. 'Outline the basics of the problem. Don't mention England. Talk about the war.' Father Henry Garnet, they knew, was always happy to indulge in theological debate. There would only need to be the slimmest of rationalisations. Catesby's regiment, already in use as a smokescreen for the acquisition of gunpowder, would provide the perfect excuse.

Catesby reached forward and filled his goblet from the flagon Father Henry had provided. The wine was Spanish; rough but full-bodied. Henry Garnet had always had good taste where alcohol was concerned.

'How are things going with it all?' the priest enquired, referring to the regiment.

'Very well. The funds are more or less in place. Sir Charles Percy has agreed to help with recruitment. We're gathering together the men at the moment. But it all takes rather a long time, unfortunately.'

Father Henry took another sip of wine. 'It's always the way,' he lamented. 'But it'll be good for you to spend some time on the continent. It may give you more of a perspective on the problems in your own country.' The Father threw a knowing look at the younger man, but he spoke with gentle affection: 'I know you get frustrated with the pace of change here, Robin, but things always turn out well in the end. And if you can help in some small way to bring about peace in the Low Countries then it's all to the good.'

'I do worry though,' Catesby said. He placed the goblet of wine back on the table and met the priest's eyes. 'About the cost. The lives that could be lost.'

Father Henry nodded sadly. 'In times of war, there is always a cost. But so long as you are assured that your cause is just, then you are right to pursue it.'

'It's not the cause itself,' Catesby said. 'It's the innocent people who get caught up in it. There are many Catholics in the Low Countries who are forced to fight against the Spanish.' Protestant extremists were trying to carve out a patch of territory in lands that rightfully belonged to the King of Spain. They had press-ganged many a reluctant Catholic to fight on their behalf. 'These men have no desire to fight for the rebels, and yet in order to defeat our enemies and capture their towns or fortresses we are expected to kill *them* as well as the Protestants.'

'It is a difficult issue,' Father Henry agreed.

'And then there are the women and children. The innocents behind enemy lines. All of our kinfolk who are caught up in the towns and cities that the rebels have taken. If we attack those cities, as we surely must, then these innocents will die. How can we ever justify that?'

Father Henry had considered this dilemma many times before. When he spoke, it was with the air of a man who had come to terms with the issue and simply wished to pass on his wisdom. 'The first thing you need to be sure of is that you are fighting a Just War. Justice in this sense means not only the objective of the war but the manner in which it is fought. It is wholly wrong to seek the death of innocents. The Catholic church is very clear on that point. Murder and rape can never have a place in a Just War. But if the deaths of innocents are a *by-product* of your cause and not the intention, then sometimes those deaths can be justified.'

Catesby nodded. This was exactly what he wanted to hear.

'For example, if capturing a particular city is to the greater good of the Catholic cause and you have no desire to harm the innocents within, then you cannot be held responsible if some of them die in the process. It is only if you *intend* their deaths that it would be unlawful.' The priest was becoming animated. Like all good theologians, Father Henry showed genuine enthusiasm in discussing his ideas. 'Think of the human body,' he observed. 'When it becomes infected, it is sometimes necessary for a surgeon to cut away healthy tissue in order to save the body as a whole. A few lives lost in war can often make all the difference to the well-being of the community at large. If that is the case, then the action taken is fully justified.'

'So…if I'm forced to kill a few innocent Catholics, in order to liberate a whole community, that would be justified?'

Father Henry nodded. 'In time of war, without a doubt.' He reached across the table and covered Catesby's hand with his own. 'Taking up arms is never easy. But you are doing the right thing, Robin. Leave England to the will of God and take the fight to a place where it is really needed.'

Thomas Percy had been left with the key to the undercroft and had come to an obvious conclusion: 'We need to buy more powder.'

Robert Catesby grimaced.

The original barrels had been transferred to the newly leased vault some weeks previously. It had taken several hours to move them all. Percy had overseen the transfer, since he was officially renting the room. Mr John Johnson had given him a hand and the two men had made sure all the drums were well covered over. Now Mr Fawkes had departed for Flanders and the rest of the plotters were preparing to leave the capital for the summer.

Catesby had met up with Percy at his lodgings on the Gray's Inn Road. They had dined together for an hour with Tom Wintour and were now going over the final details of the plan before departing the city. It would be a relief to get out of London. The stench was becoming unbearable. There was nothing they could do here now in any case until the autumn. The cellar could be locked up and safely left behind. Percy would be heading north, to break a few heads up at Alnwick. He was looking forward to it. Mr Fawkes could check up on the vault when he returned to London later in the year.

'We might as well fill the place,' Percy added, 'now that we have the space.' He leaned back in his chair and stretched his arms lazily above his head. He could just picture the explosion; the mammoth firework display erupting from beneath the Houses of Parliament. It would be a glorious spectacle, visible for miles around. He smirked, dropping his arms into his lap. They would send King James and every single one of his lords straight to Hell.

Catesby was more concerned about the immediate financial repercussions of buying more powder. He had been bankrolling the entire project for over a year now and his coffers were beginning to run low. The prospect of more expenditure was distinctly unsettling. 'If you think it's really necessary,' he said.

Tom Wintour was adamant. 'Some of the gunpowder is bound to decay, if it's left there for months on end.'

'A bit of fresh powder will balance things out,' Percy agreed, scratching the side of his face absently. 'I can organise it for you, if you want. Just lend me the money and I'll stay a few days and sort it out.'

Catesby sighed again. 'I'll see what I can do. But gentlemen, I have to be honest: I'm fast running out of cash. What with the powder; the horses; all the rents in London.'

Tom was shocked. 'Robin, you should have said!'

Catesby waved his hands dismissively. 'I'll happily bankrupt myself if it gets the job done. But we might need to look at some alternative means of funding in the very near future.'

'There's always the rents,' Percy suggested. 'I'm sure I'll be able to siphon some of that off for you.'

'That would be helpful,' Catesby agreed. The man had promised the same thing the previous year, but as yet nothing had been forthcoming. Catesby was not about to hold his breath. 'But we might need to look at widening the circle a little.'

Tom frowned. 'Is that wise?'

'Can't do any harm,' Percy thought, taking out his pipe. He filled the end quickly and lit it with the flame from a nearby candle. 'We are only a small group at the moment. A few more hands won't hurt.'

Tom was not convinced. 'But everyone who's joined us up to now has been a close friend or relative. It might be dangerous to bring anybody else in on the details of the plot.'

'If it gets the job done,' Percy affirmed, exhaling a cloud of smoke, 'it's worth the risk. Just so long as they're made to swear the oath.'

Catesby could see no alternative.

'I don't know, Robin,' Tom said. 'A lot of people might be very upset by what we're planning. There's no guarantee the oath would hold them. Even a close friend might react badly.'

'It's a valid point,' Catesby conceded. Thomas Bates, his manservant, had had severe doubts about the plot when he had first been approached to join. It was more out of loyalty to his master than faith in the idea which had finally persuaded him to become part of the conspiracy. 'At least I can tell people it *is* theologically justified.' The discussion Catesby had had with Father Henry would prove a useful reference point.

'Only an idiot would doubt it,' Percy exclaimed. 'Anyone else want another drink?'

Catesby left the lodgings soon after. Tom Wintour walked with him for a while through the grimy back streets. It was an unusually warm night. A gentle breeze carried the unwelcome aroma of the River Thames, half a mile to the south. Catesby was heading in that direction. Both men had lodgings on the Strand, some fifteen minute's walk away.

The streets were surprisingly empty. A handful of prostitutes were plying their trade on the corner of High Holborn. A one-legged beggar was picking fleas out of his hair. Muffled laughter could be heard from a nearby tavern. Many people had already left the capital. Catesby would follow suit on the morrow.

They reached Holborn and turned right.

'Why didn't you tell Father Henry everything?' Tom asked. Catesby had related to him the details of his meeting with the Jesuit Superior. 'The authorities will need to be told the truth at some point.'

'I know. But Father Henry would not approve. You said yourself: it's dangerous to let out the information left, right and centre.'

'Not to a priest. Especially under the Seal of Confession. He would be obliged to keep the secret, even if he did disapprove.'

Catesby scratched his head. 'Not every priest will keep every confession, Tom, no matter how clear the theology. They are only human, after all.'

'Father Henry would never betray a confidence,' Tom insisted, struggling to keep pace with his taller friend. 'We should tell him everything. If we can get official sanction, it will make it easier to convert others to the cause. And far easier to raise funds.'

'I suppose.'

'We should at least consider it.'

Catesby stopped dead. 'All right. I'll give it some thought, I promise.'

'That's all I ask, Robin.'

The Strand was not much further along. The streets were busier here. The cousins continued their journey in silence.

Catesby did not believe for a minute that Father Henry would approve of his plan. But a confession could prove useful in other ways. And there was one method by which he could ensure the priest would not be able to discuss the matter with anyone else. It was a risky strategy, but the rewards would be substantial.

Catesby bade his cousin goodnight as they arrived at the *Duck and Drake*; then he made his own way to the *Irish Boy*. It would be several weeks before the two men saw each other again.

By then, Catesby would have put his plan into effect.

Chapter Fourteen

Francis Tresham spun the dice across the table and let out a satisfied cry. 'Double six!' he exclaimed, with a little too much enthusiasm. 'That's another two shillings you owe me, Robin!'

Catesby groaned. 'You have the luck of the devil, Francis. That's three double sixes in a row.'

'Oh, you're just jealous. I beat you at draughts. Now I've beaten you at dice. And I'll beat you at tennis later. You see if I don't.'

Catesby could well believe it. He put a hand into his purse and produced a few coins. 'At this rate, I'll be bankrupt by sun down.'

Tresham was grinning from ear to ear. 'I wish it was always this easy to get money out of you!'

At thirty eight years of age, Francis Tresham was a good half decade older than his cousin. With jet black hair, a handlebar moustache and a long, slender nose, he had a mature appearance which masked a somewhat childish disposition.

At the mention of money, Catesby grimaced. More debts. He owed Tresham's father quite a bit of money. Sir Thomas had helped him to pay a rather large fine some years previously and even now Catesby was struggling to pay it back. Recently, what with other expenses, he had defaulted on the interest for the loan. 'I'll see your father gets his money,' he promised faithfully. 'Just give me a couple more weeks.'

Tresham looked doubtful. 'That's what you said at Whitsun!' The man was grinning benignly, but Catesby knew how seriously he regarded such matters. Tresham had served time in prison for beating up debtors. 'Don't get me wrong. It's no big deal,' he insisted. 'It's just if you don't pay up soon, it's me you're going to be owing the money to, not my father.'

Tresham's father, a wealthy landowner, was in his sixties.

'I've heard he wasn't well,' Catesby admitted sadly.

'On his way out, I'm afraid. Still, should mean I'll come into a bit of money some time soon.'

'You shouldn't be flippant about it, Francis.'

'I'm not being flippant. The old bastard never did anything for me.'

That was not fair. 'He bailed you out of prison.'

Tresham looked away. 'Only out of a sense of duty.' He picked up the dice. 'You want another go?'

Catesby held up his hands. 'I can't afford it!'

'Please yourself. I'll see if I can find Sir William. He's bound to want a game.' Lord Monteagle was one of several house guests staying at Fremlands. The man was married to Tresham's sister, Elizabeth.

Tresham bounded across the lawn and back into the house.

Catesby shook his head. He had known Francis Tresham all his life. They had been through a lot and a great deal of affection existed between them. But the man was incorrigible. He drank to excess, gambled huge sums of money and had a ferocious temper. He did not behave in a fitting manner for one of his rank.

A cough from behind interrupted Catesby's thoughts. Father Henry Garnet had stepped out onto the lawn.

Catesby smiled and gestured for the priest to take a seat. This was the first opportunity the two men had had to be alone together since arriving at Fremlands. After his discussion with Tom Wintour, Catesby was anxious to talk with the Jesuit Superior.

Father Henry seated himself on the bench and cleared his throat hesitantly. A few hours earlier, he had been entertaining the household with an extended session on the lute. Now, sitting on a wooden bench out in the grounds of the house facing away from the main building, the man seemed considerably less jovial. Evidently, like Catesby, he had a serious matter he wished to discuss. Catesby allowed the priest to open the conversation.

'I received a letter just recently from Father Claudio Aquaviva...' Father Henry began.

Catesby grimaced. The foreign Jesuit was always sticking his oar in.

'I wrote to him after our recent conversation,' Father Henry continued, somewhat uncertainly. 'It...occurred to me that you may have had some ulterior motive in seeking my advice the other week.'

Catesby frowned slightly, looking out across the moors. Fremlands was situated on top of a low hill, affording a good view of the surrounding countryside. 'I just...wished to hear your opinion,' he replied, non-committally.

'But not about the Low Countries, I fear. It pains me to say this, Robin, but I believe that you were not being entirely honest in your intentions.'

Catesby cast his eyes downwards. 'Father, I...'

'Tell me now, Robin. Are you rushing headlong into some mischief?'

Catesby took a deep breath. Equivocation was one thing. Father Henry had written much on that particular subject. But an outright lie was altogether different. Catesby had sworn to himself that he would not lie to a priest 'I...I've wanted to tell you for some time...' he began. 'I've discussed it with Tom...'

Father Henry held up a hand. Catesby had never seen such a serious expression on the face of the priest. 'The letter from Father Claudio is quite explicit. You have heard similar injunctions in the past. The Pope commands all English Catholics to suffer in silence. There is to be no insurrection. And I am commanded to ensure that these instructions are carried out.' Father Henry spoke with a quiet intensity which brooked no disagreement. It seemed scarcely credible that this was the same man who had entertained them all that morning.

'Father Claudio doesn't speak directly for His Holiness,' Catesby protested. 'And I swear to you, what we are planning would not meet with his disapproval. Not if the Pope knew all the details. Just allow me to explain it to you. We could treat it as a confession, if you like...'

Father Henry rose sharply to his feet and strode several paces across the lawn. Catesby could see his agitation. 'I'm sorry, Robin. If you really are planning something, here in England, I can't listen to you. I am forbidden by express command from His Holiness. You must understand, I *cannot* be made aware of any plot.' The middle-aged Jesuit turned back. 'But if you were considering – for example – the murder of some... great person, then you must think again. The letter from Father Claudio is quite specific. Despite what you say, Señor Aquaviva is writing directly on behalf of the Pope. I have been commanded to hinder, by all means possible, any insurrection or undutiful proceedings against His Majesty or the State. If you're planning something that might plunge this country into civil war, it is my clear and present duty to stop you in any way I can.'

'I…'

'I mean it, Robin. You must think very seriously about the lawfulness of any act you might commit. You cannot have so little regard to innocents that you are prepared to kill your own friends and those people who rightfully govern…'

Father Henry broke off. His gaze passed over Catesby towards the house. Catesby looked back. Francis Tresham had wandered back out from the main building.

'We're about to play some cards,' Tresham called. 'Would you fine gentlemen care to join us?'

Catesby glanced at Father Henry. 'Why not?' he said, rising to his feet.

If the Jesuit Superior was unwilling to listen to his confession, then there was no point in discussing the matter further. Catesby would speak to Father Tesimond instead. The younger priest would be sure to listen; and if Catesby gave his consent, Tesimond would then go straight to Father Henry. Both priests would be implicated in the plot and would have no choice but to grant their approval. Catesby did not want to force the issue in such an unpleasant manner, but Father Henry had left him no choice.

He circled the bench and followed the priest back into the house.

Lord Monteagle was already dealing the cards. 'You're looking frightfully serious,' he observed, as Catesby sat down opposite the young nobleman. Sir William Parker – the Lord Monteagle – was a respected Catholic Member of Parliament. He was a sombre, thin-faced man in his late twenties. Catesby had known him for years, though they were not close friends. Monteagle was one of those peers certain to die in the House of Lords, if Catesby chose not to warn him.

'We were discussing the discontent amongst English Catholics,' Catesby explained to him, as Henry Garnet took his seat. 'I was telling the Father how much resentment is building up. At some point, it's going to boil over.'

'Do you think there will be armed revolt?' Father Henry asked Lord Monteagle.

Sir William shrugged. 'It's possible. James is odious to all sorts of people.'

'Father Aquaviva has commanded me to prevent hostilities at all costs. But some people are not content to accept his advice.'

Lord Monteagle picked up the cards and examined his hand carefully. The man did not seem to have detected any subtext to the conversation. 'Then why not speak to the Pope directly?' he suggested. 'Get His Holiness to make an explicit statement. No right minded Catholic would ignore a direct Papal command.'

Father Henry looked at Catesby. 'Do you think that would satisfy people? If the Pope were consulted directly.'

Catesby looked away. 'I…I think it may.'

'Perhaps then we should send a representative to Flanders, to make a case in front of the Papal Nuncio at Brussels. His Holiness the Pope can be asked directly what should be done about the plight of the English Catholics. Surely that would satisfy even the most zealous of men, if the case were well presented?'

'You're right,' Catesby admitted reluctantly. 'His Holiness should adjudicate on the matter before anyone takes up arms.' He crossed himself mentally. Despite his best intentions, the priest had forced him into an outright lie.

He leaned forward to pick up a playing card from the table.

'And there is always the possibility that the new Parliament will have a more favourable attitude,' Father Henry suggested.

'Absolutely.' Catesby nodded. 'We should explore every avenue.' He kept his voice positive but his heart was beating quickly. The priest meant well but the two men were already a world apart. Catesby would have to be more forthright when he spoke to Father Oswald Tesimond.

The Jesuit arrived at Father Henry's lodging on Thames Street in the middle of the afternoon. He was in a state of considerable distress. Henry Garnet met him at the door. 'Oswald? What's the matter?' Oswald Tesimond's rounded face radiated uncertainty.

'I need to speak to you.'

Father Henry quickly gestured the younger man inside.

The priest's lodgings were modest and sparsely furnished. A Jesuit in England knew not to put down too many roots. Tesimond passed through into the main room, a plain, oak panelled chamber.

Wood had been piled up in the hearth but no fire was burning. There was a table and a few shelves but little else to draw the eye.

Tesimond glanced about nervously, making sure that the room was empty. He could not afford for this particular conversation to be overheard.

Father Henry was standing in the frame of the doorway, watching his younger friend. The elder Jesuit had acted as a mentor for Father Tesimond since his return from Rome seven years earlier. Despite the age gap, the priests had always got along well. They shared the same taste in Spanish wine and fine clothing. They liked good food and amusing company. And they were both utterly dedicated to the spiritual well-being of their flock.

Tesimond had always looked up to Father Henry. Even now, he was a little in awe of the man's great wisdom and experience. There was no-one in whom he would more willingly confide. He came straight to the point. 'I've just taken confession from Robert Catesby. He came to me this morning.'

A flicker of concern flashed across Father Henry's gaunt face. It was gone in an instant, but Tesimond was sure he had not imagined it. Did the Jesuit Superior already know something of this matter?

'Oswald, you of all people know you cannot discuss another man's confession. The Seal of the Confessional is sacrosanct.'

Oswald Tesimond looked away. He had not expected criticism over such an obvious point. And there had been an edge to Father Henry's words. 'Robin has given me permission to talk to you, under the Seal.' Such things were permitted, if the penitent was willing. 'It is a most grave matter,' Tesimond insisted. 'One which I do not feel competent to deal with.'

Catesby's confession had left the ruddy-faced Jesuit almost speechless with fear. Never in his darkest imaginings had he thought to hear such devilish words imparted under the Seal of the Confessional. It was the sort of thing one read of in textbooks.

Father Henry moved across the room to a small window, looking out onto the street. His response was startling. 'I think it is best that you keep your penitent's secret. It would serve no purpose to inform me.'

Oswald Tesimond stared at the other man, his jaw open. He had never known his friend to refuse help to anybody. Why on earth *would* he refuse? In the circumstances, Tesimond had no choice but to insist. 'I must discuss this with somebody. And I have no-one else I can turn to. Please, Father. If something is not done, a great injury will be inflicted on the Catholic community of this country.'

Father Henry looked back. His eyes were steely. 'I am under orders not to get involved with any trouble. You know that, Oswald. If you are going to divulge information concerning any potential stir in England, then I simply cannot listen.'

'But – '

'I'm sorry. I cannot.'

'Not even under the Seal of the Confessional…'

'Not even then. I'm sorry, Oswald. Truly. But you must deal with this yourself.'

'It is more than my soul can bear!' Tesimond cried.

The two men stood quietly for a moment. The sudden silence accentuated the impact of those final words. At last, the expression on Henry Garnet's face began to soften. Their friendship counted for something after all. Father Henry let out a gentle sigh, then moved across and grabbed the other priest's shoulders. 'Very well, Oswald. I will hear what you have to say.' He spoke quietly, with obvious reluctance. 'But we will have to do it under the Seal.'

Tesimond nodded. He would be breaking faith with his penitent if he discussed the matter in any other manner. This way, Father Henry would be subject to the same vow of confidentiality as he had been. The priest began to lower himself to the floor but Father Henry stopped him halfway.

'There's no need to kneel, Oswald. In the circumstances, I think we would be better served discussing this out in the garden.'

The younger Jesuit hesitated but Father Henry was adamant. 'If you are about to tell me what I think you are about to tell me,' he said, 'it is better it is away from prying ears…'

The garden was a small but pleasant square to the rear of the lodging. There was a narrow bench on which the two men could sit, but Father Henry kept to his feet and paced up and down the garden as Tesimond told the Jesuit Superior everything he had learned. He kept the details brief but he could see the darkness growing in Henry Garnet's eyes. He had felt much the same when

Catesby had spoken to him that morning. The confession had been as unexpected as it had been shocking.

Dear sweet Robin. Tesimond had always loved him. But now the man had lost his wits; had planted a ton of gunpowder underneath the Houses of Parliament and intended to blow up the King and all of the lords sometime during the next parliamentary session.

'This will be the ruin of all of us,' Father Henry said, when Tesimond had completed the story. 'His Holiness will hold me personally responsible. I'm supposed to be guiding my flock, not standing by as they rush headlong into the fires of Hell.' Father Henry halted mid-stride and swung around to face the younger priest. 'You must speak to Robin. He will listen to you. Tell him I condemn this utterly. Persuade him to seek guidance from Rome. He must inform the Pope of his intentions. Otherwise, he will send us all to the gallows.'

'I'll tell him,' Father Tesimond agreed. 'I'm sure he will understand what a difficult position he has placed us in.' Tesimond could not disguise his relief. Now at least the two men could combine their efforts. 'Robin is a good man at heart. He would not wish to cause us any undue suffering.'

Father Henry was scornful. 'That is exactly what he has done, by confessing in this manner. I wish to God he had kept this to himself. Now we can't do anything. We can't break the Seal of the Confessional but we cannot allow this atrocity to be committed. He must be made to understand the necessity of Papal approval. Even Robin would not dare persist with such a plan if His Holiness threatened excommunication.'

'I'll arrange a meeting,' Tesimond suggested. 'He will listen to you, Father. I'm sure of it.'

'I hope so, Oswald. Dear God, I hope so.'

Catesby knew exactly what to expect.

As soon as he received the summons from the Jesuit Superior he rode straight to White Webbs, the country house in Middlesex where Father Henry often stayed. Almost a year had passed since their first confrontation, at the dining table of this same country house. On that occasion, Catesby had allowed himself to lose his temper. He had not been able to hide his scorn for Henry Garnet's policy of quiet submission. Now, he felt guilty but in control. The entrapment was necessary. By informing the Jesuits of the plot, Catesby had satisfied the consciences of his colleagues, but he had also managed to pass on the information in such a way that the priests could not tell anyone else about it without his direct consent. Furthermore, the men had provided him with an officially sanctioned theological basis for the conspiracy which would prove vital in persuading new recruits of the rightness of their cause. All the Jesuits could do, conversely, was to voice their disapproval. And that Catesby could bear well enough.

He arrived at White Webbs mid-afternoon. The discreet rural house was a little way off the Barnet Road. Like Baddesley Clinton, it had been rented by his cousin Anne almost wholly for the purposes of hiding Jesuit priests. Father Henry often resided here when he was away from London.

Catesby usually received a warm welcome at the house, but this time the greetings were perfunctory.

'This plan of yours is madness, Robin,' Father Henry asserted, in a quiet back room. It was quite a shock to see the man so angry. In all the years Catesby had known him, the mild-mannered priest had never previously lost his temper. 'This is not a time of war. You cannot justify killing your own sovereign and destroying the whole apparatus of state.'

Catesby was prepared for a theological debate. 'You said yourself, Father: if it is for the Greater Good of the Catholic cause, then a few innocent lives lost cannot be allowed to get in the way.'

'This is not a time of war, Robin. And it will not just be a few innocents. This plot will condemn us all. You have a duty to your Church. Any action that you take has repercussions far beyond even the borders of this country. At the very least, the Pope must be informed of the plan. It cannot succeed without Papal approval.'

'If the Pope knew the details of this plan, he would certainly approve,' Catesby affirmed confidently. 'Why would His Holiness hinder a plan that will reverse the fortunes of every Catholic in England?'

'He will forbid this plan, as I have done. I have had a letter from Father Robert Weston.' Father Henry reached down to produce the correspondence. 'He reiterates yet again the official policy of the Pope. There should be no uprising in England. English Catholics must endure the hardships put upon them and leave the conversion of the state to Providence. It is here, in black and white.'

'From Father Weston. Not from the Pope.' Catesby waved the document away. 'I'm not going to stay my hand because of third party advice.'

Father Henry placed the letter down on the window ledge. 'But what if the Pope told you so directly?'

'He would not.'

'Then you have nothing to lose by consulting him.'

Catesby took a deep breath and allowed himself to hesitate for a moment. He had expected this tactic. The Jesuit Superior had forwarded the idea at Fremlands a couple of weeks earlier, before Catesby had even made his confession. 'Very well. You suggested I should send a letter to Rome and that is what I will do. My good friend Sir Edmund Baynham can deliver it for us.' Baynham had been the priest's preferred choice. 'I'll outline the plot in its broadest terms and will wait for Papal approval. There's plenty of time for a response. Parliament is still several months from sitting.'

Father Henry eyed his friend suspiciously. 'You will allow me to see the letter you send?'

'I will fully outline the case. You're right. The Pope should be informed. I'll send word to Sir Edmund on the morrow.'

Father Henry frowned for a moment, then nodded. 'Thank you, Robin. It is the right thing to do.'

Catesby smiled. 'Of course.'

The Jesuit left White Webbs shortly afterwards.

Catesby tarried there for a while, making the necessary preparations. He fully intended to contact Baynham. He had not lied to the priest about that. But he would make it clear to the fellow that he was not to reach the Pope until after the opening of Parliament. Baynham was easily corruptible. The man was only interested in money. He could rest up in Flanders for a few months. Then, when he got word of the explosion from Catesby, he could be sent on to Rome to inform His Holiness.

Father Henry had probably not been convinced by Catesby's sudden change of heart. The Jesuit Superior was too shrewd to be so easily fooled. No doubt he would write to Rome off his own back. But without Catesby's consent to discuss the matter, he could only allude to circumstances in the broadest of terms. If Father Henry broke the Seal of the Confessional, Father Tesimond would be honour bound to report the matter. And by the time Rome had formulated a response, it would be far too late to intercede…

Chapter Fifteen

Thomas Percy had gone to Bath to take the waters. After the discomfort of the mine and the perils of adding several barrels of gunpowder to the cellar beneath the House of Lords, he felt he deserved a short break; a time to relax and take it easy, before the quarterly grind of rent collection came upon him once again.

When a letter arrived from Robert Catesby, suggesting yet another meeting, Percy was rather put out. He had been enjoying the peace and quiet. The spa was within walking distance of the small inn where he had taken a room and he had gone each day to bathe in the natural springs. The bubbling water had soothed his aching limbs and put the middle-aged rascal in an unusually positive frame of mind. And now Catesby had to go and ruin it all. Doubtless there were things to discuss, but surely the matter could have waited a few more days?

At least Catesby had done him the courtesy of coming to Bath, rather than making Percy trek all the way up to the Midlands. If he had been forced to travel to Ashby St. Ledgers, there would scarcely have been any point coming back afterwards.

Percy poured out a cup of sack from a jug and relit his pipe. Catesby had arrived at his lodging earlier that afternoon, with Tom Wintour in tow. Percy had already spent an amiable hour drinking and playing cards with the two of them, but now that they had finished their supper it was time to get down to business.

'So what's this all about?' he asked.

Catesby cleared his throat. 'The plain fact is I've run out of money,' he admitted, sheepishly. 'I can raise a bit of cash if I sell Bushwood but not enough to see us through 'till Michaelmas. So… we need to find an alternative source of income. A bit of new blood to inject some capital into our venture.'

Percy gave a weary sigh. 'We've discussed all this before,' he said, clenching the clay pipe between his teeth. 'Obviously, we're going to needs funds to organise people in the Midlands. Any kind of uprising needs money.' Catesby had already been sounding out individuals to join the proposed hunting party on Dunsmore Heath. These men, Percy knew, would form the fighting force to kidnap the young Princess Elizabeth at Combe Abbey. 'We've gone over all this a dozen times.'

'Yes, in principle. But this goes beyond persuading a few noblemen to join a hunting expedition. None of the people I've spoken to so far have been told anything about the plot itself.'

'So what are you asking?' Tom Wintour enquired.

'Well. If I'm going to raise funds, I'm going to have to approach one or two people directly.'

'Fine. So approach them,' Percy said. 'Why bother to come here?'

'Because I swore an oath not to discuss the details of this scheme with anyone else. Not without your consent.'

'And that's what you're after?' Percy scoffed. 'Our permission to go off and talk to people on your own?'

'That's what I'm after.' He nodded. 'Obviously, I'm only talking about a handful of carefully selected individuals. But I can't pretend that it doesn't present some degree of risk.'

'Who do you have in mind?' Tom asked.

'I haven't made up my mind in every case. I'd prefer to keep some of the names private for now. But I was thinking of Ambrose Rookwood, for one.' The colourful young horseman had already helped Catesby to obtain some of the gunpowder they had stored at Westminster. Thus far, however, the man knew nothing about the plot.

'He's a good fellow,' Tom admitted.

'Bit young mind,' said Percy. Ambrose Rookwood was practically a boy at twenty-seven years old. Percy could never quite forget how much older he was than the rest of the conspirators. 'You know he was up before the magistrates earlier this year? A massive fine, so I heard. He may not have much ready cash.'

'But he does have access to a great many horses,' Catesby said. 'That will be crucial. We need to be able to co-ordinate events between London and Dunchurch. He has one of the best stables in England.' Horses could be stationed at various intervals along the way. That would be vital if news was to be got from London to the Midlands in good time. 'He'll be able to provide fresh horses along the entire route.'

'And being fined will certainly make him more sympathetic to our cause,' Tom agreed. 'I think he's a good choice.'

'Still doesn't solve the money problem, though,' Percy pointed out, taking another drag from his pipe. 'I should be able to get you three or four thousand from the rents, but that won't be until October at least.'

'Well, any time before November will help.' Catesby stood up and walked over to the window. Parliament had recently been prorogued for another month. The official state opening was now set for November the Fifth. He glanced down at the street. It was dark outside but the city centre was bustling with people. A pie man was selling hot food to a small queue of hungry workers. A child screamed from a nearby alleyway. 'I was also thinking of asking somebody a little more elevated...'

Tom was seated by the fire. 'Lord Monteagle?' He frowned. 'I'm not sure that that would be wise...'

Catesby shook his head, turning back from the window. 'No, I wasn't referring to Lord Monteagle. I don't think it would be right to approach him. I was thinking of somebody else; someone based in the Midlands.' He moved away from the window and returned to the fire, warming his hands in the flickering light.

'Lord Mourdant?' Tom guessed.

'I'd prefer not to say.'

Percy gritted his teeth. More secrets. But he didn't push the matter. Catesby's judgement had been sound up to now. 'Having a Catholic lord or even a knight on our side will certainly give us credibility,' he admitted. 'It'll be a useful tool when we need to rally support down south.'

'That's what I was thinking. And the man I have in mind will definitely be able to help with the finances.'

'That will bring the number up to twelve,' said Tom. 'Assuming they both agree. That should be enough, shouldn't it?' He looked across. 'Robin?'

Catesby took a moment before he replied. 'I did have one other person in mind. But I'm not altogether sure...'

Guido Fawkes lifted the lid from the top of the barrel and propped it up against the wall. He slid a hand into the dormant powder and sifted the material between his fingers. It was a simple mixture of fine charcoal, sulphur and saltpetre. Each of the ingredients was harmless on its own, but together – with the right trigger – the chemicals could be highly volatile. Unfortunately, the mixture had a habit of breaking down if it was left on its own for long periods of time. That was what was happening to the gunpowder in this barrel. Fawkes shook his head sadly. 'It was never intended to be stored for this long.'

Mr Fawkes had just returned from Flanders and had gone to Parliament to check up on the powder. As soon as he had discovered the problem, he had alerted Tom Wintour, who joined him now in the cellar.

Tom had only visited the place a handful of times before. The room was dark and narrow. It was not really a cellar at all – it was situated on the ground floor – but it *felt* like a cellar. There were two entrances, firmly shut, at one end of the chamber and a third along the far wall. The only visible light came from the candles the two men had brought with them. They were keeping these well away from the powder in the barrels.

The wooden containers were covered over in any case. A large quantity of fire wood had been purchased to act as camouflage. Huge stones had been planted on top of each drum, then timber and iron piled up in front of them together with the faggots and all kinds of other innocuous household items. It would take some time to dig them all out, if it ever proved necessary.

'Is it all like this?' Tom asked.

'I haven't checked every barrel,' Fawkes admitted. It would have been impractical for one man to examine them all. 'This is the sixth one I've opened. The first two were fine. Those are the ones Mr Percy delivered while I was away. The third one contained some of our original powder, which was beginning to break down. The other three barrels are essentially lost.'

Tom bit his lower lip. 'It doesn't seem that damp in here,' he observed, glancing at the thick stone walls.

Fawkes picked up the lid of the barrel and placed it firmly back on top of the powder. 'It doesn't really need to be. Time does it work, no matter what the location.' Ten years in the army had made him an expert on this particular subject. 'It wouldn't have lasted any longer if we'd left it in the house,' he said. 'And if we'd planted it at the end of our tunnel, it would have decayed in just a few days.'

Tom scratched his chin. 'We need more powder then.'

'I should say so.'

He sighed. 'Robin won't like this. I'm afraid he's on his last legs financially.'

'I only wish I could help.' Since resigning his commission, Guido Fawkes had had no independent income. He had been forced to rely on Mr Catesby to provide lodgings for him and even to pay for his passage to and from the Low Countries.

'I have a small amount of money set aside,' Tom admitted. 'I thought to hold it back for later.' Tom was better placed financially than Fawkes, but he was not exactly rich either. What little income he did have was mostly earnt in the service of Lord Monteagle. 'I was going to provide some extra horses for the hunting party on Dunsmore Heath. That's about all I can afford.'

'The hunting party won't achieve anything if the powder doesn't blow, Mr Wintour.'

Tom nodded. 'You're right. We have no choice. We'll have to get more.'

'And wood too,' Fawkes suggested. He pushed the redundant barrel back towards the others. The two men covered it over with the small bundles of firewood.

'Are you staying in London for a few days? It might take me a while to organise everything.'

'I can stay here at the house, if you think it will help.' Nobody would question Mr John Johnson remaining in the vicinity of Westminster for a week or two.

'Probably best,' Tom agreed. 'We'll have to bring the powder in by river. We can carry it up through the Cotton Garden and via the back entrance.' That was how Mr Percy had smuggled the extra barrels in a few weeks earlier. 'Hopefully then we won't be seen.'

'During the night, I take it?'

'It'll have to be. I'll send word to you when to expect me.'

Chapter Sixteen

Ambrose Rookwood was the first of the new recruits.

The flamboyant young landowner was staying at Huddington Court at the end of September. The half-timbered manor house was situated a few miles south of Droitwich. Catesby had met Ambrose on the bridge leading up to the manor and had greeted his friend enthusiastically. Ambrose was a good-natured fellow in his late twenties. He was short and somewhat lean but what he lacked in stature he made up for in style. His garish clothing and ostentatious jewellery were a constant source of amusement.

The two men had often shared a meal together. Their lodgings in London were close by and they had met up many times over the previous year. But Catesby had told his friend nothing of the plot itself and when the veteran conspirator began dropping hints about a venture he was engaged upon Ambrose simply assumed he was talking about his new regiment.

The two friends had gone out riding that afternoon. Ambrose had a passion for horses and it was this as much as his financial resources that had persuaded Catesby to approach the younger man. He had brought a prayer book with him and when they had put some distance between themselves and Huddington Court Catesby had asked Ambrose to swear the oath of secrecy. Once this was done, he revealed all: his friend had not been acquiring gunpowder for the purposes of equipping a foreign regiment. He had acquired it for the purposes of assassinating King James.

Ambrose Rookwood was understandably shocked. His eyes were wide in disbelief. 'You're not joking, are you?' he breathed incredulously. 'You really are going to kill the King.'

Catesby nodded gravely, dismounting his horse.

For a moment, Ambrose was lost for words. He jumped down from the saddle and moved away, staring out across the fields.

Catesby walked over to retrieve the prayer book. 'We have no choice,' he said. 'It's the only way things will ever change.'

Ambrose grimaced, looking round. 'But what about all the other people who'll be there? What about the Catholics?'

'They must die too,' Catesby admitted sadly.

Ambrose closed his eyes.

'I wouldn't have entered into a scheme of this kind if I hadn't been sure of the rightness of our cause,' Catesby assured him. 'Believe me, I have wrestled long and hard over the morality of it. But I have spoken to members of the Society of Jesus and they have reassured me that the death of a few innocents can be justified, if it is for the greater good of the Catholic faith. And certainly it would be no sin to kill the King.'

Ambrose frowned again. 'So…you've spoken to Father Henry?'

'I have. He knows all about the plot. Well, perhaps not the day-to-day details, but certainly the thrust of it,' Catesby said. 'I've spoken to the Father several times, at great length, and he has dismissed any doubts I may have had about the theological justification of such an act.' Catesby was being very careful with his words, but he could do so now without allowing it to sound contrived. He had had plenty of practise at the art of equivocation.

'But just the scale of it…' Ambrose breathed.

'The idea does take a bit of getting used to.'

The two friends returned to their horses and slowly made their way back to Huddington Court. The stables at the Worcestershire residence housed a number of fine animals, but they were as nothing compared to the horses Ambrose would contribute to the conspiracy, if only he would agree to join.

The sticking point for Ambrose – as it had been with Tom Wintour – was inevitably the question of the Catholic peers in the House of Lords. 'I find it hard to accept that every single one of them has to die,' he said, carefully leading his now exhausted horse up the lane towards the manor house. Many of the noblemen who would die in the blast were close friends of his. 'Couldn't we warn one or two of them to stay away?'

'Not if it puts the plan in any danger.'

'But it wouldn't, necessarily,' Ambrose insisted. 'There are *some* men in the House of Lords who can be trusted to keep a secret, Robin, even if they are in the minority.'

Ambrose was so firm on this point that Catesby was forced to backtrack: 'Maybe we could warn a couple of people,' he conceded. 'One or two friends, perhaps. But we couldn't tell them anything specific. They would have to be kept away by some… trick or other.'

That seemed to satisfy the young landowner.

'Your help is vital,' Catesby insisted. 'Not just on the financial side. We need you to deliver the message from London, to tell us when the powder is blown. You have some of the best horses in the kingdom. And you're one of the best riders.'

Ambrose raised an eyebrow. A hint of amusement had finally returned to his rounded young face. 'Only *one* of the best?'

'I hear the King's rather good on horseback,' Catesby joked.

The shorter man took a swipe at him.

They moved onto the bridge leading back to the estate. 'You may need to move a little closer to Combe Abbey, though.'

Ambrose Rookwood had a home near Bury St. Edmunds. 'You want me to *move*?' he asked, somewhat taken aback.

'Only temporarily,' Catesby reassured him, stepping off the bridge and onto the short pathway running parallel with the house. For the sake of the plan, the gifted horseman would need to be much closer to Coventry. 'I was thinking you could rent Clopton Hall.'

Ambrose scratched his neck. 'I don't know what Elizabeth would say about that.'

'It's just for a few months. That would mean that everyone involved in the plot would be within about fifteen miles of each other.' Catesby stopped at the entrance to the stables. 'So. What do you think?'

Ambrose rubbed his chin. 'I'm speechless,' he said. 'If it were anyone else, Robin, I'd think they were mad.'

'You'll consider it?'

He paused for just a moment. 'There's no need,' he said. 'I'm in.'

A proclamation was being read out in the House of Lords.

Parliament was not officially in session, but a large number of peers had still gathered in the Upper Chamber to hear the announcement. For Tom Wintour, it was a perfect opportunity to observe proceedings. He had returned to London specifically to attend the one day event. Reserving his usual lodgings on the Strand, he had made his way up to the Houses of Parliament in the company of his employer, Lord Monteagle.

The contents of the proclamation were already well known. It was the second time this year that such a declaration had been made in the Upper Chamber. In February, there had been the official pronouncement that Parliament had been prorogued until October the Third. Now, October having arrived, there was the announcement that the State Opening of Parliament had been delayed for another month. The decision to postpone the new session had been taken back in July, but parliamentary procedure dictated a public declaration on the day itself.

Nobody had been discussing any of this the previous evening. Arriving in town, Tom had shared a few pints with some old friends at the *Duck and Drake* Inn. The only topic of conversation there was the solar eclipse, which had taken place earlier that same day. Tom had caught sight of the eclipse from the coach as he was coming into London. The coachman had pulled over to the side of the road and allowed the passengers to get out and watch. None of them had seen anything like it before. The sky went completely black for almost a minute in broad daylight. One little boy, travelling with his mother, had burst into tears.

It was not the first such astronomical event. Two weeks earlier there had been a lunar eclipse. Tom had missed that, but it had caused a great deal of comment. Now, with the solar eclipse following so quickly afterwards, the response had turned from wonderment to nervous concern. Many of the patrons at the *Duck and Drake* were convinced the double eclipse was an ill omen; it could not bode well for the future, they said. Or the new Parliament.

Tom Wintour was sure of it. He had always resisted an overtly superstitious interpretation of astronomical events. Such things were predictable and well understood, though Tom did not understand the details himself. Nevertheless, as Catesby had pointed out after the lunar eclipse, it certainly heralded bad luck for the Protestants in the coming session.

A few members of the lesser nobility were allowed into the near end of the House of Lords to observe proceedings. As secretary to Lord Monteagle, Tom had little trouble gaining admittance. He had arrived side-by-side with his employer and the two men had entered the building together. Monteagle took his place in the chamber. Tom stayed back behind the bar to watch proceedings, while the rest of the lords began filing into the hall.

The House of Lords was a long narrow room. Two sets of wooden benches faced each other in the middle of the hall. At the far end sat a large throne, covered over. The peers were beginning to fill up the benches on either side.

Tom scanned the faces carefully. The great and the good of England would be here. Everyone but the King himself. Tom looked down at the floor. None of them could know about the quantities of gunpowder stockpiled directly beneath their feet. A single well placed match would kill them all.

Tom closed his eyes briefly. He did not relish the prospect. But Robin was right. This place and these people had done them all great wrong. The next session of Parliament could destroy the Catholic religion in England forever. There was no option left but to respond decisively, to protect the people of England. Destroying the House of Lords was an act of self-defence. Nothing more, nothing less.

Tom's greatest fear now was discovery. Was there any chance that the government had learnt of the plot? The gunpowder had not been tampered with. Mr Fawkes had examined it closely when they had laid down the new powder and he was certain that nobody had meddled with anything in the cellar. But what if some other information had come to the authorities? A servant confused by various comings and goings. A stray word overheard in a tavern. The conspirators had taken great pains to keep everything secret. No reference to the plot had been made in any of their correspondence. But it only took a single suspicious mind and the whole matter might be exposed.

And that would mean death for all of them.

Tom took a deep breath and scrutinized the faces as each nobleman took up his position on the wooden benches. He recognised the Earl of Northampton and the Earl of Essex. A few other faces were also familiar. The House would not be full today. Many Members would not have returned from the country. There was no reason, however, for any of the Privy Council to be absent. If the King's own advisors stayed away, it could mean only one thing: that the plot was uncovered. If the authorities knew about the powder, they would hardly risk attending Parliament; not when a single match could kill them all. If the members of the Privy Council were here, then the plot was secure. For now.

Robert Cecil was the main concern. The King's principle secretary, Cecil was the man who claimed to know everything that went on in the kingdom; the man who kept spies in every city, in England and the Low Countries; the man who had effectively been running England for the past ten years. If Cecil was here, they were safe. Tom knew him by sight. He had even spoken to the man a couple of times. Tom's position as Monteagle's secretary meant that he often socialised with members of the upper rank. Cecil, too, was an easy fellow to recognise. He was short and hunch-backed, with a narrowly compressed face and an oddly prominent nose.

And here he was, taking his place with the others on the front bench of the House of Lords. England's greatest Spy Master was in complete ignorance of the plot.

Tom Wintour grabbed the wooden banister tightly and tried to disguise the relief on his face. Everything was going according to plan. It was almost too good to be true.

Part Four
Treason

"…though there be no appearance of any stir yet I say they shall receive a terrible blow this parliament…"
- Anonymous 26th October 1605

Chapter Seventeen

Francis Tresham bit into a fruit pie and glared at Robert Catesby. 'I'm not joining your regiment, if that's what you're asking.' He swallowed a mouthful of pastry and wiped the crumbs from his moustache with the sleeve of his shirt. 'I've got enough on my plate at the moment, what with my father dying. You would not believe the state he left his affairs in. He was supposed to be one of the richest men in England, but he was up to his eyeballs in debt.'

Sir Thomas Tresham had passed away at the end of September. It was his death, in part, which had prompted Catesby to approach his cousin. 'It wasn't entirely your father's doing,' he pointed out, diplomatically. 'A lot of the money was spent covering up for other people's mistakes…' Specifically, covering up for Francis Tresham. The man had led a reckless and extravagant life. Much of the family fortune had already been squandered.

'That's in the past. I've got children now. I intend to take my responsibilities seriously.' Tresham brushed a few stray crumbs from the ruff at his neck and pushed his chair back from the table. He stretched out his legs. 'Which is why, dearest Robin, I have no intention of signing on with the Archduke Albert.'

Catesby leant forward. 'That wasn't what I wanted to ask you.'

Tresham lifted his arms above his head and gave an extravagant yawn. 'Going off the idea, are you?'

'There isn't going to *be* a regiment, Francis. There never was. It's just a ruse.'

Tresham dropped his arms. He eyed his cousin suspiciously. 'I'm not sure I want to hear this.'

Catesby was not about to give him a choice. 'I'll be blunt Francis. I need money. Something's being planned and I think you might be able to help me.'

'Now hang on,' Tresham said. 'I told you before. I'm done with conspiracies. James is King and that's the end of the matter.'

'I thought you might have changed your mind.'

'I haven't. Not under any circumstances.'

Catesby nodded understandingly. 'Fair enough. I shouldn't have broached the matter.' He looked off into the middle distance.

There was a long pause. Tresham stared at his relative. 'So what are you planning?' he asked, with reassuring predictability.

Catesby grinned. 'You'll have to swear an oath.'

'Oh, for Goodness Sake...'

'It's only fair. Everyone involved in this enterprise has sworn an oath. It doesn't commit you to anything. It's just a vow of silence.'

Tresham raised the palm of his right hand. 'All right. What is it you want me to say?'

Catesby bent over and produced the small prayer book from his bag. Tresham knelt down beside the table and quickly swore the oath. When that was done, he returned to his seat and listened carefully as the other man began to outline his scheme.

Catesby had covered this ground many times before but he had a knack for investing well-worn words with considerable enthusiasm. The same arguments he had employed with Ambrose Rookwood would be used here: the theological grounding; the knowledge and tacit approval of the Jesuits; the government's complete ignorance of the plot; the possibility of warning one or two friends. As he was speaking, an expression of horror began to form on Francis Tresham's flattened face. Catesby had expected nothing less. He knew his cousin better than his cousin knew himself. An outburst of some kind was inevitable and Tresham did not disappoint him.

'For Goodness' Sake, Robin!' he exclaimed at last, jumping to his feet. 'What are you thinking of? It's utter madness!' Tresham clutched his hands to his face. 'The whole world will turn against us. And you'll go straight to Hell. Dear God, Robin! This is the surest possible way of destroying Catholicism in England for ever.'

Catesby shook his head vehemently. 'This is the surest possible way of *restoring* Catholicism.'

Tresham returned to his chair and bent forwards across the table, his elbows resting on the polished wooden surface. 'Can't you wait a bit?' he asked, in exasperation. 'Let Parliament sit for a while and see how thing's progress before you do anything hasty?'

Catesby smiled but shook his head.

'Look, if it's money you need, I'll give you a hundred pounds. Head off to the Low Countries. Wait a while. If things don't improve, then come back and set off the powder at the end of the session.' Tresham was beginning to sound desperate.

'Things won't improve, Francis. And we can't wait. There's no point in doing this if the King isn't part of it. The only day we can guarantee he will be in Parliament is at the state opening. And that's in less than a month's time.'

Tresham threw himself back into his chair. 'But this is lunacy!' he declared.

'It's our last hope.'

'And what do you want from me? Just money, is it? Fine. Okay. A thousand pounds? Two thousand. Is that enough?'

'This is serious, Francis.'

'I'm *being* serious. Lord knows, I'm not a coward. But there's no point in taking such a big risk unless you can be certain of success.'

'I *am* certain. Look. I've taken a real chance, confiding in you like this. If you don't want to join up, that's fair enough. But I will hold you to your oath, Francis.'

Tresham scowled. 'Robin. How long have we known each other? I'm not about to stab you in the back now, am I? All right. I've promised two thousand pounds. Two thousand pounds you shall have. If I'm damned to Hell because of it, well then I'm damned. Satisfied?'

Catesby looked away. 'Yes. Thank you.'

'Now I'm going to go and get another drink.' Francis Tresham leapt to his feet and hurried out of the room.

Catesby remained seated. From the hallway, he could hear his cousin calling out to one of the servants. He grimaced. It was possible he had just made the biggest mistake of his life.

A blacksmith had ridden to Lapworth to fetch Jack Wright. The smithy arrived in the middle of the night, insisting it was a matter of some urgency. He carried with him a note written by Tom Wintour. Tom was staying at the *Bell Inn* in Daventry. Jack splashed some water on his face, mounted his horse and accompanied the blacksmith back to town. The two men rode through the night and Jack arrived at the inn shortly after seven o'clock the following morning.

Tom Wintour was just getting up.

A young maid showed Jack up to the room. The girl was stout but pretty. Jack gave her two ha'pennies for her trouble, but waited for her to leave before knocking on the door.

Half dressed, Tom Wintour admitted him to the chamber. The room was small and rather cramped. Bed sheets lay scattered across a dilapidated wooden bed. A bowl of water rested on a small table near the window.

'What's the matter?' Jack asked, lowering his head and stepping into the room. 'I got here as soon as I could.'

Tom crossed over to the table and picked up a letter lying beside the wash bowl. 'I got this yesterday. It's from Robin.' He unfolded the note and handed it to Jack.

Jack scanned the letter. It was carefully written, but the meaning was obvious. *"I have asked my cousin Francis to consider joining my expedition to the Low Countries. He has agreed to provide some funding for this venture."*

Jack looked up. 'Bloody hell.'

Tom was furious. 'What on earth possessed him to confide in Francis Tresham?'

Jack shrugged. 'He is a rich man, now his father's passed away.'

'You don't inherit common sense. The man's a loose cannon. He's not reliable. Robin should never have approached him. He should have consulted us first.'

Jack folded up the letter and handed it back to Tom. 'We did tell him he could ask anyone he wanted to.'

'I know. But I expected him to exercise better judgement than this.'

'So what do we do now?'

Tom adjusted the breeches at his waist. 'Robin wants us to meet up at White Webbs on Friday. We can go there together and thrash all this out. The letter doesn't say much, but I have a feeling Robin is regretting this already.'

Francis Tresham was infuriating. Catesby had expected him to be a reluctant conspirator, but even he had not anticipated his cousin being quite this difficult. Ever since they were children, Catesby had had the upper hand in the relationship, despite being the younger of the two. He had dragged Tresham, kicking and screaming, on many a precarious venture. But the prickly landowner had never put up this much of a struggle before. All evening, Tresham had been harping on about their friends who would be killed in the explosion. Increasingly drunk, he had argued once again for postponement and when Catesby refused point blank he had changed tack and insisted on warning just about everyone he knew. 'My brother-in-law, at least,' Tresham moaned. 'My sister would kill me if I let anything happen to Lord Monteagle.'

In the end, Catesby had managed to dampen his cousin's protestations by promising a full discussion of the matter with the rest of the conspirators. They could debate the issue collectively and decide who, if anyone, should be warned. This was a concession Catesby had been loath to give. In his own mind, the matter had already been decided.

He made his way angrily across the Savoy towards his lodgings on the Strand.

There was too much at stake, he thought. Better to let them all die, friend or foe. Ambrose could be persuaded. Even Tom Wintour was coming around to the idea. The last thing Catesby needed was for Tresham to reignite the whole debate.

It's madness, he thought. What are we supposed to do? Make house calls on every Catholic peer and say, 'by the way, your lordship, you might want to stay away from the opening of Parliament this year'? They might just as well write letters to every Member of the Upper House, saying they were planning to blow the place up. Catesby would have to be firm: nobody could be warned. Not one single solitary individual. No amount of argument would now persuade him to deviate from that position.

Across the street, a gentleman called out to him, but Catesby was too immersed in his thoughts to notice.

I should never have told him, he realised. Francis Tresham had always been unpredictable and frequently half-hearted, though up to now he had never been disloyal. If only money hadn't been so tight… He shook himself. What was done was done. They would have to deal with Tresham as best they could. His tongue would hold, Catesby was sure of it. Francis would never do anything to harm his childhood friend.

'It's Mr Catesby, is it not?'

He gave a start. Somebody had crossed the street and come to a halt directly in front of him. Catesby pulled up and took a moment to recover his wits. Then he recognised the fellow and let out a strangled yelp. 'Your lordship!' he exclaimed. It was one of the nobles he had been discussing with Tresham the previous evening; a prominent Catholic peer. 'How…nice to see you again,' he mumbled, slowly regaining his composure.

'You too, my boy,' Viscount Montague declared cheerfully. 'You're looking very well.' The viscount was a fresh faced man in black. He was clean-shaven, but for the ghost of a moustache on his upper lip.

Catesby improvised a grin. 'Thank you, your lordship. You seem in good spirits yourself.'

'Mustn't grumble,' Montague replied. He stepped to the side as a cart rattled past along the narrow street.

'You're up for the new Parliament, I presume.'

The viscount spent most of his time in the country, looking after his estates in Sussex. It was rare for him to be in London out of season.

'No, no, not yet,' Montague explained. 'As a matter of fact, I'm visiting my Aunt. But doubtless I shall be attending the House when it opens in a few weeks.' The viscount did not sound enthusiastic. He was a jovial fellow, as a rule, but his cheery disposition masked a thoughtful nature.

There was an opportunity here. Catesby had not sought it – did not want it – but he could not ignore it. He chose his next words carefully. 'Not a pleasure for your lordship, I imagine, with things the way they are.'

Montague had been rather unpopular during the first session of Parliament. His forthright condemnation of anti-Catholic legislation had earned him four days in the Fleet prison.

'Indeed not,' the viscount agreed sadly.

If any of the Catholic peers deserved to be saved from the fire, it was this man. And there would never be a better chance to warn him. But should Catesby say anything? What *could* he say?

'Perhaps His Majesty would not object too strongly if you were to absent yourself.'

The viscount frowned. 'Well, no, perhaps not.' He considered the matter for a moment. It was not unheard of for a peer to seek permission for a leave of absence. 'We shall have to see.' Clearly, any further outburst might mean another prison sentence. 'Good day to you, sir. And good health.'

Catesby bowed courteously. 'Good day, my lord.'

The viscount disappeared into the crowd.

Catesby stood for a while, his heart beating rapidly. He had made the most of the opportunity; had said far more than he should have done. Viscount Montague had received his warning. The rest would be a matter for Providence.

The debate continued across the whole of the weekend.

Francis Tresham would not listen to reason. 'We must warn our friends, at any rate,' he asserted, his eyes scanning the group. 'It's the very least that we can do.' Eight of the conspirators had gathered at White Webbs to thrash out the issue once and for all. Tresham was the most vocal. He had come up with six names; six individuals whom he felt could not possibly be allowed to attend Parliament. The list included Lords Monteagle, Montague and the less reliable Lord Mordaunt.

'I have reason to believe Montague will not be attending,' Catesby informed the gathering, without going into specifics. He had not told anyone about his meeting with the viscount. 'The same may be true of Lord Mordaunt.' It was rumoured that Mourdant had already applied to absent himself.

'Yes, but you can't know that for certain!'

'Lord Mordaunt has indicated that he will not attend,' Catesby told his cousin flatly. 'But even if that were not the case, I would never allow that man to be warned of anything. He cannot be trusted to keep a secret.'

'What about Lord Stourton? And Lord Monteagle?' Tresham had a vested interest here. The men were married to his sisters, Frances and Elizabeth. 'Surely they can be trusted. And Lord Vaux. Who do you think pays the rent on this place?'

Catesby rolled his eyes. The debate was not going the way he had hoped. Already, Tresham had Robert Keyes and Kit Wright on his side. Fawkes and Jack were supporting Catesby. The only uncertainty was Tom Wintour, who was sitting to his right. 'What do *you* think?' Catesby asked him. If Tom supported Tresham, Catesby would lose the argument.

'I would like to warn Lord Monteagle,' Tom admitted, reluctantly. 'But I have to agree with Robin. At this late stage, it's too much of a risk. His lordship has sworn an oath of allegiance. For all his sympathy to our cause, he takes that oath very seriously.'

Tresham snorted. 'Family comes first,' he said. 'If Sir William knows the people involved, he won't breathe a word to anyone. Believe me. He's as solid as a rock.'

'We're not telling *anyone* the names of the people involved,' Catesby snapped. 'The most we're discussing, Francis, is a veiled warning. And even that is going too far, in my opinion.' Catesby could feel himself shaking. He should never have agreed to this debate. If only Thomas Percy had been here. The older man would have argued the case with sufficient vehemence to stall even Francis Tresham's objections. Unfortunately, Percy was still attending to his duties in the north.

'What about Thomas Howard?' Kit Wright asked quietly.

At that, Catesby frowned. Thomas Howard was little more than a boy. He had become the Earl of Arundel when his father had died prematurely. Nobody seriously wanted the young lad dead. 'Maybe we could arrange for a small accident,' he suggested. 'Some minor flesh wound, to keep him in bed for a couple of days.'

Tresham laughed. 'That hardly sounds very practical now, does it?'

'You're the one who wants to save everybody.'

'Can you blame me? We're talking about some of my best friends here.'

Catesby gritted his teeth and forced himself to control his anger. 'There is a higher purpose involved in this, Francis. This venture is too important to be side-tracked by individual concerns. For the sake of all England, this plan has to succeed, no matter what the cost. And if that means…'

'If that means killing all our friends…'

'Better to let the innocents die, Francis, than have the plan run aground. Even if they are the closest of friends. Even if they are as dear to me as my own son. They will find their peace in Heaven. But this scheme cannot be allowed to fail. Nothing that's been said here today makes me think any differently. The innocent must perish along with the guilty. The plan will proceed and nobody will be warned. Do I make myself clear?' Catesby glared at his cousin. 'Francis?'

Tresham looked down. 'All right. Fine. Have it your own way.'

Catesby softened his voice. 'It's for the best, Francis. Believe me. It's the only way we can be sure of success…'

And that, as far as Catesby was concerned, was the end of the matter.

The next few days saw a storm of activity as final preparations were put into place. Details of the hunt in Warwickshire were finalized. A man named John Grant was gathering munitions at Norbrook, near Stratford Upon Avon. Tom Wintour, meanwhile, had returned to London to check up on the status of the royal children. Catesby wanted to know if a final decision had been made about Prince Charles. Would the younger heir be accompanying his elder brother to the opening of Parliament? If so, the plotters could safely focus all their energy on capturing the Princess Elizabeth in Warwickshire.

Tom returned to White Webbs on Friday. The news was dispiriting. 'There seems to have been a change of plan. Prince Charles definitely won't be attending the opening of Parliament. But from what I could gather, Prince Henry won't be there either.'

Catesby grimaced. Up to now, the elder Prince had not been a factor in their equations. 'So we may have to redirect our focus on him.' Thomas Percy had volunteered to kidnap young Charles as soon as the gunpowder had been blown. Now he would have to kidnap Henry instead.

'But do we know where the Prince will be?' Mr Fawkes asked.

'That I couldn't find out. Presumably, he'll be at the palace. But I don't know whether Thomas will be able to get close to him.'

'We'll find some way,' Catesby affirmed. He lifted a hand to his face and started rubbing his right eye.

'You're looking tired,' Tom said.

'I haven't been sleeping well.' Catesby sighed. 'Just nerves, I expect. But I keep waking up in the middle of the night. I get this terrible feeling there's something important that I've forgotten to do.' He shook himself, dismissing the problem. 'Perhaps we'd be better off ignoring the sons altogether. It may be safer just to focus our attention on the Princess. If we can get Elizabeth under our control, we'll still be in a position of strength.'

'How are the arrangements going in the Midlands?' Fawkes asked.

'It's all being organised. A large group of Catholics are getting ready to gather at Dunchurch. Some of them are interested in joining this regiment of mine but most are just there for the hunt. Only a couple of people know any of the specifics of the plot. And even they don't have the full details.' Catesby stifled a yawn. 'I'll be riding up to join them there on the Monday before Parliament opens.'

That was ten days away. Mr Fawkes would be in London then to set the fuse. Once the powder had been lit, a boat on the Thames would take the Yorkshireman out to sea and the safety of the Low Countries.

'Ambrose will bring the news of the explosion. Then we'll gather the party together and converge on Combe Abbey to capture the Princess.'

'Did you get much money from Francis?' Tom asked.

'Not yet. He's promised some funds by the end of next week. I have a reliable promise of arms and extra horses as well.'

'We'll certainly need them,' said Fawkes.

Events were coming to a head.

Chapter Eighteen

The information had come from an unlikely source. Tom Wintour had been dining with a friend in London; a fellow employee of Lord Monteagle. The two often met up after work, to sink a few pints and exchange any gossip. It was a pleasant way to unwind, after the stresses of the day. The mild-mannered footman invariably made good company. He had a similar political outlook to Tom and they had much the same temperament. Up until now, however, their after-hours conversation had always been trivial in nature. This time, it was different.

The intelligence his friend had provided had chilled his very soul. Tom had barely slept during the night. An echo of that fear was visible in his eyes even now. At first light on Monday morning, he had saddled his horse and ridden north out of London. Catesby was still at White Webbs, on the border between Essex and Hertfordshire. Meeting up with his cousin in the main hall, Tom had taken a deep breath. His heart was beating rapidly and the colour had drained from his face.

There was no easy way of breaking the news.

Catesby sensed that something was wrong. 'Tom, what is it?'

'Bad news,' he replied softly. 'Very bad news. Someone has sent an anonymous letter to Lord Monteagle. And he's taken it straight to the Earl of Salisbury.'

Catesby blinked. 'When was this?'

'Saturday night.'

Catesby's jaw dropped. He moved across to the fireplace. 'What did the letter say?'

'So far as I can tell, it was a veiled warning. It didn't mention gunpowder, but it did imply some kind of threat to the Houses of Parliament.'

'My God.' Catesby's voice was little more than a whisper. 'Do you know how it was phrased?'

'Not exactly. Something like "this Parliament will receive a terrible blow." The letter advised Lord Monteagle to keep his distance.'

Catesby glanced back at his cousin. 'Who told you about this?'

'Thomas Ward. We dined together last night. He mentioned it in passing.'

'Do you think he suspected you were involved in some way?'

'No. He was just perplexed by the whole thing. I think I managed to hide my surprise.'

Catesby placed his hands on the ledge above the fire and rested his head against the wall. For a second, he remained there. 'This is awful.' He pulled back and turned away from the fire. 'The letter must have been pretty damning if Monteagle took it straight to Robert Cecil.'

'That was the strange thing. According to Thomas Ward, the letter was utterly vague. He thought it was just a joke. At worst, some kind of malicious prank. He didn't draw any particular conclusions from the contents.' The only thing Ward had been confused about was the fact that Monteagle had made him read the letter out loud.

'And they have no idea who sent it?'

'A man stopped him in the street, apparently. A tall gentleman with a beard. Quite well dressed.'

Catesby looked away. 'That could be just about anyone.'

'It may have been a servant, in any case.'

Catesby moved away from the fire and returned to the centre of the room. 'Could this be unrelated?' he asked. 'Is there a chance it has nothing to do with us? It might just be some sort of ghastly coincidence.'

Tom did not think so. 'Even if it were a coincidence, it still draws attention to Parliament and to a potential threat. The Privy Council are bound to investigate.'

'So you think everything is lost?'

Tom nodded vigorously. 'I do, Robin. I think we should flee the country, while we have the chance. There's a boat on the Thames. We could be in Flanders in a few days.'

'Let's not do anything hasty. We don't have enough information to form a balanced judgement.' Catesby was clearly still trying to digest the news. 'Where is the letter now?'

'In the hands of the council. According to Sir William, they're unlikely to do anything until the King gets back from his hunting expedition on Thursday.'

'Which gives us a few days breathing space.'

'They might have already drawn their own conclusions.'

'Not without consulting the King.' Catesby was pacing the room now, thinking furiously. 'The first thing we need to do is find out who wrote this letter.'

Tom had spent most of the previous night considering the matter. 'I hate to say it Robin, but I think I have a fair idea who might have been responsible.'

Catesby stopped mid pace. The same thought had evidently just occurred to him. 'Francis Tresham,' he whispered.

'You should never have involved him in this, Robin.'

Catesby brought his hands up to his face in disbelief. Tresham had been a close friend since childhood. There had never been any question of disloyalty between them. But the idea could not be discounted. 'If Francis is responsible for this,' Catesby hissed, 'I will personally tie a noose around his neck and see him hang.' He opened his eyes. 'You're right, Tom. I should never have trusted him.'

'So what do we do now?'

Catesby drew an arm around his shoulders. 'First of all, we mustn't tell anybody about the letter. Not yet, anyway. I'll write to Francis and arrange for him to meet us here. Secondly, as you say, we need to find out if the Privy Council has drawn any conclusions from the letter.'

'They must have put two and two together by now.'

'Well, they've certainly had two days to think about it. All right. What's the worst they could do?'

Tom shrugged. 'They could search Parliament.'

'Right. So we need to check up on the powder.'

'Mr Fawkes is back in London. He has the keys.'

'I'll contact him.'

'I doubt that they'll have searched the store room. If they'd found the powder, they'd already be issuing warrants.'

'Not necessarily. They might want to catch us red-handed.'

Tom rubbed his chin. 'In which case, sending Mr Fawkes in there would be tantamount to handing him over.'

'It's a small risk. If the letter is as vague as your friend seems to think, the Privy Council may well dismiss it out of hand. And as I say, even if they are suspicious, it's unlikely they'll do anything before the King returns to London.'

'But what if they *have* found the powder?'

'If Mr Fawkes is taken, then we'll have to flee. Assuming we have time.'

'And what about the others?'

'We'll send them a warning, if we can.'

Tom shivered. The thought of being captured at this late stage was too unpleasant to contemplate. 'I couldn't bear to be taken prisoner.' He had seen too many good men tortured and executed. It was no way for a gentleman to die.

Catesby placed a reassuring hand on his friend's shoulder. 'If it comes to that, Mr Tom, we'll die fighting…'

Guido Fawkes bent over to examine the lock. He had scratched a few marks around the edges of it and inserted several splinters into the frame of the door. If anyone had turned the lock the scratches would have become misaligned and the bits of wood would have fallen to the ground. But everything seemed to be in order.

Fawkes reached down to a pouch at his waist and produced a set of iron keys. He found the appropriate key, inserted it into the lock and turned it slowly. The door scraped open and the splinters fell away to the floor. Fawkes lent over to pick up his lantern.

The undercroft had been left largely in his care since the plotters had rented it at the end of March. Extra powder had been brought in by Mr Percy and then by Tom Wintour. Since returning to London from the continent, Fawkes had checked up on the place regularly, though never more than once every ten days. It did not do to become too familiar a sight in the precinct of Westminster. Thankfully, there were so many beggars, merchants and prostitutes in the vicinity plying their wares that it was easy to pass in the street unnoticed.

This was the first time, however, that Fawkes had visited the store room at the direct request of Robert Catesby. The two men had met the previous day. Catesby had not provided a reason for the request and Fawkes had not asked for one. His sole responsibility was the security of the cellar. If Catesby had some reason to believe that security had been compromised, then the veteran soldier would take whatever risks were necessary to uncover the truth.

He held up the lantern and moved into the room. The first things to check were the other two entrances. Fawkes had never used either of these. Both doors had been firmly locked since the day the cellar had been rented, though Mr Whynniard had provided a set of keys for each one. Neither door, he quickly determined, had been opened since his last visit.

The faggots covering the barrels of gunpowder had been carefully arranged at one end of the store room. Subtle chalk strokes on the floor had been used to mark the edges of some of the bundles. Fawkes had been very careful. If any of the wood had been moved, he would know. But again, everything seemed to be in order.

Whatever worry had prompted Catesby to order the search, it had been completely unfounded. Nobody had been in the cellar. Not Mr Whynniard, not the previous tenant, not the Household Guard. The powder was untouched and ready to be ignited.

Guido Fawkes allowed himself a satisfied smile.

Parliament would meet in six days' time and Mr John Johnson would be waiting for them.

Francis Tresham had not been told about the letter. No explanation had been given for his impromptu summons, but that was scarcely unusual. There were always things which needed to be discussed and White Webbs was often the place to do it. If Tresham had any inkling of the truth, he did not show it upon his arrival at the manor house.

There was a quiet room towards the rear of the building which Catesby often used for private discussions. A servant had been in there to light a fire, but the place was now empty. He gestured for Tresham to enter the room, then followed on behind.

Tom Wintour brought up the rear, passing quickly through the door then turning back and locking it quietly.

Francis Tresham frowned as he heard the click of the key in the lock. He swung around and caught sight of the dagger Tom was gripping in his right hand. His eyes darted across to Catesby. 'Robin? What's all this about?'

Catesby drew his sword and advanced on his elder relative.

'Robin, what are you doing?' Tresham stepped backwards, his voice rising in alarm.

'Tell me you had nothing to do with it, Francis,' Catesby growled, forcing Tresham up against the far wall. With the length of his sword, Catesby pressed hard against his cousin's throat.

Tresham appeared utterly bewildered. 'Nothing to do with what?' he cried. His eyes flicked across to Tom Wintour at the door, but he found no sympathy there.

Catesby nodded to Tom. In plain language, the other man outlined the matter of the letter Lord Monteagle had received. Catesby watched his cousin closely as he digested the information. He had made a pact with Tom. If Francis admitted his guilt, he would not leave the room alive.

Tresham struggled to swallow. The edge of the sword was still pressing uncomfortably against his throat. 'For God's Sake, Robin! Why would I send a letter to anyone?'

'To warn them. To warn your brother-in-law. To save his life.'

'I know nothing about it. I swear!'

'Is it a coincidence, then?' Catesby snarled. 'You learn about the plot. You express concern for Lord Monteagle and Lord Stourton. And within two weeks this letter is sent?'

'I'm telling you, Robin, I had nothing to do with it. I wasn't even in London on Saturday.' Tresham was beginning to tremble. 'For God's Sake, Robin, I swore an oath. You must believe me. I would never betray your trust. When have I ever done anything to harm you?'

'Somebody sent that letter,' Tom pointed out, from the doorway.

Tresham glared back at him. 'You work for Lord Monteagle!' he exclaimed. 'It could just as easily be you!'

'You're in no position to throw accusations around,' Catesby snapped.

'Why shouldn't I? You come here, accusing me. Your oldest friend. Your closest relative. How dare you accuse me of this? How dare you assume I had anything to do with this treachery?'

'I dare because I know you, Francis. And because, though it pains me to admit it, I'm not sure that I trust you at all.'

Francis Tresham did not blink. He locked eyes with Catesby and held the gaze steadily. His voice now was unnaturally calm. 'I swear, Robin. I swear on my life. On the life of my children. On the Holy Bible. In God's name.'

Catesby met the gaze, but with less certainty. Try as he might, he could detect no insincerity in his cousin's manner. He moved his sword away. 'All right. On the Bible then.' He gestured to a volume lying on a table by the window. Cautiously, Tresham moved across. Tom covered him with the dagger as he picked up the book.

'I swear, on my immortal soul, that I did not do this thing. I swear on the lives of my children. On the life of my wife. And before Almighty God. I did *not* send a letter to Lord Monteagle and I have *not* warned any person of this plot.' Tresham looked up. Still, Catesby could detect no trace of deceit in the man's voice or in his manner.

He glanced back to Tom. Reluctantly, Tom nodded. The man was either a superb actor or he was telling the truth. All they could do was take him at his word. Catesby sheathed his sword. Tom stepped forward and placed his dagger on the table.

Francis Tresham closed his eyes and let out a deep sigh. He placed the Bible back down on the table, beside Tom's heavily polished knife. 'We should give this up,' he said, in a hoarse whisper. 'Whoever wrote that letter, they've opened everything up. Don't you see, Robin? It's not worth the risk…'

Catesby did not want to hear it. 'You promised me two thousand pounds.'

'I…don't have it.' Catesby glared at him. 'I mean, look, I can probably get it. But I don't think…'

'I want the money, Francis. And I want it now.'

'I haven't got it. I don't exactly carry that amount around with me in ready cash.'

'What have you got?'

'Well…about a hundred pounds. At my lodgings. But…'

'Get it. Tom you go with him.'

Tom stood aside and unlocked the door. Tresham moved hurriedly through.

'And find the rest, Francis,' Catesby added. 'We're going ahead as planned.'

Chapter Nineteen

Father Henry Garnet looked down upon the congregation with a heavy heart. The Feast of All Saints was one of the most important dates in the Roman Catholic year. Its celebration was normally one of the high points of the Christian calendar. The Jesuit Superior had chosen a hymn from the Office of Lauds to accompany the High Mass at Coughton Court. Many fine people had gathered to hear the sermon. But one man was absent. Father Henry had written to Catesby, urging him to attend the celebrations. Robin had written back, very courteously, promising to put in an appearance. But there was no sign of him this afternoon.

'From the territory of the faithful,' Father Henry intoned, in sombre Latin form, 'take away all unbelievers.' He scanned his flock again, searching for the face, in case he had been mistaken and Catesby had arrived at the last minute. 'That all beneath our One Shepherd's sway within one fold may come again.'

He had written to Rome, of course. Robin had been clever, binding him with the Seal of the Confessional. But that did not mean the priest was prevented from taking any action whatsoever. There had been some minor disturbances in Wales over the summer. Father Henry had written to the Pope, expressing concern that similar rumblings might occur in England. Not everyone, he had warned, would be kept back from rash action by a mere prohibition from the Pope. There was always the possibility that some treason might arise which would force the Catholic community to take up arms against the King. Father Henry could be no more specific than this without breaking the Seal. But he had entreated the Pope to make a definitive statement: to proclaim clearly and unambiguously that any person using force of arms against the King of England would be subject to automatic excommunication. That and that alone would be sufficient to stay Catesby's hand.

The reply had not come until late September and Father Henry had struggled to hide his disappointment. Rather than granting the censure, the Vatican had simply written back requesting more information. It was then that the priest had written to Catesby himself, demanding a meeting.

Now events were moving rapidly. Father Henry did not know the precise date on which Catesby planned to act, but presumably it would be in the early days of the new Parliament. Once the tone of the session had been set – if it continued in the same vein as the first Parliament – that would surely be the moment when the plotters would strike.

If Catesby would not come to Father Henry, then the priest would have to seek him out. The man had to be made to see reason, before it was too late.

But first the festivities would be completed.

It took less than a day for the news to reach the conspirators.

The King had returned from his hunting expedition. That much was common knowledge. According to Thomas Ward, His Majesty had been shown the anonymous letter by Robert Cecil on Friday afternoon. Tom Wintour had stuck close to the footman throughout the week. Ward was Lord Monteagle's most trusted servant and since the Privy Councillor knew all that happened in the palace it was only a matter of time before the information leaked out. And the news was not good. King James was taking the letter seriously. There was no indication of what action – if any – the sovereign intended to take, but it was certain that there would be some kind of official response. In the circumstances, that could only mean a complete search of the Houses of Parliament.

'The plot's been discovered,' Tom proclaimed sadly, relaying the information to Catesby on Saturday evening. 'They could find the powder at any time and start issuing warrants for our arrest. We have no choice, Robin. We must flee the country.'

Catesby was at a loss for words. 'Maybe you're right,' he admitted, reluctantly. 'Maybe we should just take the boat and leave.' If the government had guessed their intentions, then everything was lost. All their hard work. All the organisation. It had all been for nothing. He buried his face in his hands. It was painful even to think of it. 'I can't believe we could get this close and fail so completely.'

'Better than losing your life,' Francis Tresham asserted. 'Live to fight another day. Life isn't so bad on the continent. Ask Mr Fawkes. He's always going on about it.'

Fawkes was not there to ask. Neither was Thomas Percy. Mr Fawkes had gone north to contact the older man, who as yet knew nothing about the letter. Catesby was not sure how either of them would react to this new information concerning the King.

'We'll do nothing tonight,' he decided, raising his hand to forestall any objections from Tresham. If the plans were to be abandoned, Percy would have to know about it. 'We'll wait until tomorrow,' he decreed. 'I want to hear what Thomas thinks. If he's in favour, then we'll abandon the whole project.'

Thomas Percy was not in the best of moods. The ride from York had been interminable. Mr Fawkes had told him all about the Monteagle letter and Percy was convinced that Francis Tresham was responsible. It was the only logical explanation.

'Mr Catesby seems sure that his cousin is innocent,' Fawkes had said. 'Mr Tresham swore an oath to that effect.'

'He'd swear anything if his life was threatened.'

'Mr Wintour also seemed certain.'

Percy snorted. 'More fool him.' He would have to have words with Robin. When they had given permission for Catesby to go off and find new recruits, they had assumed he would act responsibly.

It was Sunday evening before the two men finally rode into London. Catesby and Tom had stayed up to greet them. Parliament was due to open in two days' time, on Tuesday the Fifth of November. It was therefore vital that a decision be made that evening. Should they proceed with the plan or should they flee the country?

Thomas Percy was in no doubt. 'We are not giving up now,' he affirmed, even after Tom had filled him in on the latest news. 'I haven't been working my bollocks off for the better part of two years to let it all fall apart forty-eight hours before the end.'

'But the King knows what we're planning,' Tom insisted.

'You don't know that, Tom. He may well be suspicious, but if he is, why hasn't anything been done?'

'They are waiting for us to make our move. They want to know who's involved. As soon as anyone shows up to light the powder, they'll be arrested. Then we'll all be taken.'

'But Guido said he'd already checked the powder.'

'That was last week. Anything could have happened in the last couple of days.'

Percy growled. 'We should have stuck with my original plan. It would have been so much simpler if I'd just killed the King myself. I've been close enough, these past few months.'

Mr Fawkes coughed politely. 'I am prepared to visit the cellar a second time to see if anyone has been in there.' All eyes focused on the Yorkshireman. 'We have come this far. We will never have another opportunity. I agree with Mr Percy. It is better to take the risk. If you gentlemen wish to flee, I do understand. But for my own part, I am determined to stay here and light the powder. If that means I am taken, then so be it. It is the will of God.'

Catesby eyed the pious soldier with renewed respect. 'You are a very brave man,' he whispered.

Percy was grinning broadly. 'So it's agreed then…'

'Not by me!' Tom Wintour exclaimed. 'Thomas, this is lunacy. The government may already have issued our arrest warrants. We only stayed in London for an extra day in order to warn you about everything that was going on. Otherwise, we'd have been halfway to Flanders by now.'

'They're hardly going to come for us this evening,' Percy snapped. 'In any case, it's me they'll be after. It's my name on the rental form for the cellar.'

'That's all the more reason to flee!'

'Not if everything's quiet. I'll ride up to Syon house tomorrow. I have to go anyway, to report back to the Earl. If anything's going on, Northumberland will know about it. Robin can take a horse and meet up with the hunting party at Dunchurch, as arranged. And Mr Fawkes can check up on the powder. You can leave town as well, if that's what you want. That way, only Guido and I will be in the firing line.'

'And Ambrose,' Catesby added. 'He's in town too.'

Ambrose Rookwood would carry the news of the explosion. 'And once the powder is fired,' Fawkes said, 'I can take the boat to Flanders.' His face was grim. 'I am resolved to do this, gentlemen.'

Percy was in full agreement. 'What do you say, Robin? We've come this far. We're never going to get another chance.'

Catesby took a moment to consider. There were two possible courses of action. If they went ahead, they would almost certainly be caught. If they did not, it was likely that they would be caught in any case. The decision was obvious. 'Very well. We go ahead as planned.'

Tom looked away.

'I'm sorry. Tom. If you want to leave, I'll understand.'

Tom Wintour shook his head. 'I think you're insane. But it's your decision. And whatever you decide, I'll stand by you.'

'Good man.' Catesby rose. 'It's getting late. We should get some sleep.' He glanced across at Percy. 'But you should find new lodgings for tonight, Thomas. Just in case…'

The Earl of Northumberland was not in the least perturbed. Percy had sent a letter, explaining his sudden return to London and it had been accepted without question. Northumberland seemed delighted to see him. 'I have a few friends in. Would you care to dine with us?' he asked, when Percy arrived at Syon House.

Thomas Percy had been fearful of his reception. Despite his bravado in front of the others, the news of the letter had shaken him badly. Arriving at the door, he had half expected to be arrested on sight. Whoever the scoundrel was who had sent Lord Monteagle that letter, Percy would seek him out and throttle the bastard.

As a Privy Councillor, it was almost certain that Northumberland knew about the anonymous letter. If he had suspected his relative in any way, it would have been obvious at once. The Earl was not a subtle man. But his reception had been cordial and Percy could detect no awkwardness in his employer's behaviour towards him.

After they had eaten, Northumberland took him aside and for a short while they discussed business. Percy had been as rigorous as ever in securing the rents but the message from Fawkes had necessitated a return to London before he had completed his task.

'I gather you had some other matter you wished to discuss,' Northumberland commented, after he had checked the partially completed accounts.

'Yes, my lord.' This was the excuse Percy had provided in the letter. It was also the pretext for his visit this morning. 'I got into a bit of trouble in York,' he explained. 'The Archbishop wanted to have me arrested. He suspects me of being a papist.'

The Earl laughed. 'All England knows you're a papist, Thomas! But that fool of an Archbishop should know better than to interfere in my affairs.'

'I may need to pay a few bribes here and there to soften the situation,' Percy said. 'That was the matter I wished to discuss with you, my lord.'

'You want a loan, do you?'

'If you were agreeable, my lord. Purely as an advance on my wages, of course.'

Northumberland yawned expansively. 'I don't see that that should be a problem. You've served me well, Thomas, these past few years.'

Percy bowed his head. 'I'm very grateful, my lord.' And he was. He was more grateful than the Earl could possibly know, for now he knew that all was well. The Privy Council did not suspect him and that meant they had not discovered the cellar. Northumberland had given him the reassurance he needed.

A little voice in the back of his head began to whisper. It was the irritating and unwelcome voice of Francis Tresham. You should warn him, Tresham said. Tell him to stay away from Parliament. You owe him that much. But Percy dismissed the idea. There was no place for sentiment when the future of England was at stake. The plot had come too close to failure already. Let Northumberland burn, if that was God's will.

There would be no more warnings.

Chapter Twenty

Sir Everard Digby was not the first to arrive at Dunchurch. He would not be the last, either. The small Warwickshire village was practically under siege. Horses filled the stable yards. Hunting dogs strained at the leash outside half a dozen taverns and inns. The settlement was a regular stopping off point for coaches but it was rare that it played host to such a remarkable collection of immaculately dressed gentlemen, with all their attendant servants and animals. The villagers would make a fair sum of money, but they would have to work hard for every shilling earned. There were gun-dogs to kennel and servants to house; suckling pigs to roast and ale to quench the thirst. And each gentleman had his crates of clothing, muskets, powder and shot.

Digby was easily the most impressive of the new arrivals. The dashing young knight had reached Dunchurch that afternoon and had quickly settled in at the *Red Lion*. He was now twenty-seven years old, a handsome aristocrat who carried himself with the dignity and stature of a much older man. His white doublet was lined with the finest purple. Voluminous breeches reached down to the knee and colourful satin hose were deeply encrusted with gold lace. Digby was a pillar of the local community. Many of the gentlemen descending on the village were coming here at his invitation, though it did not take much to persuade men of quality to join a hunting party, even in early November. The nearby heath was ideal ground for a hunt.

It had been arranged for the assembled gentlemen to meet up at the *Red Lion*, once they had all found suitable accommodation. Some of the new arrivals Digby scarcely knew. Others were all too familiar. There was his uncle, Sir Robert Digby. There were the Littleton brothers, Stephen and Humphrey. And there was the Catholic priest, Father Hammond. None of these men knew the true purpose of their expedition. The hunters had been selected because of the likelihood of their sympathy to the cause, but there was no guarantee that any of them would sign up when the moment came.

Digby had taken a great deal of persuading himself. He had made no bones about his disillusionment with Parliament when

Robert Catesby had first approached him down in Buckinghamshire a few weeks earlier. But the idea of killing so many people, even people who had committed the vilest of crimes, had struck him as an act of pure wickedness. How could any good Catholic possibly contemplate such slaughter? But the anger Digby had been trying so hard to suppress had gradually reasserted itself and he had allowed himself to be persuaded. The Jesuits knew all about the plot, he was told; Father Henry Garnet in particular. Digby would not have consented to be involved if that had not been the case. An outline of the theological argument was also shown to him in a book by Martin Del Rio. But it was his friendship with Catesby himself that tipped the balance. There was something utterly compelling in the man's deep brown eyes. Digby could not refuse to help.

Each new arrival at the *Red Lion* was greeted with elaborate courtesy. Drinks were ordered for everyone present. Digby's most reliable servant was sent out to organise an extravagant supper for everybody that evening. The people would eat, they would drink and tomorrow they would hunt.

Combe Abbey was little more than eight miles away. It was here that Catesby's puppet queen currently resided. As yet, the young Elizabeth had no inkling of her part in the plan.

The dogs would not be hunting game on the morrow. They would be hunting a princess.

Thomas Percy took a large slurp from a tankard of ale and wiped his hand across his mouth. 'They don't suspect a thing,' he declared, glancing up at Tom Wintour. 'I saw Northumberland. I visited Richmond. I even went to Essex House. There's not a whisper of anything.' The whole of London seemed completely oblivious to the plot. If the authorities had known anything about the powder in the cellar, they would already have acted. 'We can go ahead,' he asserted, with dubious confidence. 'Nobody knows anything at all.'

Jack Wright bit his lip and scratched himself on the chest. 'Either way, we're committed now. Guido's already set himself up at the house. He won't leave Westminster until the powder's blown.' Mr Fawkes had left the others in the early afternoon. They had promised to send him word if all was well.

'He's a good man,' Tom affirmed. 'God help him.'

'We can't lose!' Percy exclaimed. 'Why are you all looking so bloody depressed? We're about to strike the biggest blow against Protestantism the world has ever seen. This time tomorrow, the King, his government and all the lords will be as dead as a doornail and the whole world will be flocking to our side. We should be celebrating!'

Celebrating.

That last word seemed to hang in the air for a moment.

Tom Wintour broke the awkward silence. 'Did you get the watch?' he asked.

Percy nodded. He grappled inside a pouch and produced a small disk of shiny metal. This was the signal the group had agreed upon. If Fawkes received the watch, all was well and they could proceed as planned.

Robert Keyes had been delegated to take it to him.

The watch was purely symbolic. Fawkes would use a slow burning fuse to ignite the powder. He would set it alight as soon as the King arrived in the Upper Chamber on Tuesday morning. The fuse would give him fifteen minutes to get clear of the cellar before Parliament was engulfed in flames.

Percy handed the time-piece across and Keyes pocketed it without comment.

'Robin will be leaving shortly,' Tom advised.

'He's at the *Red Bull*,' Jack said. 'I'll go and give him the good news, shall I?' The cheerful swordsman would be riding out of town with Catesby that evening. Together they would be the first to reach the hunting party at Dunchurch. News of the explosion would follow on behind. Ambrose Rookwood stood ready with his horses to deliver confirmation of their success.

'I'd better be going too,' Percy declared, rising to his feet. As with Tom and Ambrose, he would be staying in London until the powder was ignited. He had taken Catesby's suggestion, however, and acquired new lodgings for a couple of days. He lifted up his tankard. 'Gentlemen,' he proclaimed, with a huge grin on his face. 'The next time we meet, the King will be dead!'

Either that, Tom thought, or we will be.

Light rain was spattering the cobblestones outside the *Red Bull*. The candlelight from the inn only partially illuminated the street. Muffled sounds from inside the building were amplified as the main doorway swung open and Robert Catesby appeared in the door frame. He stood for a moment, silhouetted in the dim light, fastening the wine red cloak at his neck and then pulling a large connacled hat down onto his head.

It was a dreary night outside, wet and overcast; but despite the hour, Drury Lane was choking with life. Carts were clattering down the road with their usual disregard for pedestrians. Street traders were loudly proclaiming their wares to all who would listen, though doubtless they would soon be packing up for the night. And every public house in the vicinity – and there were many – was overflowing with customers.

Catesby stepped out into the street. It was never easy to leave the comforting warmth of a good inn. Especially on a night like this. He had sent his manservant, Bates, to collect the horses. Jack Wright, who had walked to the *Red Bull* from the Strand after the earlier meeting, had popped out the back to answer a call of nature.

For a moment, Catesby was alone in the street. The sounds of London seemed to fade into the background. He stood for a moment, his mind numb. This was it. Within twenty four hours, the outcome would be known: either total success or abject failure. It was a strange feeling. So many separate incidents had led him to this point. The death of his wife. The persecution of his father. And the shocking idea that had struck him one quiet afternoon at Ashby St. Ledgers. Catesby tried to recapture the anger and despair he had felt at that time. It had sustained him for many months. But now he did not seem to feel anything at all. His mind was frozen, like the Thames in winter. Events would follow their course for good or ill. There was nothing he could do now but play out his hand and trust to providence.

A cart clattered past him on the cobblestones. A spray of mud across the ankles awoke him from his melancholy.

The door of the inn swung open and Jack Wright bustled through from behind. The voices of the drinkers wafted out into the night air but were quickly cut off as the door swung backwards.

Jack looked up at the rain, which was falling more steadily now. He grimaced and pulled his hat down tightly. The black felt did little to keep the head dry but the brim did at least keep his eyes clear of water 'Lovely night to be out,' he remarked, cheerfully.

From an archway, Thomas Bates appeared, booted and spurred like his master. Behind him came two servants, who were leading a trio of horses out from the stables. The geldings were powerful animals, but docile. They trotted out onto the street and pulled up obediently beside the large window of the *Red Bull*. One of the horses belonged to Bates. It was smaller than the others, but had strong, firm legs that could easily keep pace. The servant reached down into a small purse and produced a few pennies to pay the grooms for their effort. He had already settled the bill at the inn.

Catesby took the reins of his horse and patted the animal gently on the neck. The horse nickered playfully.

'Are we ready then?' Jack asked. They had a long journey ahead of them.

Catesby nodded. There was nothing left keeping them in London. He pulled himself up into the saddle and kicked the horse into a steady trot.

They would have to travel slowly until they reached the outskirts of town. The horses could easily slip on the wet cobblestones and there were no replacements to be had for some miles.

Jack Wright and Thomas Bates mounted their own horses and followed behind.

Slowly, the three men disappeared into the darkness.

And the rain continued to fall.

Part Five
Flight

"Stand by me, Mr Tom, and we will die together."
– Robert Catesby, 8th November 1605

Chapter Twenty One

There were footsteps in the corridor.

Guido Fawkes fastened his cloak tightly around his neck and listened intently. There had been enough of a gap since he had locked the cellar door to allow for the possibility that he had not been seen entering the building. It was nearly midnight now. The streets outside were quiet. There had been no one about as he had slipped into the vault from the Whynniard house. It was just as well. In daylight, Fawkes had had a credible excuse for being here. After dark, he could offer none whatsoever.

The footsteps faded into the distance.

A few minutes passed and there was no further noise. Fawkes breathed out quietly. The silence was reassuring. He bent over to pick up a lantern he had brought with him. As he did so, a scraping sound reverberated along the outer wall. Fawkes froze, holding his breath for a second time. There were more footsteps moving about, but he could not locate the source of the noise. They might have been coming from anywhere along the outer corridor.

After a few seconds, the movement stopped. Fawkes waited a beat. A trickle of sweat had formed on his brow. The sound started up again but gradually it faded away.

For five minutes more, the old soldier kept perfectly still. There was no further noise. Whoever it was, they had gone. But nobody should have been there at all.

He moved across to the main entrance. Crouching down by the door, he looked for signs of light from the other side, but there were none. His own lantern was covered over on the store room floor where he had left it. Nobody outside the vault could possibly have seen the light.

Fawkes fumbled for the keys at his waist, then reached forward slowly and felt for the lock. He inserted the key and gently pulled at the door, opening it just a few inches, listening carefully all the while. There was no sound to be heard, apart from his own quickened breathing. He opened the door further and stepped out into the familiar corridor.

'There's someone in there!' a voice exclaimed suddenly.

A hand grabbed Fawkes from the side.

'Take hold of him!' another man yelled abruptly.

Fawkes felt his arms being pulled hard behind his back. He let out a yelp and struggled to break free, but the two men had gripped him tightly and he was unable to get away.

'Over here, sir!' one of them called out.

A light appeared at the end of the corridor. A lantern was being held aloft. A tall figure bounded around the corner, followed by two burly yeomen in their distinctive metal helmets and breastplates. The man with the lamp was clearly in charge. A magistrate, perhaps, or a Gentleman of the Privy Chamber. He pulled up in front of the old soldier.

'Who are you?' he demanded. 'What are you doing here?'

Fawkes' reply was automatic: 'John Johnson, my lord.'

The magistrate glanced at the two guards restraining him. These men were also yeomen. Their hands gripped Fawkes' body as tightly as a vice. 'He was inside the room, Sir Thomas,' one of them explained. 'It was locked from the inside.'

Fawkes blurted out the obvious excuse. 'It's my master's cellar,' he explained, awkwardly. 'I was… collecting firewood.' It did not sound convincing, even to his own ears.

'After midnight??' Sir Thomas exclaimed. 'I hardly think so!' The indignant knight peered into the gloom. 'Hold him tight, Mr Doubleday,' he ordered. 'You two, follow me.'

Fawkes was pulled to one side as Sir Thomas pushed open the door to the cellar. He watched with trepidation as the magistrate moved forward. Two yeomen followed dutifully behind, entering the undercroft. Then Fawkes was dragged inside as well.

Sir Thomas was holding up his lantern. The dim candle light was barely sufficient to illuminate the interior. Perhaps he would not look too closely.

'It's just a store room,' Fawkes said, struggling to keep his voice calm. 'My master lives close by.'

'Who is your master?' Sir Thomas asked.

Fawkes hesitated for a second. He could not fail to answer the question and there was no point in lying. The information could be checked easily enough. 'Mr Thomas Percy, my lord. He rents a property on Parliament Place.'

Sir Thomas stepped forward to examine some of the wood stock-piled at the near end of the chamber. 'That's a hell of a lot of firewood for just one house.' He gestured to one of his men. 'Let's dig into it.'

The yeoman moved forward and began to pull away some of the bundles of wood. The faggots clattered across the floor and in a matter of moments the guard had unearthed buried treasure. 'There's a barrel of something here,' he advised his superior.

Guido Fawkes closed his eyes. That was it then. Everything was lost.

Sir Thomas Knevett moved closer. 'What's in it?'

The guard removed a heavy stone from the top of the barrel, then lifted the circular lid underneath. 'Careful with the lantern, my lord. It's gunpowder.'

The magistrate spun around and glared at Fawkes. 'Search him!' he ordered. 'Search him from head to foot.' He turned back to the guard. 'And see if there's any more of it.' The yeoman dutifully obeyed.

Fawkes stood quietly and allowed himself to be frisked by the guards.

Sir Thomas moved back to him and held the lantern up close to the man's beleaguered face. 'Well, Mr Johnson. What have you to say to this?'

One of the yeomen had found the watch Robert Keyes had brought him earlier in the evening. He had also discovered some bits of kindling and three fifteen minute fuses. 'He meant to blow up the whole of Parliament,' the fellow exclaimed, unable to hide the incredulity in his voice.

Sir Thomas Knevett struck Fawkes a glancing blow across the face. 'What have you to say for yourself?' he demanded again.

Guido Fawkes felt strangely calm. 'If I'd known you were outside the door, my lord,' he replied, with brutal honesty, 'I'd have blown the powder then and there...'

The knock was barely audible.

Tom Wintour lay sprawled on his bed in a darkened upper room at the *Duck and Drake*. He was dead to the world. He had been sleeping badly of late – the constant anxiety was beginning to take its toll – but accumulated tiredness had finally overwhelmed him and Tom had fallen into a deep slumber. The tapping continued – someone was knocking quietly at the door to the bed chamber – but Tom was oblivious. Only when the sound was punctuated by the whisper of a voice did it finally penetrate his dormant consciousness. 'Mr Wintour!' the voice hissed. A second later, there was another soft knock.

Tom opened his eyes groggily. The room was in complete darkness. It was the middle of the night. How long had he been asleep? Not long enough, he decided vaguely, stretching out on the uncomfortable bed.

From the door, there was another gentle tap.

Tom sat up suddenly. Someone had spoken his name. Who could it be, at this hour? He rubbed his eyes. Whoever it was, it did not bode well. Not at this time of the morning.

He pulled back the bed sheets and stood up. The wooden floor was cold beneath his feet. Moving away from the bed, he narrowly avoided tripping over the chamber pot. Thankfully, it was empty. He fumbled slowly towards the door. 'Who's there?' he whispered.

'It's Kit,' a voice came back. 'Kit Wright.'

Jack's younger brother. It was definitely bad news.

Tom unlatched the door. His eyes took a moment to adjust to the light. An awkward giant stood in the hallway, illuminated by a dim candle. Kit Wright. Tom gestured him into the room. 'What's going on?' he demanded, closing the door quietly and keeping his voice low.

The tall visitor moved across to the window and looked out furtively onto the street. 'There's some kind of commotion,' he explained. 'In the vicinity of Lord Monteagle's' residence. A gentleman called on Sir William scarcely half an hour ago. Dragged him out of bed.'

'What for?'

'Taking him to Essex House. I don't know why. I think they were looking for Northumberland. But it looks bad, Tom. I think the matter is discovered.'

Tom brought a hand to his mouth. Something very bad indeed must have happened if the Privy Council were being roused at this ungodly hour. 'What time is it?' he asked.

'A little after four.'

Tom took a deep breath. 'Go to Essex House. See if you can find out anything more. I'll get myself dressed. Meet me back here as soon as you can. We need to find out exactly what's going on.'

Kit nodded and made for the door.

'Good luck,' Tom called after him.

He sat down on the edge of the bed. If the plot had truly been uncovered, then Mr Fawkes must have been arrested. If that was the case, they would know about Percy too. Tom buried his head in his hands. They were all dead men.

Kit returned to the *Duck and Drake* within half an hour. The man's face was drained of colour. He sat down on the bed next to Tom and confirmed his worst fears. 'They are definitely searching for someone. I saw John Lepton at Essex Gate.' Lepton was a Groom of the Privy Chamber. 'He spoke to the lords and then rode up Fleet Street as if he were possessed by the devil.'

'It's Mr Percy they're after,' Tom realised. Thank God they had persuaded the old rascal to stay away from his usual lodgings. It would take the authorities some time to track him down, even though he was sleeping within walking distance of the *Duck and Drake*. 'Somebody needs to warn him.'

'I'll go,' Kit volunteered at once. 'I'll warn him.'

'Ride together. Get out of London as fast as you can.'

'What about you?'

Tom shook his head. 'Somebody needs to find out exactly what went wrong. I'll follow on as soon as I can. If possible, I'll meet up with the rest of you at Dunchurch, as arranged.'

Jack's younger brother shuddered. 'Take care of yourself, Tom.'

'I'll be fine. Don't worry about me. Just warn Thomas Percy.'

The Palace of Whitehall was in uproar. Yeomen were running from room to room. Bewildered peers and other noblemen were arriving from their lodgings. Guards were being stationed at all the entrances and exits. People were barking orders but hardly anyone seemed to have a clear idea of what was happening.

At the eye of the storm, Guido Fawkes watched events unfold with a peculiar detachment. It did not seem real.

After his arrest, he had been dragged up from the vault into Parliament itself, and then to Whitehall, where the King had been roused and was waiting to question him.

Fawkes had never seen King James up close. Shorn of his usual robes of state, the sovereign was less than impressive. He had obviously dressed in a hurry. His hair was unkempt, his eyes tired and baggy. The man's natural authority was fogged over with the remnants of an abruptly disturbed sleep.

In any other circumstances, put in chains and forced onto his knees before the King of England and Scotland, Fawkes would have felt cowed. But his adrenaline was flowing now and when James confronted him before the members of the Privy Council he answered with defiance. 'I regret nothing,' he declared boldly. 'Except that I failed in my task.'

The King's jaw dropped. There were shocked murmurs from the assembled lords. 'We thank God that you did!'

'It wasn't God,' Fawkes stated firmly. 'It was the Devil who allowed this discovery.'

'Who helped you in this?' King James demanded, trying to regain the initiative. His accent, though mild, was unmistakably Scottish. 'There must have been others.'

Fawkes did not reply.

'Answer me, man!'

'You have no authority to examine me.'

That was too much for the King. 'No authority?!?' he exclaimed. 'I am your sovereign!'

'I do not believe that, my lord. You were not anointed by God. You are nothing but a heretic and a tyrant. I owe you nothing.'

There were gasps from the other lords. They were not used to hearing the King addressed with such disrespect. But Fawkes did not care. He had nothing to lose now.

'You did not act alone in this,' the King insisted. 'Who were the other conspirators?'

Fawkes did not blink. 'There were none but myself.' The Yorkshireman had no intention of implicating his friends. 'I brought the gunpowder into the cellar. My master knew nothing of it.'

King James stared at him. 'And you really would have set the powder alight?'

Fawkes smiled slightly. 'I would.'

'And killed us all?' The King's eyes were wide in disbelief.

'That was the intention, my lord.'

'*Why*, for God's sake?'

The answer was simple. 'To blow you Scottish beggars back to your native land.'

The King's face reddened suddenly. 'And what of the lords?' he demanded, gesturing to his companions. 'All those other souls who have done nothing to offend you? Her Majesty the Queen and the Royal children? Would you have killed them too?'

'If they were there, I would have done nothing to save them.'

James looked away, aghast. 'I cannot believe any man could conspire so hideous a treason.'

At that, Fawkes shrugged. 'A dangerous disease requires a desperate remedy.'

Chapter Twenty Two

Thomas Percy was fleeing for his life.

He swore at his horse and kicked the animal savagely. Behind him, Kit Wright was struggling to keep pace. 'Faster!' Percy cried, and kicked again. Everything had gone wrong. John Johnson had been taken into custody and now all of London was looking for Thomas Percy. He had to get out of the city. He had to put as much distance between himself and Parliament as possible.

Kit Wright had broken the news and the two men had left the inn together. Percy had barely stopped to dress himself. He had sprinted to the stables like a madman, almost colliding with a startled groom. 'I am undone!' he had exclaimed. The servant just stared at him, open-mouthed.

There had been no time to gather his things. He had probably left half his possessions lying scattered across the bed chamber. At a time like this, material wealth was of no concern whatsoever.

The two men had ridden out of the stables in the pre-dawn light and headed North West. Nobody had stopped them as they galloped through the back streets of old London town. Even the slippery cobblestones had failed to check their flight.

Out of the city now, Percy whipped his horse even harder. There was still a chance they could make it to safety. Thank God for Tom Wintour, he thought. That young man had nerves of iron. Thank God, too, that he had chosen to lodge in a different tavern the previous evening, as Catesby had suggested. And thank God he had thought to have his horse already saddled for the morning ride.

Percy had been so certain that everything would go according to plan. Mr Fawkes had taken his place in the cellar and there was no reason to believe that Parliament would not open as scheduled that very morning. Percy had expected to rise at first light and then to take a leisurely ride out of town. What had happened to make things go so badly wrong? He would find out in time.

All that mattered now was speed.

Percy whipped the horse again.

'Faster, you stupid animal!'

Further north, Catesby was making slower progress. His companions had been riding with him for some hours in the dark, through muddy country lanes, and their horses were beginning to grow tired. Thankfully, the rain had now dissipated but the early morning sky was still overcast.

Jack Wright led the way on his large chestnut gelding. He was an impressive figure, tall and confident in the saddle; clearly at home there. Catesby was glad to have him along.

Off to the right, sunlight was beginning to flicker between the leaves of the trees. Dawn was breaking.

Catesby allowed himself the indulgence of a smile. By now, their lordships would be waking in London, he thought. King James would be attending to his toilette. The peers would be dressing and breaking their fast. And then the sovereign and his many lords would be making their way slowly towards Parliament House, just as they had done the previous year. And as they did so, Guido Fawkes would be crouched there, waiting patiently beneath the Upper Chamber, all set to send them to oblivion.

Fawkes was a brave man. Catesby hoped he would get away safely. The only regret Catesby had was not being closer to London. It would have been reassuring to hear the sound of the gunpowder going off. But he could imagine it well enough. Any time now.

Up ahead, Jack Wright had slowed to navigate an awkward curve in the track. Catesby began to slow down as well but just then his horse hit a pot-hole at the edge of the road and the animal staggered slightly. Catesby felt something give and the horse slowed itself abruptly. It was starting to limp on one of its front legs. 'Hold up!' he called out.

Jack pulled up his reins. 'What's wrong?' he shouted, turning his horse and trotting back along the path.

The manservant Bates came to a halt behind them.

Catesby bent forward in his saddle and peered down at the animal's front legs. 'I think he's thrown a shoe.' He dismounted the horse and grabbed a foot to confirm the diagnosis.

Jack scratched his head. 'We're only about a mile from Daventry,' he said. 'We can get it fixed there. It won't take long.'

Catesby grimaced. They would have to find a blacksmith. That would slow them down even further. Still, it had to be done. He grabbed the reins and pulled them over the horse's head.

The yeoman would not let Tom Wintour pass.

He had been walking down King's Street towards the Houses of Parliament. A burly palace guard had stepped into the middle of the road, blocking his path. 'You can't come down here,' the man announced, tersely.

'What's going on?' Tom asked.

The response was unhelpful: 'Orders.'

It had been the same at the Court Gates. Tom had gone there first. The whole place had been completely locked up. Everywhere was the same. The sun had barely risen on a new day and already the whole of London was being systematically shut down.

The guard lowered his pike threateningly. 'Go about your business!' he barked.

Tom had no option but to turn tail and make his way back towards the Strand. It was dangerous for him to be in London now. Known Catholics would be under immediate suspicion. It would only be a matter of time before warrants were issued for the arrest of Mr Percy and the others. Fawkes would hold his tongue for the first few hours but beyond that it was impossible to say.

People were milling about on the streets. Various traders were setting up their usual stalls but other people had clearly come out, as he had, to discover the cause of all the commotion.

On the far side of the road, some scoundrel was updating his friend. 'It's treason!' Tom heard the young fellow exclaim. 'Somebody was plotting to blow up the King and all of the lords.'

He closed his eyes and kept walking. So it was true. The plot had been uncovered. Robin had gambled and he had lost.

There was nothing more to learn in the capital.

Ambrose Rookwood sheathed his sword and prepared to mount a powerful black stallion. The young horseman had stayed in London until eleven o'clock, running hither and thither to discover the exact details of Mr Fawkes' arrest. As soon as had gathered all the information he could, he had returned to his lodgings and prepared to leave the capital. The black horse he had saddled was the best in his entire stable. Probably, it was the fastest animal in the entire country. Speed was of the essence now.

Ambrose fastened his cape around his neck, an extravagant purple affair. It matched the brightly polished sword at his waist. He clutched the hilt of the new blade and smiled grimly. The sword had been hand forged by John Craddock of the Strand. Ambrose had commissioned the blade some time earlier but it had only been delivered the previous evening. The hilt was skilfully engraved with the image of Christ carrying the Cross. It had cost Ambrose almost twenty pounds. The weapon had been intended as a celebration of success. Now it could only be a symbol of triumph in adversity. The plot had failed, utterly.

Ambrose rode out of London with reckless haste. He had lined the route to Dunchurch with a succession of fine horses. His reputation as a first class equestrian had been well earned but this would be his greatest challenge yet. There could be no time for dallying. He would swap rides every couple of hours and would overtake the others well before sun-down. Catesby had to know what had happened in London.

As midday drew close, Ambrose was already thundering through the home counties. In Bedfordshire, at Brickhill, he caught up with Thomas Percy and Kit Wright. The two men had just past through the village when he reared up behind them. Kit Wright, who was in front, heard Ambrose call out and he slowed to a halt.

'What news?' Kit called back.

The younger man rode up beside them. 'Mr Fawkes was caught red-handed in the cellar,' he announced. 'He was taken at midnight. The King was woken and a proclamation has been issued for your arrest.' This last was directed at Percy.

Thomas Percy shuddered. 'There's no point wasting time here then.' He rounded his horse. 'The sooner we reach Dunchurch the better.'

At the Palace of Whitehall, Guido Fawkes had held his nerve through several hours of interrogation. A dozen different lords had bombarded him with a hundred different questions. Essentially, however, they all wanted to know the same thing: who was he and why had he planned to kill them? In the space of twelve hours, Fawkes had faced more peers of the realm than he had encountered in the rest of his thirty-five years. And none of them seemed to have any idea who he was.

'What was your aim in destroying Parliament?' a Scottish lord demanded in the early afternoon.

His response was simple. 'It was done to bring about the restitution of the Catholic religion. And to prevent the Unification of Scotland and England.'

Fawkes felt like an actor performing a role. The peers had accepted his assumed identity without question. He was Mr John Johnson, servant to Mr Percy. And the more he was forced to repeat the lie, the more convincing it sounded, even to himself. There was confusion, however. He did not act like a servant. He addressed the lords – and even the King – with cool but barely disguised contempt. Their lordships had no idea what to make of him. And the more unsettled they became, the more confident Fawkes began to feel. They would put him on trial and execute him as a traitor. It was not a question of if, but when. Once that fact had sunken in, Fawkes had been able to concentrate on his one remaining responsibility. The lords were anxious for him to start naming names. He insisted that he had acted entirely alone. All that mattered now was buying time for Catesby and the others.

The blacksmith at Daventry had proved remarkably efficient. The man had managed to re-shoe Catesby's horse in a matter of minutes. It was not long, therefore, before the three riders were back on the road, a chill breeze cutting through their damp clothing. The horses were still tired, of course, and Catesby had decided not to push the animals too hard. There would be no fresh mounts before Ashby St. Ledgers and that was still some hours away. By then, he hoped, they would have news from London.

'It's Mr Rookwood!' Bates exclaimed from behind. 'Mr Rookwood is coming!'

Catesby swivelled around in his saddle. Sure enough, in the far distance, a horseman could be seen galloping down the hill towards them at phenomenal speed. Ambrose was easily recognisable. Even at such distance, the bright purple and gold of his elaborate doublet served to mark him out.

Jack pulled up beside Catesby and grinned from ear to ear. 'There's no-one faster than Ambrose,' he declared.

Catesby was tense. 'Let's hope it's good news.' Raising a hand, he waved to the distant figure. Ambrose did not wave back.

The next two minutes were interminable. Jack could not keep himself from smiling. He at least was convinced that all was well. Thomas Bates was nervous. Catesby was merely hopeful. There was no reason to suppose that anything had gone wrong.

Even when the trio saw the whites of the man's eyes, they could not discern what he was about to say. The young rider pulled up his horse and took a moment to recover his breath.

'Well, come on,' Jack insisted. 'What news?'

Ambrose took one last breath. Then he told them everything.

Jack's smile quickly disappeared.

'They're looking for Mr Percy already,' Ambrose concluded. 'I don't know how long it will be before they have the other names. It all depends on how long Mr Fawkes can hold out.'

Catesby felt cold all over. 'Where are the others now?'

'Thomas and Kit are just behind me. They should be here in a few minutes. Mr Keyes has gone to be with his wife. Tom Wintour was in London when I left, but he'll be on the road by now.'

'What about Francis?' Jack asked.

'That I don't know. I haven't seen him at all.'

Francis Tresham was supposed to collect funds from his home in Northamptonshire and then meet up with them at Dunchurch.

'So what do we do now?' Ambrose asked.

Catesby looked away. On the hill, he could see two men appearing over the horizon. Jack's brother was riding just ahead of Thomas Percy. 'I…don't know,' he admitted.

They waited in silence for the two men to arrive.

'Why are we dawdling?' Percy demanded, pulling up in the middle of the road.

It was Catesby who replied. 'We were just…digesting the news.'

'It changes nothing,' Percy snapped. 'We ride on to Dunchurch, as planned. We should have a small army waiting there, ready to rise up on our behalf.'

'A rebellion?' Bates asked, his eyes widening.

'That was the idea.' Percy unclipped his cloak and threw it into the bushes. Speed would be vital now. 'Let's see how many of them are willing to join us…'

Chapter Twenty Three

The half-timbered tavern at Dunchurch was bubbling over with enthusiasm and good cheer. A roaring fire kept the patrons snug and warm, though heavy rain was visible through the criss-crossed windows at the front of the inn. Supper had already been served. The *Red Lion* was a good place to eat. Sir Everard Digby had sat himself down to dine with a large group of fellow Catholics. A great deal of ale had already passed their lips and everyone was looking forward to the hunt the following day.

Everyone except Sir Everard.

The jovial young knight had managed to cover his distraction well. No-one dining with him would have guessed that Digby was in any way preoccupied. He had joined in with the general merriment, delivering his fair share of improbable anecdotes and laughing uproariously at the stories delivered by others. Beneath the mask, however, his mind was wandering. Catesby and his associates would be well on the way to Dunchurch by now. Hopefully, they would bring good news. But it was a bad night to be out.

Digby prayed silently for their safety. He took another swig of ale and glanced across at the door. It was a little after eight o'clock now. He had been keeping a close eye on the entrance to the *Red Lion* throughout the evening. At last, the door swung open, revealing six tired and bedraggled individuals. A cry went up across the saloon. 'Robin!' Digby exclaimed, rising to his feet.

A gaggle of servants had already enveloped the travellers, removing the hats and cloaks from those who still had them. The new arrivals were wet through. The rain, which had let up during the day, had now returned with avengeance.

'You've just missed supper, I'm afraid,' Digby said, coming forward. He wore an amiable grin on his face, as much for the benefit of the other diners as for his fellow conspirators. 'But I'm sure the ostler can arrange something…'

Catesby embraced him warmly but Digby immediately sensed that something was wrong. He broke off to greet the other new arrivals. 'Is Tom not here?'

'He'll be following later,' Catesby said, with convincing assurance. He leaned his head towards Ambrose Rookwood. 'Mingle with the others. I need to speak to Sir Everard.'

Ambrose nodded. He gestured to Kit Wright and the two men moved forward towards the bar. 'So where's the ale?' the young horseman demanded as the crowd cheerfully enveloped them.

Digby gestured Catesby into a side room. Jack and Percy followed them in. And here the new arrivals broke the bad news to their noble friend.

'According to Ambrose, they mounted a search of the whole parliament building,' Catesby said.

Digby's jaw dropped open. 'We must have been betrayed.' He glanced up. 'Why else would they have bothered to look?'

'We *were* betrayed,' Catesby confirmed. He told Sir Everard briefly about the letter.

'And we all know who sent it,' Percy snarled. 'You should have slit his throat while you had the chance.'

'If Francis *was* responsible, he'll be punished for it. If not by us, then by the Holy Father. Francis will be damned to the eternal torments of Hell.'

Percy grinned sourly. 'It couldn't happen to a nicer gentleman.'

Digby was still in shock. 'This is not what I wanted to hear.'

'We're not beaten yet,' Catesby insisted.

'But what do we do now?' asked Jack.

Thomas Percy gave a blunt response: 'We carry on as planned.'

'There seems little point in making a raid on Combe Abbey,' Digby reflected. 'And it won't be long before the authorities learn everything there is to know.'

'Agreed. "But though the field be lost,"' Catesby quoted theatrically, '"all is not lost". How many men do you have gathered here?'

'About a hundred.'

'That's a start. If we can persuade all these good Catholics to come together and fight, there's no knowing what we could achieve.'

Digby looked away. 'An armed revolt?'

Percy was enthusiastic. 'Why not? That was what we originally planned. People will flock to the cause. We have munitions at Norbrook. John Grant's gathered a ton of stuff, so Robin says. And the people here must have muskets and powder. Plenty of horses, too.'

Catesby nodded. 'We have nothing to lose.'

Sir Everard Digby rose up from the table. His expression was grave. 'There's no other remedy,' he agreed. They were in too deep to turn back now. 'A gentleman does not desert his friends. But we will have to break the news to the others.'

'It might come better from you than from me.' Catesby suggested. 'We must hurry though. The sooner we can get going, the better. Do you have fresh horses?'

Digby nodded. 'Of course.' He moved towards the door. 'Let's see how many will join us…'

Two yeomen had been detailed to escort Mr Fawkes to a nearby cell in the bowels of Whitehall. He was weary after an intense day of interrogation. 'You'll be off to the Tower tomorrow,' one of the guardsmen warned him. 'That'll loosen your tongue.'

Fawkes grimaced. So far, the examinations had been surprisingly civilised. There had been no threats, intimidation or violence, just unending repetition. He had responded to the relentless cycle of questions with a succession of lies and half truths. In so doing he had bought his compatriots the better part of a day. Nobody had mentioned torture, as yet. At the moment, the lords were primarily concerned with discovering the truth. But it was only a matter of time. Torture was a blunt and unreliable instrument but it would be used eventually – as a last resort – when the authorities had exhausted all other options. And then, sooner or later, they would break him.

Beyond the walls of the palace, there was the distant sound of cheering crowds.

'You hear that, Mr Johnson?' the second guard jeered. 'They're celebrating.' The yeoman grabbed Fawkes by the scruff of the neck and forced him up against the nearest window. 'All of London is celebrating the failure of your devilish scheme.'

In the distance, Fawkes could make out the flicker of firelight. *Bonfires*. A dozen of them were in view even through the narrow slit. The fires seemed to form a crude thread across the London skyline.

'They won't forget this day in a hurry,' the first guard observed.

Fawkes was certain of that. He closed his eyes.

'We ought to throw *you* on a bonfire,' the second yeoman growled. He pulled the prisoner away from the window and shoved him forward along the corridor. 'It'd save us all a lot of trouble…'

The *Red Lion* was jam-packed. More than a hundred men were squeezed into the main bar, drinking, gaming and pontificating loudly on a dozen different subjects. Few of them noticed when Sir Everard Digby returned to the chamber. 'Gentlemen,' he called out, lifting his hand to attract their attention. 'If I could have a few words.' His voice was lost amidst the general chatter. Digby clambered up onto a nearby table and banged a tankard for quiet. That got their attention.

'Bit late for speeches,' somebody yelled.

'Gentlemen,' Digby called again, his head brushing against the low ceiling. 'I gather many of you are interested in joining Mr Catesby's regiment.'

There were shouts of acknowledgement and a few drunken cheers. All eyes were upon him now.

'Mr Catesby is intending to form the regiment this very evening. But it is not the heretics in the Low Countries we will be fighting. It is the heretics in our own land.'

This last remark was greeted with puzzled silence.

'What are you going on about?' one of the men asked. It was Digby's uncle, Sir Robert; an overdressed bear of a man. 'Are you drunk, Everard?'

'What we are proposing,' Catesby interjected, 'is an army gathered together against the forces of Protestantism in our own country.'

'A rising?' somebody exclaimed.

'Armed rebellion!' Percy confirmed loudly.

The tavern exploded in a cavalcade of contradictory opinions. A dozen different voices were struggling to be heard. Digby, from his higher position, signalled for silence. Calmly, without exaggeration and unnecessary rhetoric, he explained what Catesby was proposing. They would ride to Norbrook that very evening to gather arms. From there they would head east, rallying the local communities. They would seek help from Sir John Talbot, a rich landowner with his own private regiment. They might even join forces with the Welsh rebels over the border. And then they would seize the whole of the Midlands and eventually march on London to overthrow the King.

It was an audacious plan. For some, even in their drunken state, it was too much. 'This is treason!' Sir Robert Digby exploded. 'Treason and murder against our sovereign lord. This will set back the Catholic cause forever.'

Others disagreed. 'He's got it coming to him, the Scotch bastard!'

The landlord and servants looked on with growing consternation as raised voices angrily clashed across the bar room.

Catesby looked up at Sir Everard.

'Gentlemen!' he called. 'We have no time to discuss this. If we are to make our move, we must do it tonight.'

'Who's with us?' Thomas Percy demanded.

To Sir Everard Digby's surprise, more than half of those gathered cried out their approval.

Sir Robert Digby looked on in horror and disgust.

Chapter Twenty Four

The Catholic warriors streamed drunkenly out of the *Red Lion* Inn. Horses were quickly saddled and weapons located. Reluctant servants were press ganged into accompanying their masters. And within minutes, a small column was winding its way out of Dunchurch, with Sir Everard Digby at the head. It would have been a magnificent sight, but for the rain and the cold and the darkness. The Catholics of England were finally doing something to recover their country from the heretics.

They rode for some hours along slippery mud-drenched tracks. Visibility had been reduced to just a few yards, but the men were in good spirits. Catesby kept close behind Sir Everard Digby. The two men had set a healthy pace, but the rain was falling heavily and gradually the enthusiastic chatter of voices faded into silence. The convoy continued on its way regardless.

If the journey was uncomfortable for the riders, it was exhausting for the horses. The animals had been whipped into such a frenzy of speed upon their departure it was hardly surprising they soon began to tire. The problem was that much greater for those horses that had been out earlier in the day. The brief pause at Dunchurch had done little to revitalise them.

Thomas Percy's grey-brown gelding was practically on its last legs. 'Stupid animal!' he snarled, wiping the rain from his brow and whipping the horse as hard as he could. It was all right for Ambrose. That smug little bastard had his own horses on standby at every conceivable location. But for the rest of them, beyond Dunchurch, there were no replacements to be had. 'These bloody animals won't get us much further,' Percy growled. It was already midnight and the column had slowed considerably. 'Maybe we could grab some fresh horses at Warwick. There are stables near the castle. We could slip in and out at this time of night without anyone being any the wiser.'

Tom Wintour's elder brother was riding to his left. 'Are you serious?' the hunched figure exclaimed. 'You want us to mount a raid on Warwick Castle?'

'Not a raid!' Percy snapped. 'Just a bit of quiet horse rustling.'

Catesby drew up beside them. 'Actually, that's not a bad idea.' He scratched the side of his face and glanced back at the long line of bedraggled young men. The cold and the rain had already dampened much of their enthusiasm. 'The way things are going, we'll be lucky to reach Norbrook by midday.'

'If at all,' Percy muttered. 'But with a handful of fresh mounts we could probably be there in a couple of hours.'

Tom's brother was still not convinced. 'We're rebels, not thieves,' he protested. 'We shouldn't be party to theft. We could get ourselves into real trouble.'

Catesby laughed. 'What? You think we're not in real trouble at the moment, rising up against the King of England?'

'*You* may be, Robin, but as for the rest of us...'

Catesby lifted a hand to cut off any further dissent. 'Anyone who knows anything about this is already a dead man in the eyes of the law. A bit of horse rustling is neither here nor there.'

The casting vote went to Sir Everard Digby, who gave cautious approval to Percy's scheme. 'We will leave our own horses in exchange. Once they are rested they will be more than adequate compensation.' Fair exchange, after all, was no robbery.

Ambrose Rookwood had been listening carefully to the debate. 'If you're going off to Warwick I might as well head to Norbrook on my own. I've got another gelding waiting about three miles from here.' He grinned. 'Just the one, I'm afraid. I can start getting the arms laid out as soon as I get there. It'll save us all a bit of time.'

Catesby nodded. It made sense to have one of them arrive at the manor house ahead of the rest. Ambrose grabbed the keys from John Grant and disappeared rapidly into the night. Catesby turned to the others. 'We'll leave the pack-horses here.' The heavily encumbered animals would be of no use in the raid. 'Mr Bates, get a couple of servants to keep an eye on them.' The party would need to be quick once they got inside the city walls.

Bates nodded and set about the arrangements.

If they could find enough horses, they could replace the pack-animals as well.

Sir Everard Digby drew up beside him.

'Ready?' Catesby asked.

Digby took a lungful of air. 'Ready,' he agreed.

'All right. Let's get going. But quietly!' Catesby kicked his horse into a slow trot. 'Let's see if we can get in and out without attracting any attention.'

The stables Percy had in mind were adjacent to Warwick Castle. The owner was a man named Benock. Like Ambrose, he was famed for the quality of his horses. At this time of night, however, the fellow was bound to be fast asleep.

The streets of the city were deserted. It took only a few minutes to locate the stables. Catesby drew his sword and approached cautiously. The other riders were trotting slowly behind. Almost a dozen men had ventured into the city at Catesby's behest.

A rickety wooden gate guarded the entrance, but it was not chain-locked. Sir Everard Digby dismounted his horse, reached through the gate and swung the door open. The dashing young knight gestured to his companions and they followed him cautiously inside.

The new horses were tied up in a long line of small stalls. They were expensive animals – strong and well-bred; perfect material for the newly assembled rebel band.

The party fanned out and each man found himself a suitable mount. There were saddles nearby, which could be quickly thrown onto the new horses. The old saddles could be left behind in payment. It would take too long to untie them in any case.

Jack Wright was already strapping a fresh saddle into place. He winked at Catesby. 'Better than my old nag,' he whispered.

The other man had just opened out the front of a stall and was leading a strong brown gelding onto the cobbles towards the open gate.

Out in the street, the servants were waiting.

Sir Everard Digby, to his left, was addressing a couple of the grooms. 'Mr Fowes, Mr Conyers,' he whispered. 'Take the old horses and tie them up inside. Then get yourself and the others a fresh set of legs. But be quick about it.'

'Yes, sir,' Mr Conyers replied, nervously.

Catesby patted his new horse, grabbing hold of the mane and pulling himself swiftly up into the saddle.

The last of the replacements were now being led out through the gates.

Just then there was a loud cry.

'Thieves!' somebody yelled. 'Someone's stealing the horses!' It was a young voice. A stable boy, perhaps.

Seconds later, a bell rang out.

'Bloody hell!' Thomas Percy swore. 'Let's get out of here!'

Catesby grimaced. This was just what he had been hoping to avoid. The rest of the rebels struggled onto their new mounts, whipping the befuddled animals into a reluctant gallop.

The abandoned older horses, which had just been led into the stable, started to panic at the noise. A desperate servant managed to grab hold of one of them, which he mounted awkwardly and rode out through the gate. Others, however, were not so lucky.

Local men were starting to appear in the street. Within seconds, they were converging on the stables.

Sir Everard Digby was heading in the opposite direction. He was following close on the heels of Catesby and Thomas Percy, who were already hurtling out of Warwick as fast as their stolen animals would carry them. It was not until they were well outside the city walls that any of them could afford to pull up and take stock of the situation. The rest of the troop, who had stayed behind with the pack horses, was less than half a mile away.

'Is everyone here?' Digby enquired anxiously.

Thomas Percy scanned the faces of the riders who had pulled up beside him. 'We're all here,' he said.

Catesby let out the breath he had been holding. They had been lucky to get away at all. And they were not out of danger yet.

'Somebody's bound to follow us,' Sir Everard Digby pointed out.

That much was obvious. 'But it'll take them time to organise a posse.' Thankfully, nobody in the city could know who they were or where they were going. 'Gather the supplies,' Catesby ordered. 'We need to...'

'Excuse me, sir.' One of the servants had come forward to address him. 'But what happened to Mr Conyers and Mr Fowes?'

Catesby frowned. Two of the grooms who had been with them at the stables. 'I'm sorry,' he said. 'They must have been taken.' He wondered briefly if the servants might know anything that could compromise the group but it did not seem likely. 'I'm afraid there's nothing we can do.' The men would have to take their chances.

Catesby had more important matters to consider. 'We ride on to Norbrook!' he declared.

And now they had the horses to get them there.

Ambrose Rookwood ate feverishly. The servants had provided a simple meal of bread and sweetmeats, with cider to wash it down. Ambrose felt ravenous. There had scarcely been time to order food at the *Red Lion* and the handsome young gentleman had not eaten properly since leaving London the previous morning.

He had arrived at Norbrook long after midnight.

The servants, who had been asleep, were courteous if somewhat confused. It was unusual to receive visitors in the middle of the night, but Ambrose was a good friend of the owner and had visited the manor house many times before. One of the grooms had recognised him at once. Ambrose had told the man that his master was on his way back and the elderly servant had roused the rest of the household.

Food would need to be prepared for the whole group.

The groom had insisted that Ambrose eat something too. Reluctantly, he had seated himself in the dining hall, though he could barely keep his eyes open as he ingested the food. The mud-spattered equestrian had pushed himself to the limit to get to Dunchurch the previous evening and the weight of his fatigue was beginning to catch up on him.

After he had finished the meal, one of the servants led him down to a stone vault some distance from the dining area. It was guarded by a heavy wooden door. Ambrose pulled out the set of keys John Grant had given him and quickly opened the door. A secret cache of arms had been stored here, in readiness for the revolt. He lifted his lantern and moved quickly into the room. There were matchlocks here – long, slender muskets – carefully stacked alongside several bags of powder and boxes of shot. Ambrose had donated a substantial sum on joining the cause and it was clear that Catesby had put the money to good use. There were enough weapons here to outfit a small army.

He put down the lantern and grabbed a musket with each hand. They were cumbersome devices, taller than he was from top to tail. The gunpowder was piled up around the edges of the room. 'We need to get all this up to the dining hall,' he said, calling back to the groom, who was waiting patiently outside. The servant nodded.

It would take some time to transfer the weapons from the vault to the main hall. The other servants would have to lend a hand.

'We'll need wagons, too, at the front of the house. There's a lot of equipment to be transported when we leave here.'

'Several carts have already been prepared,' the groom announced. 'They're out by the stables.'

'Good man!' Ambrose beamed.

John Grant had obviously thought everything through in advance. Norbrook had always been part of the plan.

'Let's get to it then…'

At three o'clock in the morning, the rest of the rebels arrived. Thomas Percy thundered into the dining area with Catesby close behind. Catesby let the older Catholic pass on all the news to Ambrose, while he surveyed the armaments his friend John Grant had purchased. The man himself was reassuring the servants.

Matchlocks had been laid out on the dining table, together with a basic meal of cold meats and ale. The servants were dismissed, but the conspirators crowded together and ate hungrily. Catesby watched them as they dined, carefully taking stock of the group. There were about forty-five men in all. Less than they had hoped for; and less than they had started with. A handful of recruits had slipped away after the raid on Warwick Castle. Servants, thankfully. But enough people had remained to make a credible core. These fine men, with these fine weapons, were an army in embryo. When other Catholics learned that they were rising up against the King their numbers would surely begin to swell.

Thomas Percy was tucking into a meat pie 'If we can persuade Sir John Talbot to join us,' he mumbled, between mouthfuls, 'we'll have half the Midlands on our side!' There were murmurs of agreement from around the table. That was certainly the plan. Talbot was a substantial landowner, with his own private regiment. The man was also father-in-law to Tom Wintour's elder brother.

There were, however, more pressing concerns. 'We can't stay here long,' Catesby announced, placing a matchlock down on the hard wooden table. The diners groaned. 'We'll have to move on within the hour.' If the Sheriff had been woken at Warwick, there was a chance that the authorities might send men out to try and apprehend them. Nobody at the Castle could know anything about the Westminster plot – there hadn't been time for any messengers to arrive from London – but the High Sheriff was unlikely to overlook a direct assault on Warwick Castle, even if it was just to steal a few horses. Catesby did not want to risk a confrontation at this early stage. He had no doubt that his men could defend themselves, but it was better to wait until more of them had rallied to the cause.

There was another possible source of help, which had been mentioned back in Dunchurch. There were many in Wales who would be sympathetic to their objectives. After Huddington, that is where they would head.

Catesby checked his pocket watch, then glanced over to the corner of the room. His manservant, Thomas Bates, was sitting quietly, picking at a crust of bread. The poor fellow had scarcely said a word since leaving London. He had always been a reluctant conspirator. But he had done his duty by his master and Catesby was grateful. He stood up and walked over to the servant.

'I'll have an errand for you to run, once you've finished.'

Bates swallowed a mouthful of food. 'Of course, sir. What do you want me to do?'

Catesby frowned. 'I need you to take a letter to Coughton Court...'

Chapter Twenty Five

It was impossible to cross London Bridge without catching sight of the shrivelled heads. A line of butchered craniums had been put on display on the south side of the bridge. Lifeless eyes stared blindly across the River Thames. The decapitated bodies of these recently executed outlaws had been buried without ceremony beneath the chapel of St Peter's, within the confines of the Tower of London, but the bloodied heads had been thrust onto sharp spikes and erected along the Thames as a warning to others. The King's justice would be swift and severe.

'That'll be you in a few weeks,' a yeoman remarked cheerfully.

Guido Fawkes looked away. He was not afraid. He had already resigned himself to his fate.

The guards had come for him before first light. They had tied his arms behind his back and bundled him onto a small rowing boat. Four yeomen were accompanying him downstream. One unlucky fellow had taken to the oars while the other three kept careful watch over the prisoner. There was no possibility of escape. With his arms and legs chained, Fawkes would not be able to swim for it. But the guards were not about to let him drown either. That would be too clean a death. They needed him alive, for now.

Passing under London Bridge, busy with the sounds of the street traders and early morning traffic, Fawkes caught sight of the Tower in the distance. It was a sombre, grey stone edifice with long crenulated walls; tall and forbidding. Beyond the castle, further up the north bank, was Tower Hill. There, presumably, Fawkes would meet his end.

The five hundred year old castle was surrounded by a moat fed with water from the Thames. There were several entrances, on land or by river. It was a Royal Palace and King James was often in residence there. But there was only one entrance for the likes of Mr Fawkes. The vessel pulled close to St. Thomas' Tower.

Traitor's Gate.

An iron double door had been pulled back and the water flowed through into a shallow quadrangle. The boat pushed inside, passing underneath a heavy iron trellis. Steps at the far edge led up out of the water. One of the guards stood up and jumped onto them with a tow rope in hand. Quickly, he fastened the boat to the jetty.

Fawkes was prodded to his feet. He stepped onto the slippery steps and moved up onto a gravel pathway which ringed the inside of the castle wall. A circular tower stood immediately to his right. Away on the left he recognised the imposing form of the Bell.

The guards prodded him straight ahead, towards a narrow archway. Rising above it, his new home.

The Bloody Tower.

The drawing room at Coughton Court was comfortable if a trifle contained. A stone chimney piece stretched up to an arched ceiling. Coloured glass topped the far window. An elaborate carpet lined the stone floor. It was a quiet, graceful room in a quiet, graceful house a short distance from the Forest of Arden.

Father Oswald Tesimond closed the book he had been perusing and put it down on the table by the fire. The rotund Jesuit had taken to reading a little each day. There was usually a brief lull after breakfast which afforded the perfect opportunity.

He stood up as Father Henry Garnet entered the room. The elder priest was clutching some documents in his bony white hands. His expression was grave.

'What is it?' Tesimond asked.

Several days had past since the Jesuit Superior had delivered his sermon at the Feast of All Saints and in that time the Father had been understandably preoccupied.

'I've just received word from Robin,' Father Henry said, holding up the letters. Behind him, moving through the doorway, came the tall, dishevelled figure of Thomas Bates.

Tesimond's mouth fell open. Catesby's groom was the last person he had expected to see at Coughton Court. 'Thomas!' he exclaimed. 'What are you doing here? Where is your master?' Robert Catesby rarely went anywhere without his loyal servant.

Bates looked down at his feet. The man had never been comfortable in the presence of the clergy, though there were few serving men as pious. 'He was at Norbrook this morning, Father,' Bates replied. 'He left there a few hours ago. For Huddington.' The groom had obviously been on the road for some time. His clothes were speckled with mud, his hair seemed ragged and the sleeve of his shirt was torn. Tesimond had seldom seen him in such a poor state. And it was obvious from the haunted look in his eye that there was something seriously amiss.

'The letter explains everything,' Father Henry said. He handed the document to his friend.

Tesimond opened it with some trepidation.

The letter was brief and to the point. It was addressed to Father Henry Garnet. It said that Mr Fawkes had been arrested, but that the rebels planned to carry on regardless, rising up in rebellion against King James. Tesimond's hands began to tremble as he read. It was just as Father Henry had feared.

"Forgive my rashness," Catesby wrote, *"but believe me when I tell you I have complete faith in the rightness of this action."* He begged Father Henry to join the rebels. *"You must lend us your support or we will all be lost. Help us gather together an army, in England and in Wales. Your influence will be pivotal. If you refuse to help us – if you allow us to perish now because of personal scruples or to free yourself and your fellow Jesuits from blame – then you too will quickly perish, as will all Catholics in this land."* The letter was signed simply *"Robin"*.

Father Tesimond looked up. 'Dear God. We are all utterly undone.'

'We will be held accountable,' Henry Garnet agreed. 'Robin is right about that at least.' The priesthood would be blamed for everything. People would claim that the plot had been instigated by the Jesuits, even though the Society was forbidden from interfering in political matters. Nowhere in England would be safe for them now.

'I should go to him,' Tesimond suggested. 'It would not be right to abandon dear Robin in his hour of need.'

'Oswald, we cannot support him in this. I will write to him. I will tell him to give himself up. This madness cannot continue.'

'I thank God at least that Parliament was saved.'

Father Henry nodded gravely. 'There is…further bad news. Sir Everard Digby is also involved in the plot.'

Tesimond slumped back down into his chair. 'I can scarcely believe it.' Digby was one of the brightest stars in the Catholic firmament. The house in which they stood – Coughton Court – was currently rented by the charismatic young knight.

'Sir Everard has also sent me a letter,' Father Henry explained sadly. 'He has joined the conspiracy and asks that his wife sends on some horses and extra supplies.'

'Mary knows nothing of the plot,' Tesimond said. 'How are we going to tell her that her husband has conspired to murder the King of England?'

'I will have to show her the letter. Sir Everard asks that I do so. But it will come as a terrible shock.'

It was not just Mary that would suffer. Digby's children would be disinherited and their property seized by the crown. The whole family would be rendered destitute.

'This is a bad business,' Father Henry said.

Thomas Bates stood silently by the door. The frightened and exhausted groom had stood by his master in the gravest of circumstances. He at least was doing the right thing. If only his employer had had the same sense.

'Get yourself cleaned up, Thomas,' Father Henry ordered. 'I will write a reply to your master. You can take it to him, if you are willing.'

Bates nodded. 'I will, Father.' He bowed his head and slipped out of the room.

Tesimond moved across to the door. He glanced down at the letter Sir Everard had sent them. 'I'll go and talk to Mary…'

The interrogations continued throughout the day much as they had done at Whitehall. Fawkes was conducted across to the Queen's House, a pleasant half-timbered building overlooking Tower Green and was escorted in chains to the Council Chamber on the first floor. Awaiting his arrival was the King's principal secretary, Robert Cecil.

Cecil was an ugly fellow, short and hunch-backed, with a compressed face, beady eyes and a prominent forehead. Aside from King James, he was the most powerful man in England. Cecil watched silently as Guido Fawkes was prodded forward into the room. The minister was comfortably seated behind a large wooden desk, but Fawkes would be made to stand for the duration of the interview. 'Good morning,' Cecil began.

Fawkes met the man's eyes and returned the greeting with exaggerated confidence. He felt nothing but contempt for Robert Cecil but he was not about to let his feelings show. He needed to keep a cool head. The fact that the principal secretary had come to the Tower to interview him in person was a statement of the importance they placed on breaking him. That made Fawkes even more determined to resist.

The interrogation followed a predictable pattern. The same questions were asked over and over again. 'Where did you sleep on Wednesday last?'

'I can't remember.'

'What about Thursday? Where did you sleep on Thursday night?'

'I forget.'

'Where did you sleep on Friday and Saturday?'

'I don't know.'

Cecil conducted the proceedings with a quiet precision, at times cordial, at times aggressive. Fawkes responded politely to each question, but he rarely answered truthfully.

In the afternoon, the secretary produced a special document which had just arrived from Whitehall. This time he was in no mood for prevarication. 'His Majesty has prepared a list of formal questions he wants answered.' Cecil looked up from the paper. 'It's in your interests to co-operate.'

Fawkes raised an eyebrow. 'I will consider it, my lord. It will depend on the questions.'

Cecil glanced down at the list. 'Firstly, your name.'

'You have that already, my lord. My name is John Johnson.'

'And where were you born?'

'In Yorkshire, my lord. At Netherdale.'

A scribe carefully noted down the responses, but the information he was giving them was nothing new.

'Your parents?' Cecil asked.

'My father is Thomas Johnson. My mother's name is Edith Jackson.' The last statement, at least, was true.

'How old are you?'

'Thirty six years old.' John Johnson was thirty six, Fawkes told himself. He was thirty five.

'And where have you lived since your birth? We have no records of any Catholic by the name of John Johnson.'

'I grew up in Yorkshire and went to school there. Then I was in Cambridge. Afterwards, I was in…other places.'

The secretary narrowed his eyes. 'What other places?'

'I prefer not to answer.'

Cecil let that pass. 'What was your trade, originally?'

'I was a farm hand.'

'Those scars on your chest. How did you receive them?'

'I suffered from pleurisy, my lord. It leaves such scars.' Actually, the wounds had been earned in battle, but Fawkes did not want Cecil to know that he had been a soldier.

'Very well. You were in service to Mr Thomas Percy. Were you in service to anybody else before that?'

'No, my lord.' Yes, as a young man.

'Then you had no reference. How did you come into Mr Percy's service?'

'I approached him myself. He's a Yorkshireman, as I am.'

The questions continued in a similar vein, with Cecil working his way methodically through the King's interrogatories. Most of this covered old ground. The authorities were still trying to pick up on any inconsistencies. But Fawkes was careful not to deviate from his earlier statements.

Cecil seemed particularly interested in his knowledge of French. A letter had been found on him, written while he had been abroad. There were further questions about foreign travel. Then the secretary asked him bluntly: 'Are you a papist?'

'I am a Catholic,' Fawkes responded proudly.

'How did you become a papist? Are you a convert?'

'I was not converted, I was raised a Catholic.'

And suddenly, Cecil's intention was clear. They did not know who Mr John Johnson was, but they suspected him of being a priest. More than that, they *wanted* him to be a priest. The questions about France were intended to determine if he had studied abroad, as most Catholic priests were forced to these days. If they could prove that he was a priest or that he had a strong connection to any priest it would be a tremendous propaganda coup. Fawkes was determined not to let that happen.

He was a layman and a manservant and he had acted alone.

Even Robert Cecil would not get anything more out of him.

Chapter Twenty Six

Tom Wintour was the last to arrive at Huddington Court. He had travelled a hundred and ten miles from London to reach his ancestral home and the poor horse that had carried him – a noble grey-white gelding – was on its last legs. After two solid days on the road, Huddington Court was a welcome sight; but the normally tranquil Elizabethan manor was now choked with activity. The hunting party from Dunchurch had arrived earlier that same afternoon and the small bridge covering the moat was blocked with carts piled high with weapons. Horses were being led away to the stables. Raised voices were directing the activities of various servants. And a group of familiar faces were gathered on the nearside of the moat. Catesby was the first to catch sight of Tom Wintour. He raised a hand in greeting. Tom dismounted his horse and led the exhausted animal over to his younger cousin.

The two men embraced.

'It's good to see you,' Catesby said. 'I was worried. Ambrose told me you were still in London when he left.'

Tom nodded. 'I left shortly after he did. The whole city was being shut down. I was glad to get out when I did. How did you get on at Dunchurch?'

'Surprisingly well.' Catesby filled him in on the volunteers who had joined at the *Red Lion*. 'In the circumstances, we were lucky to get so many. Having Sir Everard on our side made all the difference.' There was more news to relate: the raid on Warwick Castle and the arrival at Norbrook. Tom listened eagerly. There was clearly a lot to catch up on. 'I wrote to Father Henry at Coughton Court,' Catesby said. 'Bates got back about an hour ago.'

'What did the Father say?'

Catesby looked down. 'What you'd expect. He can't believe we would enter into such wicked actions. He says we should give ourselves up. Father Tesimond was more supportive. He's here at the moment. Bates brought him along. He wanted to see us all one last time.'

'He's a good man,' Tom said.

'I can't persuade him to ride with us, though.'

That was hardly surprising. Tom looked up and caught sight of his sister-in-law, Gertrude, peering down at him from a first floor window. He stepped up onto the bridge and waved at her. Gertrude waved back, but her expression was grim. Tom's elder brother, Robert, would be in the house too. He grimaced. The whole family was implicated now. Tom would have preferred to keep them out of it, but that was never going to be possible. Relatives shared culpability, financially if not criminally. As soon as he had joined the conspiracy, he had placed his entire family in danger. It was too late now for regrets.

Catesby joined him on the bridge.

'Where are we going next?' Tom asked.

'Hindlip House. Then Hewell Grange. Possibly Holbeach. We're planning to contact Sir John Talbot, when we get into Staffordshire.' Talbot was Robert Wintour's father-in-law. 'He has men who could help us.'

Tom was dubious about that. 'I'm not sure Sir John would want to get involved.' The old knight was prickly at the best of times.

Catesby was too tired to debate the matter. 'We can at least try. I've been trying to persuade your brother to write us a letter of introduction. He isn't being very helpful.'

'He's worried for his family, Robin. We all are.' Tom sighed, thankful that he at least did not have a wife to worry about. 'I could approach Sir John, if you really think it's a good idea. But I'm not sure he will listen. He's committed to King James now.'

'That's what your brother said.'

'And after Holbeach, what then? We can't keep running forever.'

'We're not *running*, Tom. We're trying to gather support. If Sir John won't help us, we'll carry on to Wales. We can pick up more men there, if we have to.'

Tom glanced down at the moat, a narrow sliver of water clinging tightly to the fringes of Huddington Court. 'How many do we have here?'

Catesby frowned. 'Less than forty. Including servants. We've lost a few people along the way.' He looked up. 'Get something to eat. We'll be here for a few hours yet. Rest up if you can. You look exhausted.'

'So do you.' They had all been on the road for the better part of two days.

'I don't think we're going to get any more rest, Tom,' Catesby admitted sadly. 'Not in this life, at any rate.

Guido Fawkes was pushed through a doorway in the Bloody Tower and was made to descend a narrow spiral staircase. Two yeoman stood back and allowed Sir William Waad to pass through in front of them. Waad was the Lieutenant of the Tower. Fawkes knew him by reputation, if not by sight. He was one of the King's henchmen, invariably brought in to do the royal dirty work. Waad had sat in on the interrogations that day. Doubtless, since the man was in overall charge of the Tower, he would conduct any further sessions himself. Robert Cecil had too many affairs of state to deal with and Sir William was a reliable deputy.

'You're going to break eventually,' the man sneered, descending the stairs immediately behind him. 'Why not make it easier for yourself and start naming names?'

Fawkes kept his eyes on his feet. It was rare for the lieutenant to accompany one of his charges, but making conversation in transit was a traditional ruse. It was hoped that the informality of the situation would trick the prisoner into letting something slip.

'I swore an oath, my lord,' he stated simply, coming to the bottom of the stairs.

'Oaths can be broken.'

Fawkes shook his head. 'I took the oath in company. It was reinforced by the taking of the Sacrament. I do not hold these things lightly.'

Waad raised an eyebrow. He was not a handsome man, but he had an expressive face. 'So some Jesuit scoundrel was in on it!' he exclaimed, triumphantly.

Fawkes was adamant. 'That is not so, my lord. The priest knew nothing of our pact.'

'But who were the other men?'

'That, my lord, I will not tell you.'

Waad prodded him forward along a narrow corridor. It was damp and badly illuminated. 'You might as well know, the King has granted formal authorisation for the use of torture.' He waited for a reaction but Fawkes was unwilling to give it. 'We'll start with the manacles on the morrow. If that doesn't loosen your tongue then we'll move on to the rack.' Still, Fawkes kept himself from volunteering a response. 'Now is probably your last chance to avoid all that.'

'I will not give you the names.'

Waad shrugged. 'It's your choice, Mr Johnson. Ah, here we are.' The lieutenant had stopped at a narrow wooden door. It was scarcely three and a half feet tall. He gestured for the warders to come forward and unlock it. 'This is a cell we reserve for our more difficult prisoners. We call it the Little Ease.'

Fawkes lent forward and peered through the doorway. The room was a small cube, barely four feet high and the same distance across. It was scarcely fit to kennel a dog.

Sir William Waad gestured to the door.

Fawkes kept his expression pleasant. 'I wish you good night, my lord,' he said, as he bent down and clambered into the tiny prison cell. The door was slammed shut and locked by the guards.

Waad bent over. His battered face filled the tiny grate. 'Sleep well, Mr Johnson. And think on what I said.'

Fawkes clasped his knees to his chest and sat up against the wall. The cell was uncomfortable, but he would make do. He was not about to let petty unpleasantness erode his spirit. He had managed to hold his tongue for two whole days. Even now, the authorities did not know his real name. If they broke him tomorrow, so be it. He had at least brought his friends a little time.

'The body of Christ,' intoned the priest, 'the blood of Christ.' Catesby swallowed the wafer and took a sip of wine from the proffered goblet. Jack was knelt quietly to his left. Tom was also there, with Percy, Sir Everard Digby and many others. It was probably the last chance they would have to celebrate Mass together. There were two priests at Huddington Court. Father Tesimond had arrived that afternoon but it was Father Hammond, the resident priest, who conducted the service in the early hours of Thursday morning.

Catesby had been awake for scarcely an hour. An uncomfortable, troubled sleep had been abruptly cut short by Thomas Percy.

'We're being followed!' the white-haired rascal had bellowed. 'The High Sheriff of Warwickshire is on our trail!' A Catholic well-wisher had sent a messenger from Warwick to deliver the news. According to this man's account, the two servants left behind at Warwick Castle had been captured and had given the authorities the names of the men responsible. The High Sheriff had organised a posse and even now was in pursuit. Luckily, the grooms had not known where the hunting party was headed and it was taking the posse some time to pick up the trail. But they would discover the truth soon enough. At best, the rebels could only hope to be half a day ahead.

'We should stop and fight,' Percy declared. 'There are enough of us. If we took the High Sheriff the locals would be falling over themselves to help us.'

Tom Wintour, roused but still half asleep, proffered the usual note of caution. 'It would be foolish to risk a confrontation without more men. We have no idea how large this posse is. Better to stick with the original plan. Fly to Wales. Or at the very least, contact Sir John Talbot, as Robin suggested.'

For once, Catesby decided to follow Tom's advice.

The others were woken. Nobody felt much like leaving Huddington Court. It was after midnight and the rain was falling heavily once more. It was then that Father Tesimond had suggested holding the Mass. It would be a welcome distraction for the men, he said, buoying up their spirits before departure. 'We should also organise a confessional. It might be the last opportunity for many of your supporters to unburden their souls.' Neither Tesimond nor Father Hammond would be accompanying the rebels when they left Huddington Court, but the men would surely feel better about their departure if one of the priests had first granted them absolution.

Catesby made his confession to Father Tesimond. The ruddy-faced Jesuit had been his confessor for nearly seven years. It would be hard to say goodbye to the man. They were of the same generation, more or less, and had been good friends even before they were priest and penitent. Catesby was grateful he had made the effort to be here. The priest disapproved of the plot, just as Father Henry did, but he had shown true loyalty in coming to Huddington to see them all one last time. In so doing, he had placed his own life in considerable jeopardy.

'Get abroad, if you can,' Catesby had insisted, when Tesimond had again refused to join him on their departure. 'Tell them the truth about us. Don't let the government distort everything.'

Tesimond had promised to do what he could.

The confessions were necessarily brief. A score of men had sought absolution from only two sanctified priests. Father Hammond and Father Tesimond did the best they could in the circumstances, but each sinner could be spared only a few minutes to unburden his conscience.

Then Father Hammond had presided over the Mass and the taking of Holy Communion.

Tom Wintour was the last in line to receive the sacrament. Catesby watched him sip from the silver goblet. For Tom, leaving Huddington would be particularly painful. This was his home. His family were here. He had been brought up here. Tom's elder brother may have inherited the estate, but Tom was no less a part of it. At least the man would have a chance to say goodbye.

Catesby had not said goodbye to his family. There had been an opportunity to visit his mother, on the way to Dunchurch, but he had not taken it. What would he have said? Father Hammond completed the service and Catesby rose wearily to his feet. The only person he wished to speak to now was the one person he could never speak to again. His wife Catherine had always understood him better than anybody else. She would have consoled him; but she would have admonished him too. How then could he look his own mother in the eye? Better for her to remember him as he was in happier times; not as a desperate fugitive on the run from the authorities. For that, in essence, was what he now was. The forces of the law were on their trail and – short of a miracle – they would all soon be taken.

If it came to it, Catesby resolved, they would fight and die in battle. Better that than a traitor's death.

Chapter Twenty Seven

Daylight never troubled the stone chamber at the base of the White Tower. Candles burned continuously, providing a gloomy light, but they were little comfort to the lost souls forced into the bowels of the Earth at His Majesty's Pleasure.

Guido Fawkes was hanging from a large wooden pillar midway across the chamber. They had escorted the Yorkshireman here from the Bloody Tower at first light. The Little Ease – where he had slept – had been a paradise in comparison to this darkened room. Here, with little preamble, his wrists had been forced into iron gauntlets. He had been pushed onto a set of wicker steps and an iron bar had been placed between the rings of the gauntlets to secure them. His arms were then lifted above his head and attached to an iron staple driven into the wood at the top of the pillar. Then the steps had been removed and he had been left suspended in mid-air.

Time passed slowly and the iron cuffs gradually began to cut into his wrists. The pain spread through his arms to his shoulders and upper torso. Then his wrists began to swell, pressing against the iron manacles. But the real pain hit him in his chest and belly. And the sweat poured from his brow. This was what the authorities referred to as "gentle torture".

Fawkes had dealt with his fair share of pain in life but this was altogether more extreme. He did not know how long he would be able to endure it. Every few hours – or minutes, maybe – one of the guards came forward with a set of steps, climbed up to wipe his forehead with a cloth and then tightened the manacles further, cutting off the blood to his hands and intensifying the pain. He needed all of his energy just to stop himself from fainting.

And then the questioning began again.

Thomas Percy drew his sword and advanced on the trembling servant. 'Show me to the armoury!' he demanded angrily, 'if you value your life!' The elderly groom backed away, his eyes wide with fear. Percy was a vision of hell, a white devil, wet through, his eyes glaring viciously.

Catesby placed a restraining hand on Percy's shoulder. 'There's no need for threats, Thomas.' He stepped forward and addressed the ageing servant in a more respectful manner. 'We won't harm you, I promise. Just show us where Lord Windsor keeps his armaments.'

The groom regarded him suspiciously. 'His lordship is not at home,' he mumbled, for the third time.

'We know that!' Percy snapped.

Catesby shot Percy a warning glance and the older man reluctantly sheathed his sword.

A cluster of frightened servants had gathered at the entrance of Hewell Grange, a large country house not far from the Staffordshire border. Lord Windsor, the owner of the estate, was a boy of fourteen. He was absent from the property but many of his servants had been left behind and were staring open-mouthed at the new arrivals.

Tom Wintour had not wanted to come here. It did not seem right. Lord Windsor did not deserve to have his house desecrated in this manner. He had said as much when the idea had first been mooted but Catesby had overruled him.

Now his cousin gestured for the groom to lead them inside.

The servants were huddled together nervously on the far side of the courtyard, the heavy rainfall cutting through their ragged clothes. 'I'll keep an eye on the supplies,' Ambrose Rookwood volunteered. The young horseman drew his sword while Catesby and the others disappeared inside the building.

The elderly groom led the small group along the hallway and down towards the cellar where the armaments were stored. Catesby kept close behind him. It was a blessing to be somewhere dry, even for a few minutes.

It had rained continuously all morning, as the rebels made their way slowly north west from Huddington. Some of the servants had become restive during the journey and Catesby had been forced to box them in to prevent anyone else from deserting. They had lost too many men already.

The groom fumbled nervously with a set of keys and opened the bulky wooden door that protected the armoury. Catesby moved inside. There were muskets and powder here, stacked up along the walls; far more than they could carry, though there was plenty of space left on the carts.

Jack Wright moved forward to examine the weapons. 'How much do you think we should take?' he asked.

'A couple of dozen muskets. Concentrate on the powder.' The bags they had carried from Norbrook had probably been compromised by all the rain. If they wanted to fire any of the matchlocks, they would need fresh powder. That was one of the reasons the group had been forced to stop at Hewell Grange, despite Tom Wintour's objections. They could not fight anyone without gunpowder.

Catesby helped the others to carry some of the weaponry back out into the courtyard. A few men from a nearby village had gathered in the rain, perplexed at all the noise. They were exchanging nervous words with some of the servants, though Ambrose was keeping them all well away from the wagons.

Back at the armoury, Jack had made a discovery. He called Catesby over to a large chest at the far end of the vault which he had managed to force open. 'It's full of cash,' he observed.

Catesby peered inside. The chest was brimming over with small coins. 'How much do you think is there?'

'I don't know.' Jack grabbed a handful of the coins and ran them through his fingers. 'A thousand pounds. Twelve hundred maybe.'

Catesby bit his lower lip, remembering what Tom had said. 'It wouldn't be right to deprive Lord Windsor of his inheritance.'

'We could do with the money though.' The more currency they carried with them, the easier it would be to draw new recruits once they had crossed over the border.

Catesby shook his head. 'Take sixty pounds. That should see us through to Wales.' That and the money Sir Everard Digby had provided. 'Make sure the trunk is properly locked up. We don't want anyone else riding off with it.' Jack nodded.

When the armoury had been cleared – or at least when the rebels had taken everything that they needed – Catesby instructed the elderly manservant to lock the place up and accompany them outside the house.

Despite the inclement weather, a couple of dozen villagers had congregated in the courtyard to watch their departure. The men were curious as well as fearful. It was unusual to see so many gentlemen gathered together on horseback, especially when the lord of the manor was away from home.

'Who will join us?' Catesby demanded, addressing the assembled rabble. 'We fight for God and Country.'

The locals had already guessed some of their intentions and wanted nothing to do with them. 'We are for King James as well as God and Country,' a rough voice called out from the crowd.

'You're wasting your time,' Percy spat. 'They're no use to us. We need real men.'

Thomas Percy was up to his knees in fresh water. It was some hours later and the small band of wet and weary men had been trying to cross the River Stour for the better part of an hour. A cartwheel had jammed in the flowing water and the sudden jolt had dislodged some of the munitions.

'This is ridiculous!' Percy exclaimed angrily.

Struggling against a relentless current, he waded forward to help Jack Wright secure the supplies on top of the cart. With several others, they took hold of the dilapidated wagon and slowly lifted the front wheel a few inches above the ground, shuffling it over the unseen obstacle and placing it back in the water.

Thomas Percy shook his head in disbelief. It was a little after eight o'clock in the evening. 'We've been going since dawn and we've scarcely covered more than twenty miles!' he lamented. The light had faded mid afternoon and they had travelled the last few miles in complete darkness. The roads from Hewell Grange had been particularly bad. The rain had turned the tracks to mud and the horses had been slipping all over the place, trying to drag the rickety wooden carts through the awkward slush. The wagons had been getting stuck in the mud long before they had reached the ford. And the rain was still falling heavily.

'We've certainly picked the right time of year,' Jack laughed, wading towards the far bank.

The River Stour was flowing fast and the ford was at its highest point. If it had risen any further it would have been impossible to cross without ruining the contents of the wooden carts. As it was, the passing spray could still soak some of the material, rendering even the newly requisitioned gunpowder all but useless. And they would not be able to check up on it until they reached the security of Holbeach House.

The unencumbered horses had been led across the river first, ahead of the wagons. These animals were being looked after once again by Ambrose Rookwood, with the help of a few servants, while the others were struggling with the munitions. The last of the carts was now lurching across the river behind a particularly stubborn mare. Sir Everard Digby, in his shirt sleeves and little else, was having to drag the horse in order to make it pull the wagon. Several others, including Catesby, were pushing the cart from behind.

'Come back here!' Ambrose yelled angrily, from the far bank.

Jack Wright peered ahead. 'What's happening?'

'I think a couple of the servants have bolted,' the young man replied. 'Grab that horse, will you?'

Jack rushed forward and caught hold of the abandoned animal. It was his own grey-white gelding. He had left it in the care of a groom he had considered reliable, but the man had obviously taken fright. Only a handful of the lesser sort remained now. Thomas Bates and five or six others. Catesby's manservant would be the last to run out.

Sir Everard Digby brought the remaining horses up onto the far bank. The battered wagon was now free of the river. Digby gave the reins to Tom Wintour and strode quickly back to the water to give Catesby a hand up onto the muddy bank.

The men stood together for a moment, looking back at the Stour. It was too dark to see the far side. The moon was obscured by clouds and they had crossed the river without even torch light to guide them. Catesby took a moment to recover his breath, then came forward and retrieved his horse from Thomas Bates. 'Not far to Holbeach now,' he said, wiping the water from his eyes. 'Just another few miles. Then we can bed down for the night.'

'We've lost a lot of time, Robin,' Tom Wintour observed. 'The Sheriff's men may be getting closer by the minute. They'll have made better time than we have.'

'They couldn't have made worse time,' Percy snarled.

Fawkes' strategy had been a simple one: let out the information a bit at a time. Give them some of what they wanted, satisfy them for a while, then pull back. He had been absurdly confident in his ability to resist these "gentler" tortures. But after countless hours hanging from a cold wooden pillar like the Lord Jesus himself on the Cross, that confidence was beginning to disintegrate. With every moment that passed, he was coming closer to cracking.

Whenever he passed out, they would untie him, bring him around and then put him back exactly where he had been before. Fawkes had lost count of the number of times he had fainted.

And still the questions came.

Sir William Waad was a merciless interrogator. He would repeat the same questions over and over again. And for the first time, Fawkes was beginning to provide some of the answers.

He had told them his real name, for one. That had shocked the arrogant lieutenant; and it could do no harm now. Then he had outlined some of the early history of the plot. He had even admitted to the existence of other plotters, though he had refused to provide any of the names. Mr Percy they already knew about. The other names, Fawkes was determined, would not come from him.

Then, in the evening – he assumed it must be evening – the Lieutenant of the Tower changed tack. 'We already know the names,' Waad announced nonchalantly. 'Your friends are trying to drum up support in the Midlands. We've had word of them from there. We know who they are. We know everything about them. So there really is no need for you to endure any more.'

Fawkes spoke through gritted teeth. 'I will endure anything for the sake of the Cross.'

Waad was unimpressed. 'Very laudable, Mr Fawkes. But as I say, we already have the names. This is merely a formality. Why not do yourself a favour and confirm the information?'

It was a bluff, Fawkes thought. It had to be. 'If you know the names already, my lord, then you do not need to hear them from me.'

The lieutenant sighed. 'You leave me no alternative then.' He stood up and exchanged a few words with a nearby guard. 'We'll have to move on to the rack...'

Chapter Twenty Eight

Matchlocks were piled high in the back of the wagon. Thomas Percy pulled off the blankets covering the supplies and took hold of a musket, sliding it clear of the rope fastening the weapons to the back of the cart. The gun was nearly six feet long, made of wood and iron. Percy slid a hand along the barrel. It was well-crafted, but cumbersome. Rain splattered onto the polished metal. Percy grimaced. He had never liked matchlocks. They were useful in combat, but they were not reliable. And they took far too long to load. There were more muskets here than they could possibly need. The group had been anticipating collecting supporters as they made their way westwards, but so far not one single person had agreed to join them; not since Dunchurch, at any rate. Everywhere the rebels went, they had been spurned. It was almost as if they carried the plague. Sir John Talbot would be the last hope.

Percy removed a third blanket, covering the far end of the cart. Boxes of shot were stacked together against the sides of the wagon. Ammunition for the muskets. The powder had been stored in bags on another cart. Bates and a few others were attending to that. Percy pulled out a knife and cut the already fraying rope holding the boxes in place. He grabbed a few containers and another matchlock, then made his way across to the porch.

The lights of Holbeach House were warm and inviting. The owner of the estate, Stephen Littleton, was standing in the doorway. He was a tall, clean shaven man of about thirty. One of the servants was listening patiently as he explained the manner of their arrival. Littleton had joined the plotters at Dunchurch and so far had proved loyal. Doubtless, after the horrendous journey from Huddington, he would be pleased to see his home. For everyone else, it would simply be a relief to get out of the rain.

Holbeach House was a perfect place to hole up. It was a veritable fortress. Percy had been here several times before. It was not a big estate, but the grounds were surrounded by a high wall and the main building had almost a dozen windows facing to the front. That would give them an advantage, if the Sheriff's men happened to arrive during the night. Guards would need to be posted at the front gate, to give warning of any approach. And marksmen could be positioned at the windows to pick off the attackers, if any attempt was made to storm the building. Muskets would be useful here, if nowhere else.

Littleton stepped back to allow Percy into the hallway.

The supplies were being carried through into a nearby dining area. Percy followed behind. A servant was just stoking the fire. Another was lighting extra candles. In the centre of the room, on the dining table, an impressive collection of muskets had already been piled up. The long, slender weapons dominated the large oak surface. Catesby was standing by the fire, warming his hands.

Percy off-loaded the matchlocks and the boxes of shot, then moved across to the hearth to join his friend. He held out his arms. His clothes were dripping water onto the smooth stone floor but the warmth of the fire was more than adequate compensation. 'This will be a good place to stand and fight,' he asserted cheerfully. 'The speed we're going, we're never going to outrun them.'

'It depends how close they are,' Catesby said. 'And whether we can get reinforcements.'

Percy was not worried about that. 'They'll come, Robin. And how many men can the Sheriff have with him? A couple of dozen? Fifty, maybe?' It was unlikely to be more than that. 'We can take them. I'm sure we can. And a victory here could be all we need to change our fortunes.' If a small band of Catholics could capture and kill a High Sheriff, then surely hundreds would rise up to join them.

'Or it could be the end of us,' Catesby pointed out.

Percy shrugged. 'Better to die fighting.'

'We'll stay the night at any rate,' Catesby resolved. 'Hopefully, the rain will ease off by tomorrow. You might as well get out of those wet rags. Stephen has offered us some fresh clothes if everything of yours is saturated.'

'You could do with some clean clothes yourself. Is it just me or do we all stink to high heaven?'

Catesby smiled tiredly. 'It's just you, Thomas.'

Percy crouched down, moving closer to the fire. 'We'll need to post a guard at the front gate. Just in case. I'll take first watch, if you like.'

'We could get one of the servants to do it.'

'You must be joking. They'll run for the hills at the first sign of trouble.' He rubbed his hands together and gazed at the flickering flames dancing across the hot coals. 'Better if we do it ourselves.'

'Agreed. But do get some sleep, if you can.'

Percy shook his head. 'Sleep is for the dead. There's too much else to do.'

It was a ten-mile ride to Pepperhill. Without the wagons to slow them down, Tom Wintour and Stephen Littleton had managed to cover the distance in little more than an hour. Dawn was breaking as they pulled up at the edge of the estate. Littleton was proving a reluctant companion. He had voiced his scepticism about the mission before they had even departed. Tom shared his misgivings and was surprised the man had agreed to travel with him. Presumably, he wanted to get away from Holbeach. It was almost certainly safer on the road than it was at the manor house. Too many people had known the rebels would be stopping there.

Tom had managed to get a few hours sleep, but not enough to refresh him. Guards had been posted at the gateway and along the walls of the estate. Everyone had had to take a turn. They could not rely on the servants, less still on Stephen Littleton's household. Luckily, there had been no sign of the Sheriff's men during the night. But the posse could not be far away. That was why this mission was so important.

Tom spotted Sir John Talbot coming out of his house. Pepperhill was situated on a high promontory, amid the rural landscape of Shropshire. The ageing nobleman had risen early and was making his way towards an adjacent lawn, which served as a bowling green. Sir John stopped when he saw the riders approaching. Tom had not expected the man to be awake at this hour, less still up and about. The greeting he gave them was not in the least bit cordial.

'What are you doing here?' he demanded, coming forward to confront the two visitors. 'Are you insane?'

Tom was taken aback. Sir John had cut him off before he had managed to utter a single word. 'Why...shouldn't I be here?' he asked, in complete bewilderment.

'I've heard all about your devilish schemes. I want nothing to do with them.'

Tom and Stephen exchanged worried glances. Evidently news was spreading fast; if not about the powder plot then at least about the raid on Warwick Castle.

'You shouldn't have come here. Don't you know the Sheriff is on his way? It's more than my life is worth, even talking to you!'

'We need help,' Tom pleaded. 'We're walled up at Holbeach. All we need is a few extra men. Then we can flee to Wales and unite with the rebels. Your assistance could be all that's needed to tip the balance.'

Sir John Talbot grasped the hilt of his sword with his right hand. 'Didn't I make myself clear? I want nothing to do with this. Leave now, for God's Sake. I'll not be hanged for your stupidity.'

'Come on, Tom,' Stephen said. 'We'll get no help here.' He pulled on the reins of his horse and circled the animal around. Reluctantly, Tom did likewise.

He could feel the angry glare burning into his back as the two horses made their way back down the hill. Tom had not really expected Gertrude's father to offer them any help, but he was shocked to have been so angrily rebuffed. Robin had clearly misjudged the mood of the local Catholics. Nobody wanted anything to do with them. Not villagers, not gentlemen, not peers of the realm. And from what Sir John had said, the High Sheriff had to be within a few miles of the estate. It was even possible – Tom shuddered at the thought – that the Sheriff had arrived at Holbeach House during their absence.

'It might be better if we didn't go back,' Stephen Littleton suggested, quietly. 'Without Sir John we won't have enough men to defend ourselves.'

'I'll not desert my friends, Stephen,' Tom replied angrily. 'We're committed to this now. And we have important news to deliver.' He kicked his horse into a trot. 'I just pray that we're in time.'

Catesby looked up as Ambrose Rookwood entered the dining room. 'The Sheriff is less than five miles away,' Ambrose declared solemnly. Thomas Percy ducked down under the frame of the door behind him. The two men had been keeping watch at the main gate since dawn. A messenger had just come to them there; one of the Sheriff's men. The posse was on its way. 'The Sheriff wants us to surrender. He says if we give ourselves up voluntarily he will plead our case before the King and see that our lives are spared.'

'He thinks we're just a bunch of horse thieves,' Percy sneered.

'Is he still at the gate?' Catesby asked.

Percy shook his head. 'I told him to go fuck himself. If I'd had a musket, I'd have shot the little bastard then and there.'

'He's on his way back to the Sheriff,' Ambrose said.

Jack Wright was standing over by the table. 'Who's watching the gate?'

'Your brother. And Sir Everard.' Percy grinned. 'You should have seen that man's face. I told him straight: if he thought some local Sheriff with a handful of men could take Holbeach House, he was out of his tiny mind.'

Catesby was standing by the fire, keeping watch on a metal tray that had been laid out a short distance from the flames. 'Five miles,' he reflected. 'So they'll be here in less than an hour.'

That was it, then. They had run out of options. There was no time left to flee; not with Tom Wintour away seeking help.

'This is where it's all going to happen,' Percy agreed, with barely disguised glee. The man had been itching for a fight ever since the raid on Warwick Castle.

Jack walked over to the window. 'I'm glad someone's happy,' he commented dryly, glancing out across the lawn. 'I suppose there are worse places to die.'

'We're not going to die,' Percy insisted. 'With any luck, Tom'll be here soon with reinforcements.' He reached out and picked up one of the matchlocks from the dining table. 'Even if Sir John doesn't play ball, there are enough of us here to hold a Sheriff at arm's length. We have weapons, we have a defensible position. He'll never risk a full-on assault. We'd cut them down before they were halfway across the courtyard.'

Jack stifled a laugh. 'You live in a world of your own, Thomas.'

'I tell you, we can't lose!'

Jack smiled quietly to himself.

Percy cocked the musket. They had plenty of ammunition, true, but there was a question mark over the powder. Several bags had been left open in the main hall during the night, in the hope that some of it would start to dry out, but the combination of continuous rain and the river crossing the previous evening had rendered almost all of the powder unusable. And without gunpowder, none of the matchlocks would fire.

'We'd have been better off with crossbows than muskets,' said Jack, glancing back from the window.

'We'll use swords if we have to.' Percy placed the musket back on the table and patted the hilt of his blade with a fatherly affection.

Catesby had laid some of the powder out on a small tray in front of the fire in a last ditch effort to dry it out. They only needed a small amount for the matchlocks. It was probably foolish placing the gunpowder close to a naked flame but the risk was a calculated one. The substance had been spread very thinly across the metal platter. It could not explode but a stray spark from the fire might still cause it to ignite.

Ambrose Rookwood walked over to the grate. 'How's it coming along?' he asked.

Catesby looked up. 'See for yourself.' He was keeping the tray at a respectable distance.

Ambrose bent over to examine the powder. 'Not some of the better stuff,' he observed. The flames were beginning to die away in any case.

'John Grant's gone to get some more coals,' Catesby said.

The heat did seem to be having some effect, though. Ambrose leaned in closer. The gunpowder looked as if it was beginning to dry out. Perhaps they would be able to use it after all.

Grant arrived with the hot coals to stoke up the fire. Catesby stood back and allowed the man room to access the chimney. Grant moved in, kicking against the coal scuttle. He emptied the coals onto the fire. A stray coal fell towards the nearby platter.

And the gunpowder flashed into life.

Chapter Twenty Nine

It had stopped raining during the early hours of the morning but the roads were still muddied and difficult to traverse. Tom Wintour kicked his horse urgently. It would have been safer to avoid the roads altogether, but speed was essential now. Stephen Littleton was struggling to keep pace behind his older companion. The two riders were scarcely a mile from Holbeach House. It was imperative they got back there before the Sheriff arrived.

In the distance, a bugle sounded. Tom let out a growl of frustration. The posse was getting closer.

He struck his horse again, forcing the animal to increase its pace. Stephen Littleton endeavoured to follow suit. The two men were already pounding through the countryside at a breakneck speed.

Suddenly a man jumped out of the undergrowth, darting across the muddy track directly in front of them. Tom scarcely had time to react but his horse had swifter reflexes and swerved to avoid a head on collision. Tom gripped the reins tightly as the muscular gelding galloped past the unknown figure.

'Mr Wintour!' the man cried, as the animal sped away down the track.

Stephen Littleton's horse had also swerved to avoid the sudden obstacle, but Littleton had more room to manoeuvre and was able to pull up almost at once. Ahead of him, Tom was struggling to reassert control. The hooves of the brown gelding were slipping dangerously in the mud, but the animal managed to keep its feet and gradually it slowed. Tom pulled the horse to a stop and then turned it awkwardly, directing it back along the pathway.

Now that he could see the fellow clearly, Tom recognised the groom as one of his own, a young servant he had left behind at Holbeach that morning. The last of them, in fact. He pulled up in front of the exhausted looking young man. 'What are you doing here?' he demanded. 'Are you running out on me?'

The groom shook his head vehemently. 'There's been a terrible accident!' he exclaimed.

Tom jumped down from his horse. 'What do you mean, an accident?'

'At Holbeach, Mr Wintour. It was terrible. Half a dozen people are dead.'

'What are you talking about? How can anyone be dead?' It was not possible. Not so soon. 'Has there been an attack on the house?' Were the Sheriff's men there already?

'No, sir. It was an act of God. They were trying to dry some of the powder close to the fire. There was an explosion. Mr Catesby was killed outright. And Mr Rookwood too.'

Tom brought a hand up to his mouth.

'A few others were badly injured. Everybody is fleeing the house.'

Stephen Littleton dismounted and joined the two men. 'Are you absolutely certain of this?' he asked, addressing the groom.

'I'm sure, sir. God has abandoned us. It's every man for himself.'

Tom shuddered. He took a moment to regain his composure. 'You're leaving?'

The manservant nodded. 'With your permission, Mr Wintour.'

'Of course.' Tom reached down into his pouch and produced a few coins. 'Take these. God be with you.' He placed the coins in the young servant's hand. The groom mumbled his thanks and darted into the undergrowth on the other side of the road.

Tom turned back to his companion. He opened his mouth, but no words came. Could it be true? Robin dead? He had to get back to Holbeach. He had to find out for himself exactly what had happened.

Stephen Littleton had other ideas. 'You heard what your man said. Everything's lost. We have to think of ourselves now, Tom. We must get away from here.'

Tom gritted his teeth. 'You go, Stephen, if you must. I'll not abandon my friend.'

'Didn't you hear? He's already dead. There's nobody left at Holbeach to mount a stand.'

'If Robin is dead, then he deserves a proper Christian burial.' *If* he was dead. 'I want to see his body with my own eyes. Whatever the risks. I owe him that much, at least.'

Stephen shrugged. 'It's your life.' He returned to his horse and pulled himself up into the saddle. 'Good luck, Mr Tom,' he said, raising a hand in farewell. 'I'll see you in the hereafter.' So saying, he turned his horse and galloped off into the distance.

Tom watched him go. He could not bring himself to blame the man. Littleton was no coward. He had come this far with them, after all. Better that he departed now. There was no need for Stephen Littleton to sacrifice himself at Holbeach, if there was a chance he could get away. It was, in any case, only the smallest of chances now.

Tom pulled himself back into his saddle. He had unfinished business at Holbeach. His friends needed him there, now more than ever. Dead or alive, he could not abandon them. And there was only one way to discover the truth.

The wall surrounding the fireplace was a blackened mess. Chairs had been knocked over. Several of the muskets had clattered to the ground. And there was blood on the stone floor of the dining hall.

Thomas Percy crouched down with a damp handkerchief and wiped the blood from Catesby's scorched face. The dazed conspirator was sitting up against a wall on the far side of the room, facing inwards from the windows. Across the room, Jack Wright and his brother were tending to John Grant. 'Look after Ambrose,' Catesby croaked. 'He needs it more than I do.'

Percy nodded and made his way across to the shivering horseman. Ambrose Rookwood had been close to the fire when the hot coal had hit the platter. The powder had ignited in a rapid burst, sending a shower of sparks flying up through the air. Catesby had been a little further back, but he too had been caught up in the sudden ignition. Percy and Jack, standing closer to the window, had got by unscathed.

It was a miracle none of them had been killed. Sacks of gunpowder were lying scattered across the room. They had been left open deliberately during the night. If a stray spark had fallen into any of these, the explosion would certainly have killed them all and doubtless would have destroyed the greater part of Holbeach House. As it was, their friend John Grant – the man who had gathered most of their arsenal at Norbrook – had now been completely blinded. His face was burnt away, his muscles visible where skin had once been stretched and his charred eyeballs hanging loose from their sockets.

Catesby had got off lightly in comparison. His skin was burnt and the searing heat had almost rendered him unconscious, but he had at least been able to stand up and move away from the hearth. He had staggered across to the far wall and promptly collapsed.

It was at this point, with Catesby lying dazed, that many of the rebels had decided to cut their losses. Catesby could not blame them. There could hardly be a clearer signal than this. God had spoken. It was not His will that the rebels would succeed. All they could do now was to throw themselves upon His mercy.

A figure appeared in the doorway. Catesby struggled to focus. It was Tom Wintour, back from Pepperhill at last. The short, stocky Catholic stood for a moment, staring back at his friend, unable to hide a mixture of relief and sudden horror. 'They told me you were dead,' he whispered, coming forward into the room.

Catesby put a hand on the window ledge and struggled to his feet. Tom rushed over to assist him. 'I very nearly was,' he rasped. His hands were bloodied and dark with soot. He grabbed onto Tom's shoulder for support.

'Everyone's flying from the house,' Tom said.

'Your brother's gone,' Percy confirmed, from over at the fireplace. 'And Sir Everard Digby.'

'Sir Everard's gone to get help,' Catesby croaked. He clutched a hand to his head, feeling suddenly light headed.

'He's gone to give himself up,' Jack corrected.

'We couldn't keep them here. Not after this.'

Tom took a moment to survey the damage to the room. The dining area was all but unrecognisable. Scorch marks covered the ceiling and the far wall. Boxes of ammunition lay scattered across the floor and there was soot everywhere. The gunpowder had done its work here, if not in Parliament. Tom stifled a cry as he spotted John Grant over by the Wright brothers and took in the man's terrible injuries. He looked away quickly, unable to meet Grant's vacant and bloodied eye sockets. 'Stephen's gone too,' he murmured to Catesby. 'The Sheriff is on his way. I heard the bugle calls as I was riding in. He could be here at any moment. And no-one's guarding the main gate.'

Catesby nodded. 'We know, Tom.'

Tom stared back at his cousin. The man's brow was raddled like burnt paper and blood continued to drip from the blackened ruff at his neck. 'What do you mean to do now?' he asked, quietly.

Catesby looked him straight in the eye. 'We mean to die.'

Tom swallowed nervously. It was the answer he had been expecting.

'Are you with us, Mr Tom? You can leave now, if you want. There may still be time to get away. No-one will think the less of you.'

Tom shook his head.

'Bates went,' Catesby pointed out. 'His loyalty is to his family. Your brother's gone too. I wouldn't blame you if you wanted to join them.'

Tom was vehement. 'I will do whatever you do,' he insisted. 'I'm not going to leave you now.'

Catesby nodded wearily. 'You're a good fellow, Tom.' He glanced back at John Grant and Ambrose Rookwood. 'You can help Thomas look after the wounded. Jack, you and your brother get up to the front gate. Take a couple of matchlocks. Let us know when the Sheriff arrives.' Catesby was beginning to recover some of his authority. 'Thomas, load up as many of the other muskets as you can. We should be able to cover most of the courtyard from the first floor windows.'

'Will the powder work?' Tom asked.

'We'll have to chance our arm. If it doesn't, we'll just have to resort to old fashioned methods.' Catesby patted his sword.

Jack and Kit moved past him into the hallway and out into the courtyard.

Tom walked across to the slumped figures of John Grant and Ambrose Rookwood. Jack had tied a bandage around Grant's head. 'Get them upstairs,' Catesby instructed. 'If the matchlocks do work, they can provide cover from the upstairs windows. If you're up to it, John.'

'I can't see a bloody thing,' John Grant muttered.

Ambrose was more positive. 'I'll take a couple of them with me,' he affirmed. The young horseman still had one decent hand, after all.

Tom helped John Grant to his feet. The poor man's face had all but disintegrated. Tom would not have known who it was, but for the voice. Supporting him at the shoulder and waist, the two men moved into the hallway.

From outside the house, the bugles could still be heard. Closer now. Jack Wright was already sprinting across the courtyard, trying to reach the gate before the entrance was breached. Kit Wright was not far behind. Tom could see them through the open doorway. Time was running out, but the brothers reached the entrance before the Sheriff's men came into view. They closed up the gate and fastened it as best they could.

Tom Wintour moved to the stairs with John Grant and helped the blind man to climb up to the first floor. Behind them, Thomas Percy was lending an arm to Ambrose Rookwood. Ambrose could at least still see, but his leg had been badly scorched and he found it difficult to walk without assistance. Percy would position Ambrose to the right of the main porch. The man would be able to give covering fire through the upper window, if only the muskets could be made to work.

At the top of the stairs, Tom froze. A single gun-shot rang out from the courtyard.

The Sheriff's men had arrived.

Sir Everard Digby waited in silence.

The roads were crawling with troops.

The young knight had led his two companions slowly down a steep incline. It was an awkward manoeuvre but it was the only practical way to keep out of sight. The riders had got away from Holbeach just in time. Digby would have preferred to travel alone but two of his servants had insisted on accompanying him. They were good, loyal men but already they were slowing him down. He had tried offering them money but they had refused to leave his side. Then, less than a mile from the estate, they had run into the militia. Fortunately, it had not been a head-on collision. Digby had caught sight of some troops on the periphery of the group and had immediately cut away from the main road. The Sheriff's men had seen them, however, and had given chase. They had had to leave the established tracks altogether, hurtling through woodland in order to make their escape.

There had been more men gathered together than anybody had expected. Glimpsing the posse from the outskirts, Digby was quite convinced that several hundred soldiers were advancing on Holbeach House. Troops from Worcestershire and Warwickshire. The numbers were far in excess of what Thomas Percy had been anticipating. The poor men back at Holbeach would not stand a chance. Not that they expected to live.

Catesby had known the end was near. He had wanted to die at Holbeach House, rather than allowing himself to be taken alive. Digby felt guilty about leaving them behind, but he had done so for the best of reasons. His intention initially had been to fetch help, like Tom Wintour, but that was clearly impossible now. He had not anticipated the Sheriff's men being quite so near. Now he would have to flee; if he could. Or perhaps it would be better to give himself up. He did not want to be hunted down like an animal. Sir Everard Digby had done his best to give his pursuers the slip, but the men were still on his trail and were unlikely to desist. His best chance was to hide out in the undergrowth until nightfall and then to break out under cover of darkness.

The plan, Digby knew, had only a slim chance of success.

The gateway had been forced open but there was no sign of movement from the militia. The Wright brothers had retreated to the main house. The Sheriff's men were holding position just outside the grounds of the estate. At the window on the first floor, Ambrose Rookwood struggled to keep his musket level. The barrel protruded some feet through the open window and it was proving difficult to hold the weapon steady. The powder had ripped the flesh from Ambrose's arm as well as his leg and the pain was excruciating.

John Grant was sitting on the floor out of sight of the window. His suffering was even greater, Ambrose knew. Yet here the man was, completely blind, sat purposefully alongside a small stack of preloaded matchlocks, ready to hand them to Ambrose as and when required. The bravery of the fellow beggared belief.

Ambrose swallowed uneasily. He hoped he would show the same courage when the moment came.

It would not be long now.

A flash of movement by the gate caught his attention. A man had sprinted through the gateway and was now speeding across the lawn. Ambrose struggled to aim his musket. At this distance, he was certain to miss. Matchlocks were not renowned for their accuracy. He was not even sure that the weapon would fire. Powder, he thought, always powder.

Ambrose pulled the trigger. The musket fired and a single ball of metal tore across the courtyard. The shot was far from the mark, but at least the powder had ignited. The invader disappeared behind a nearby tree. Another fellow was running through the gate. Grant handed Ambrose a second musket. He shoved the long barrel awkwardly through the window and let off another shot. The Sheriff's man dived for cover behind the nearest bush. Three or four others were coming forward to take up positions on the lawn. Ambrose pulled the trigger on a third musket. It fizzled but did not fire. Then a ball smacked into the brickwork just below the window. He ducked down out of sight. The sharpshooter behind the tree was now returning fire. Ambrose grabbed another gun from John Grant. It would take the marksman some time to reload. He lifted his head to see what the others were doing. To his surprise, there was no-one in view.

The Sheriff's men had taken up their positions.

On the ground floor, Tom Wintour had observed the cross-fire through a small window to the right of the front door. The remaining conspirators were gathered together in the hallway. Jack, Kit, Percy and Catesby. They had been anticipating a full-on frontal assault. The Sheriff had more than enough men to storm the building, but seemed unwilling to do so. Presumably, he did not wish to sacrifice any of his subordinates without first attempting to shorten the odds. The sharp shooters had taken up positions within the grounds of Holbeach House and doubtless they would take pot-shots whenever they saw any kind of movement inside the building. 'He's hoping to pick us off one by one,' Jack guessed.

Thomas Percy was unperturbed. 'If that's the way he wants to play it.'

Tom Wintour glanced out of the window a second time, but he could not see any sign of life in the courtyard.

'They're holding position!' Ambrose called from the first floor. A minute passed, without a sound from anyone. Muskets had been carefully aimed on both sides but no shots were being fired.

'It's stalemate,' Jack realised. 'He won't come any further forward. He's waiting for us to make a move.'

Percy grinned. 'He won't know what's hit him!'

The other rebels did not share Percy's bravado. It was the end of the road and every one of them knew it.

Percy glared at his friends. 'It's better than being taken alive!' he snapped.

Catesby raised a hand. The others looked at him quizzically. 'It's time to make our peace with God,' he said. The conspirators nodded solemnly and the five men knelt down together on the cold stone floor.

Catesby closed his eyes and began to pray, his lips whispering the litanies he had been taught as a child, his hands fingering the golden crucifix hanging at his neck. Finally, he brought the cross up to his lips and kissed it reverently. 'Everything I did,' he murmured, 'I did for the honour of the Cross and the True Faith which venerates this Cross.' Now he would give his life for the same cause. If God had decreed that the plan must fail, then Catesby would not question His judgement.

He opened his eyes. Tom Wintour was by his side, praying silently. Catesby placed a hand on his friend's arm. 'Gentlemen,' he said. 'It's time.'

Chapter Thirty

The horse was balanced precariously on the side of the incline. Sir Everard Digby remained mounted, out of view, but he was ready to make his escape the instant he was discovered. The grooms were having more difficulty with the steep slope. That was hardly surprising. Serving men rarely had the opportunity to become accomplished riders. In the distance, Digby could hear the sounds of his pursuers. One particular voice stood out. 'Look over here!' some scoundrel was bellowing, in a crude, guttural accent. 'He must have come this way. Look at the tracks!'

Sir Everard Digby kept very still. The ground everywhere was muddied after the rain. It was inevitable that the horses would have left tracks. But Digby did not wish to be captured by ordinary militia men. There was no telling what they would do. They might kill him outright, even if he attempted to surrender. Common soldiers had been known to murder their prisoners just to steal their swords and take all their money. It would not be a dignified way to die. He gestured quietly to the grooms. There was only one way out and that was straight through the line of his pursuers. He faced his horse up toward the bank.

A head popped over the horizon; a man on foot, a grubby soldier with a pike. 'Here he is!' the man called, waving frantically to his comrades, who were out of sight. 'Here he is!'

'Here he is indeed!' Digby replied, kicking hard.

The horse leapt forward, up onto the level ground, causing the soldier to fall backwards in alarm. There were a dozen men beyond him, some of them on horseback. Without hesitation, Digby hurtled straight at them. If he could pass through this threadbare militia, he could veer any which way and lose himself a second time in the forest.

The men stood their ground.

Digby quickly scanned the terrain around them. In the trees, beyond the small party, he spotted more horses. More troops. A couple of dozen, perhaps. They were splitting into two sections and cutting off the edges either side of him. The men in front, meantime, had raised their pikes. A man on a horse had lifted a musket. Digby had a split second to decide what to do.

He pulled hard on the reins and brought his horse to a sudden halt. Then he raised his hands. The soldiers approached him cautiously.

In the depths of the White Tower, the candles continued to burn. Mr Thomas Norton, the rack-master, stood at the side of a large wooden apparatus, awaiting instructions from Sir William Waad. 'Another turn,' the lieutenant ordered, his voice flat and apparently uninterested.

Guido Fawkes was stretched out across the rack. It was a crude rectangular device, with two wooden slats across the middle and three large drums tied together with thick rope. Fawkes' weakened body was suspended between the two ends of the mechanism, his ankles and bloodied wrists strapped to the upper and lower drum. A lever either side of the central roller controlled their movement. The left lever would turn the bottom drum. The right, the top. And with every movement, his body was being pulled further apart.

There was only one rack in England and often just the threat of it was enough to loosen a man's tongue. But Guido Fawkes was no ordinary man.

Mr Norton pulled the lever and the lower drum turned another quarter of an inch. Fawkes screamed out and Sir William Waad nodded contentedly. 'Much more of this, and you'll be maimed for life,' he explained in a matter of fact tone. 'We'll need to carry you up to the scaffold. It won't be very dignified.'

Fawkes spluttered. He was having difficulty speaking now. 'I...I don't care how I die.' His bravado could not last, however. Another turn of the drum and he would be forced to capitulate. Nothing in his entire life had prepared him for the torment of this crude wooden apparatus. Fawkes had been injured as a soldier, nearly killed on occasion; but he had never experienced anything like this. It felt as if his very soul was being torn apart and he knew he could not endure it any more. A final turn of the drum elicited another scream and at this point something in his mind broke. 'All right! All right!' Fawkes cried out desperately. 'I'll tell you! Just let it stop! Please let it stop!'

Waad examined the prisoner critically. A scribe in a corner stood ready, quill in hand. 'The names, Mr Fawkes. That is all I ask. The names.'

Fawkes could barely move his head. 'I'll tell you everything,' he whispered.

Sir William Waad smiled condescendingly.

The iron blade had been specially wrought. Jack Wright lifted the sword up to his face. Ambrose had insisted he take it. The young horseman would not be able to wield the weapon now, but it was right that it saw some action. It was a beautiful object, encrusted with emeralds and diamonds. The perfect weapon. Jack had wielded a great many swords in his life, but none like this. He kissed the cross of the blade and murmured a last prayer. Matchlocks were for barbarians. He would die a gentleman, with sword in hand.

Beside him stood Tom Wintour, his hand placed on the hilt of his own sword. Slowly, Tom drew the blade from its sheath. Then he moved towards the door.

Jack followed behind, with his younger brother Kit. It was fitting the two siblings should die together. They had always been alike in so many ways.

At the rear, Thomas Percy stood ready, with Catesby at his side.

All was quiet in the courtyard of Holbeach House. The Sheriff's men stood their ground calmly, most of them at the gate, some behind the line of trees which speckled the lawn, all of them waiting for any sign of movement from the house.

They did not have to wait long.

Tom Wintour pulled open the front door and ran out through the porch way onto the damp gravel. Behind him, the Wright brothers came yelling, their swords raised but their heads ducked down as they moved out into the light. Tom sprinted forward, scanning the lawns for an enemy to attack. Behind the foliage, several marksmen were taking careful aim. 'Over in the trees!' Jack called out, catching sight of one of them. Before Tom could react, a crossbow bolt leapt through the air and thudded into his right shoulder. The force of the bolt knocked him backwards. He screamed. His sword clattered to the ground and his body smacked into the hard gravel surface.

Jack Wright had his own troubles. A marksman had singled him out. Jack's face exploded in a crunch of blood and bone as the musket ball hit him square on.

As Jack fell away to the ground, Tom was struggling to get back on his feet. Behind him, Catesby was hurtling through the porch way, with Percy at his side. Another shot hit Kit Wright, knocking the young man backwards onto the gravel.

At the window, Ambrose Rookwood was attempting to provide covering fire. He let off one shot, but a marksman had spotted him and returned fire. By pure fluke, the musket ball caught Ambrose in the upper arm and he dropped out of sight.

Tom Wintour was trying to recover his sword, but his shoulder was completely dead. 'I can't move my arm!' he cried out, as Catesby reached his side.

'Stand by me, Mr Tom!' Catesby bellowed, helping him to his feet, 'and we will die together!'

Percy skidded to a halt in front of the shorter man. He stood back to back with Catesby, the two of them masking Tom Wintour as the Sheriff's men began to move forward from their position at the gate. Percy raised his sword and took a deep breath. The marksmen on the lawn were holding their positions. Some had reloaded. A musket ball thudded into Percy's chest. At the same moment, Catesby was struck, seemingly by the same shot.

The Sheriff's men rushed towards them. Tom struggled to pick up his sword with his left hand. His friends had fallen either side of him. Before he could grab hold of the blade, a pike was thrust into his belly. Hands grabbed him from behind.

Catesby lay bleeding on the cold gravel, his head facing back towards the house. Percy lay next to him, his eyes vacant. Blood was dripping from his mouth.

'Take him alive!' a voice yelled. 'The King will need someone to answer for all this.' Tom Wintour. They were talking about Tom. Catesby watched helplessly as his cousin was manhandled back into the house. Poor Tom, he thought. The man had been so desperate not to be taken alive. Now he would be tortured. Tried. Hanged, drawn and quartered. Just like Guy Fawkes.

Poor Tom.

Troops were storming through the building. Another shot rang out. Ambrose, presumably, trying to defend himself. But they would take him too.

Catesby pulled himself onto his knees. His body was completely numb. He looked at the blood on his stomach, but it did not feel like his own. None of it seemed real. Crawling on his hands, Catesby began to move back towards the house.

He passed Jack Wright. The Yorkshireman appeared to be breathing still. The younger brother was more fortunate. Kit had joined Percy in death. Already, the soldiers were stripping the body, removing the boots and fine silk stockings. They would take anything of value.

The troops were everywhere. One of them kicked at him as he moved towards the porch. Catesby rolled to one side and his eyes caught sight of a painting hanging on the wall at the far end of the hallway. It was a portrait of the Virgin Mary. He reached out a hand towards the painting.

Soldiers were already ransacking the interior, stealing and destroying. Anything of value would disappear. Anything Catholic would be smashed. Books. Crucifixes. A passing trooper grabbed hold of the portrait and threw it across the hallway.

The men were animals. Nothing more.

With the very last of his strength, Catesby crawled across the threshold of Holbeach House. Every second was a lifetime of agony. At any moment, he knew, a passing soldier might grab him and finish him off. But at last, his fingers took hold of the frame.

Catesby clutched the holy image to his chest.

And the Virgin Mary watched, impassively, as the light faded from his eyes.

Author's Note

The first question I always want to ask when reading a work of historical fiction is: how much of this is actually true?

It's an awkward question but an understandable one.

Unfortunately, the only response an honest author can give is: 'I haven't the faintest idea.'

Every character in this book is based on a real person; almost every scene is adapted from contemporary records and much of the dialogue (though updated) is derived from eye-witness accounts.

But that doesn't make it true.

There is admittedly a wealth of documentation available to historians and writers of historical fiction – original confessions, trial transcripts, secret letters, proclamations and even an official government account of the discovery of the plot. But the records are inconsistent. Some documents contain obvious errors; others distort the truth. Even hand written accounts by the conspirators themselves cannot be taken at face value, since they were obtained using torture.

The problem any author has is that although some of these documents are undoubtedly unreliable, in many cases they are the only sources of information available. How else can we discover what happened in the early days of the plot, aside from the accounts given by the plotters? Nobody else can tell us. No-one else was around at the time. All we can really do is to take the evidence at face value and try to piece together the most likely sequence of events.

That is what I have endeavoured to do in this book.

It is a work of fiction and doubtless many historians would take issue with certain decisions I have made. I have however tried very hard not to impose my own viewpoint on the narrative. There are already more than enough grandiose theories in circulation. There are probably as many ideas surrounding the gunpowder plot as there are surrounding the assassination of John F. Kennedy. For my part, I have opted to follow a roughly orthodox chronology. If this were a book about the murder of JFK, it would be the story of the lone gunman.

The narrative is told almost exclusively from the point of view of the plotters themselves. It therefore presents only a partial picture of the Gunpowder Plot. We do not discover, for example, who sent the Monteagle letter, for the plotters never found out either (though it is only fair to point out that – despite what Catesby and the other conspirators may have felt – it is unlikely that the letter was written by Francis Tresham).

We do not have a Protestant perspective on events. Catholics may have been in the minority in England but where they formed a majority – such as in France or Spain – they behaved just as badly towards the Protestants as any Protestant did in England towards the Catholics.

We never learn how much the government knew about the plot in advance. Some academics believe that Robert Cecil was aware of the conspiracy well before the delivery of the Monteagle letter and there is certainly some evidence to support this view. Others believe Cecil instigated the entire plot, though they are in the minority. Certainly, the principal secretary manipulated events to secure the maximum propaganda value, but how late in the day is anybody's guess. All that we can say for certain is that – once again – Catesby was also completely in the dark.

There are other issues concerning the gunpowder plot where I have been forced to take a particular view.

The largest decision I have made concerns the existence or otherwise of the mine dug beneath the Parliament building. This is referred to extensively in the confessions of Tom Wintour and Guido Fawkes. However, a tunnel was never found and the authorities apparently never bothered to look for one. This fact, combined with the uncertain geography of the mine, the absurdity of it being dug at all by such tall and unskilled gentlemen, not to mention doubts about the authenticity of the Wintour confession, have led some historians to conclude that the entire thing was a fiction, concocted by the government for propaganda purposes.

The geography of the mine is, admittedly, difficult to determine, but for the purposes of this book I have chosen to assume that it did exist. The balance of probability – it seems to me – is in its favour. The conspirators must have had some plan to get the powder close to the building before they rented the Whynniard cellar. Perhaps they considered digging a tunnel – even started it –

but then gave up on the idea as impractical. The authorities then picked up on it during interrogation and exaggerated the idea's importance. That seems to me the most likely chain of events. In this book, however, I have gone further, following the account of the mine as given in the confession of Tom Wintour. In the absence of conclusive evidence either way, I felt this made more sense dramatically.

There are other minor uncertainties which I will not bore you with here. Needless to say, wherever there is doubt, I have used that same "balance of probability". Where even that is insufficient, I have gone for the most plausible and/or most interesting scenario.

On a handful of occasions, I have deviated slightly from established fact. Father John Sugar was arrested in July 1603 rather than April 1604 as implied here. Sir Everard Digby did not witness the hangings in Warwick. Guido Fawkes probably did head north to see his mother in the summer of 1604, but not in the company of Jack Wright. Catesby was not at the state opening of Parliament (so far as we know) and there is no reason to suppose Sir Everard Digby was there either. There is also no reference to the mine collapsing on top of Tom Wintour, though the story of the coal sacks being moved is taken from the confession of Guy Fawkes.

The sources of information for this book are too numerous to list in their entirety, but I am particularly grateful to the Gunpowder Plot Society (www.gunpowder-plot.org) and to the Internet Archive (www.archive.org) for providing digital copies of contemporary documents and numerous out-of-print books. Of the primary sources, *The Narrative of Father Oswald Tesimond* and the *Autobiography of Father John Gerard* were especially useful. Of the modern history books, *The Gunpowder Plot: Terror And Faith in 1605* by Antonia Fraser is surely the definitive work. Useful alternative commentaries were found in *What Was The Gunpowder Plot?* by John Gerard SJ (exploring the possibility of government complicity in the plot) and *A History Of The Gunpowder Plot* by Philip Sidney (exploring the possible involvement of the Jesuits). *What Gunpowder Plot Was* by Samuel Rawson Gardiner was also extremely helpful.

In the aftermath of the siege at Holbeach, the remaining conspirators were easily rounded up. Tom Wintour was executed on 31st January 1606 alongside Ambrose Rookwood, Robert Keyes and Guido Fawkes. Sir Everard Digby, John Grant and Thomas Bates had been hanged the previous day. Father Henry Garnet was arrested on 27th January and was executed at St. Paul's Churchyard on 3rd May. Francis Tresham died in the Tower, without being brought to trial. Father Oswald Tesimond escaped to Europe where he wrote a book about his experiences.

Could the Gunpowder Plot have succeeded? It is doubtful but not impossible. Perhaps if Parliament had opened on 7th February 1605 – as originally intended – there is a chance that things might have gone well for the plotters. The powder was still fresh and the number of conspirators was in single figures. After that, with the expansion of the plan to involve a rising in the Midlands, it was always going to be more difficult. The more people who know about a plan, the more likely information is to leak out. When Parliament was prorogued until the autumn, the conspiracy was essentially scuppered.

There are always plots. The vast majority fail but occasionally one succeeds. And when it does, it has the power to change everything.

Remember, Remember the Gunpowder Treason
The Murdering Papists unleashing their Plot
The King and His Subjects all Killed for No Reason
The Jesuit Plotters Surrounded and Shot.

Would England have been a better place if the Gunpowder Plot had succeeded? It seems doubtful. Would England have accepted a Catholic government? That is equally doubtful. At best, the plotters would have been hunted and killed by the survivors, at worst they would have plunged the country into a bloody civil war.

Michael Dax
5th November 2012

Also Available On This Imprint

The Pineapple Republic
by
Jack Treby

Democracy is coming to the Central American Republic of San Doloroso. But it won't be staying long...

The year is 1990. Ace reporter Daniel Parr has been injured in a freak surfing accident, just as the provisional government of San Doloroso has announced the country's first democratic elections.

The Daily Herald needs a man on the spot and in desperation they turn to Patrick Malone, a feckless junior reporter who just happens to speak a few words of Spanish.

Despatched to Central America to get the inside story, our Man in Toronja finds himself at the mercy of a corrupt and brutal administration that is determined to win the election at any cost...

Also Available On This Imprint

The Scandal At Bletchley
by
Jack Treby

"I've been a scoundrel, a thief, a blackmailer and a whore, but never a murderer. Until now..."

The year is 1929. As the world teeters on the brink of a global recession, Bletchley Park plays host to a rather special event. MI5 is celebrating its twentieth anniversary and a select band of former and current employees are gathering for a weekend of music, dance and heavy drinking. Among them is Sir Hilary Manningham-Butler, a middle aged woman whose entire adult life has been spent masquerading as a man. She doesn't know why she has been invited – it is many years since she left the secret service – but it is clear she is not the only one with things to hide. And when one of the other guests threatens to expose her secret, the consequences could prove disastrous for everyone.

For more information, visit the website:
www.jacktreby.com

Printed in Great Britain
by Amazon